# The Midlife Crisis of COMMANDER INVINCIBLE

YELLOW SHOE FICTION
Michael Griffith, Series Editor

# The Midlife Crisis of COMMANDER INVINCIBLE

A NOVEL

NEIL CONNELLY

LOUISIANA STATE UNIVERSITY PRESS
BATON ROUGE

Published with the assistance of the Borne Fund

Published by Louisiana State University Press

Manufactured in the United States of America
Louisiana State University Press Paperback Original
First printing

Designer: Barbara Neely Bourgoyne
Typefaces: Calluna, text; Franklin Gothic Demi Freehand, display
Printer and binder: McNaughton and Gunn, Inc.

Library of Congress Cataloging-in-Publication Data
Connelly, Neil O.
The midlife crisis of Commander Invincible : a novel / Neil Connelly.
pages cm
ISBN 978-0-8071-5317-8 (pbk. : alk. paper) — ISBN 978-0-8071-5318-5 (pdf) — ISBN 978-0-8071-5319-2 (epub) — ISBN 978-0-8071-5320-8 (mobi) 1. Superheroes—Fiction. 2. Vigilantes—Fiction. 3. Midlife crisis—Fiction. I. Title.
PS3603.O546M53 2013
813'.6—dc23

2013012567

The paper in this book meets the guidelines for permanence and durability of the Committee on Production Guidelines for Book Longevity of the Council on Library Resources. ♾

*For Chris N.,*
*truest of friends in the darkest of hours*

# The Midlife Crisis of COMMANDER INVINCIBLE

# ONE

*Masks like Me. Noble Intentions. What the People Wanted to Believe.*
*A Missing Star. The Thing about a Falling Baby.*
*The Nothing That Can't Wait. Code 26.*

I'm flying high over this city that was supposed to be mine. Once, the mere sight of my black and bronze cape fluttering above would've stopped traffic, spun the heads of all the stunned citizens. Nowadays, even if I streak through Center Circle at rush hour, I'm lucky if a half-dozen tourists snap cellphone photos. So I spare myself the indifference and stay above the neon glow, up here among the low-floating clouds and the blinking tips of skyscraper antennae. On a moonless evening like tonight, I doubt any civilians can even see me in the darkened sky, and that suits me fine. Tonight, I'm just not feeling like much of a superhero.

Two miles ahead, straight across the west river, a cone of light shines from a hovering police helicopter. I cruise in the general direction, over a Cuban American Pride street fair and past a church spire. As I near the water, I can tell the trouble's in Washington Park, and I try to tune in my ultrahearing to learn more. Above the whirling blades, I can't figure out the nature of the emergency, and I'm legally obliged to keep my distance. There was a time when I would've automatically assisted, when helping peace officers was a matter of honor and duty, a knee-jerk instinct. But with the agreement the unions signed back in '98, masks like me aren't supposed to interfere in police affairs unless officially requested. They have a form that requires two signatures. So I hang suspended over the rippling river and glance down at my Danger Ring, hoping for it to glow with the promise of certain purpose. It remains dull. In the center of my chest, the dying thing grows a bit more.

The only real action I've had tonight, the only distraction I've been able to find since flying away from the HALO, involved a fire on the East Side. I crashed feet first through the window of a burning two-story on South Holland and plucked free a family of four. Safe on the street outside, behind the fire engines, the woman planted a kiss on the dusty cheek of my bronze mask. The man gave me a dirty look and pulled his wife back into his arms. Their two kids, a girl and a boy with blankets tossed over their shoulders, stared at me wide-eyed. I hacked a few times from all the smoke I'd sucked in, and one of the firefighters offered me some oxygen. I waved the plastic mask away and said, "Give it to them."

"We're OK," the wife said.

The pure oxygen was good, and when I sat on the curb I no longer felt dizzy.

"What's wrong with Mr. Magnificent?" the boy asked.

"That's not him," his sister said. "He's one of the other ones."

"Oh," the boy said.

Sheila always used to tell me I should try to be more upbeat, that it's all about positive attitude.

I leave the helicopter behind and follow the river south. Since my surgery, flying puts a hell of a strain on my lower back, but the brace Dr. Hippocrates gave me looks like a girdle. I refuse to wear it out of principle. I just take my time, slow floating under the Continental Bridge, over the docks of Irishtown, finally easing myself onto the top of a tenement on 36th. I can't explain why, but spots like these are where I feel right lately. Out-of-the-way places where I'm alone and no one expects anything of me and I can keep an eye out for some small good to do. I stand on the northwest corner and look down on all the normal people, ten stories below. They hustle along the sidewalk, wait for a break in traffic to cross. I focus on a couple walking arm in arm and imagine them smiling. Once, my ultravision could've confirmed this, but now it comes and goes. I wonder where the couple is heading and hope it is home to bed. I hope they make love that wakes the neighbors.

I fold my hands behind my back and roll my knuckles into the knotted muscle on either side of the base of my spine. I think about the empty pill bottle in my shaving kit back in the HALO and Dr. Hippocrates's lecture about chemical dependency. Despite my lingering pain, he refused to refill the prescription. Some nights after my shift, I can convince Debbie to give me a back massage, something that takes the edge off. I picture her, probably just finishing Nate's nightly bath. I wonder if she's still angry. If my quarters were empty—as they were for almost a decade—I might call it an early night. But if I come in now, before my watch has ended, she'll know something is wrong. Being a good wife, she'll ask me. I hate to lie, and I can't think of how to tell Debbie the truth.

Another copter, this one carrying the KQEP Action News crew, clatters north toward the river. Back in the late '80s, when Sheila anchored the evening edition for QEP, they usually opened with some story trumpeting the team's exploits. It was always "Guardians Save City from Ferocious Five" or "Atlantean Plot to Flood City Thwarted by Guardians." Sure, some part of it was fueled by Sheila's feelings for me, the budding romance between an energetic reporter and a mysterious new hero on the scene. But more, the coverage was a sign of the times. We were what the people wanted to believe in. Infallible heroes with miraculous powers and noble intentions. Two decades later those days seem like a hallucination cooked up by Duchess Dreamo. Sheila left Kingdom Town years ago. The truly dangerous supervillains have all been rounded up, or they've disappeared so deep nobody thinks about them anymore. As for the press coverage, a few weeks, Hal Hightower at KQEP did an exposé on Gypsy's most recent attempt at rehab. This one is court ordered.

The copter disappears, and I'm so itchy for action that I consider risking a jurisdictional violation and following it, but I know nothing sinister is happening back in that park. Nothing sinister happens anymore. Probably some drug punk on the run or a gang fight. I've got nothing against helping out with everyday crimes. I'm not above that. But frankly the cops, who went on strike to force those concessions about noninterference, don't want our help, and usually they don't need it. There was a time when every day brought some threat that could only be handled by me and the other Guardians. What I wouldn't give for a Communist scientist with a stolen nuclear sub, a mutated rhino on the loose, a rampaging robot to smash to bits. I'd die for a baby falling from the sky. I'm not proud of this, but on the verge of my fortieth birthday, I'm coming to know just who I am. The thing about a falling baby is that you don't have to call a committee meeting or deliberate the moral implications or question the long-term consequences of your actions. A wailing infant plummets from a high-rise balcony—you catch it. A rogue state's nuclear missile streaks toward your hometown—you knock it into outer space. A prehistoric two-headed creature that sank an oil platform lurches from the choppy North Atlantic with twin jaws snapping—you kill the bitch.

But things just aren't like they used to be. It seems there are no more monsters, no more damsels in distress, no more falling babies. Nobody needs me to save them.

I step back from the edge and walk the perimeter of the rooftop just to keep my legs from getting stiff. More and more, they fall asleep when I'm in flight for too long, something that often makes for tricky landings. I rub at my neck and wish there were a way to get some coffee. My shift lasts three more hours, and without something to wake me up, I'll never make it through this night. The familiar pain at the base of my skull grows sharper. Even worse, I feel the edge of that craving coming up on me. As I've learned to do more and more often lately, I push the pain and the hunger away. I'm a better man than that.

As unheroic as it seems, I'm considering curling up in a corner and just resting my eyes for a few minutes. I've found the cape makes a decent blanket. But then I hear scuffling over the side, down below in the alley. I peer into the blackness, barely able to detect movement, then step off the ledge and let my body descend.

What I find, as my feet settle to the cracked asphalt, is a white-haired man standing in an industrial dumpster, hip deep in debris. The Majestic, an ancient movie house, is being gutted. The man uses his arms as rakes and flails garbage everywhere. "Seventeen seventy-six," he says, bent over. "That was a big year in the history of history."

I clear my throat, and he looks over his shoulder. We make eye contact, and he straightens, then comes to the side of the dumpster and drapes one arm on it like it's the top of a neighbor's fence. "I was born in Opelika, Alabama," he tells me.

I nod and say, "Good evening. I am Commander Invincible."

"Dressed in that getup, you best be somebody."

"I'd like to help you," I offer. "Why don't we head over to the shelter on 8th Avenue? They'll have some warm food."

"Sally never has pepper. And I'm not going anywhere on a date with you."

"I won't hurt you," I say. "I'm a hero."

"I know what you are. Could be I'm nuts, but I'm far from stupid. You the one shoots laser beams out your fingertips?"

I shake my head. "I'm Commander Invincible—the Undefeatable Man."

His other arm comes up from his side, and he spikes a brick at my face. It breaks in two across my forehead, and one piece drops on my foot. I curse and wipe the dust from my eyes. The man shrugs and says, "Just confirming your credentials. Sorry about Sparkplug."

"Me too," I say. Twelve years, and total strangers still apologize.

In my prime, I'd have dodged that damn brick. Or caught it barehanded. Despite my fancy name, I feel pain more and more every day, and it's been a decade since I could instantly heal any wound. So now, in addition to my back killing me, my head throbs. I could use a cold beer, a handful of ibuprofen, and Debbie's magic massage. Of course what I really need is a good bit stronger, but I made my wife a promise. Good men keep their promises.

"Look," I say, "just come on and sign in at the shelter. It's not smart to be out on the street."

"You want to play Good Samaritan, help me find my goddamn star."

I glance up, but the clouds and city lights blot out the constellations.

"My star," he shouts. "The one that hung on my dressing room door. They had it in a glass case in the lobby, kept it all these years as a memento. I'm sure it's in here somewhere, and I want it."

"You used to be an actor?" I ask.

"I'm still an actor," he says. "I'm between engagements. But it just so happens that I once did four years here at the Majestic as King Lear. Standing room only. Long before your time."

The theater being demolished showed movies, but it's an old building, a place that could have once housed plays, I suppose. I try to calculate the possibility that this man is telling the truth. He senses this and says, "I don't especially give a rat's fuck if you believe me or not. My life doesn't depend on what others think."

This line rattles me, but I don't linger on it. "You shouldn't be out here," I tell him. "It's not safe on the streets."

"It's safe for me," he says. "Nobody wants to fuck with a crazy man. You haven't learned that yet?"

I'm bothered by this imparted wisdom more than anything, and suddenly I'm not at all sure what I'm dealing with here. I wish Gypsy were with me so she could read his mind and confirm his story. Then the man says, "Hey, your ring's going off."

The Danger Ring flashes red on my hand. I tap the inside with my thumb and raise it to my face. My best friend Ecklar's voice crackles through the static. "This is HALO Command. What's your status?"

"I'm peachy keen. You got something for me?"

"Negativo," he says. "The board is clear. Just checking in." Ecklar's only three feet tall, which he tells me is about average for the planet Andromeda. On that world, he has seventeen children and three wives, each of whom has at least one other husband. He was a physicist there, working on a way to end his civilization's war with the planet Malkovia, until an interstellar vortex experiment went wrong and threw him halfway across the galaxy.

"Nothing happening here," I tell him.

The white-haired actor says, "That's nice."

"No offense," I say. Then I cup the ring as if King Lear won't hear and ask, "Any chance Deb's in central control?"

Ecklar clears his throat. "No. Deb's not here. She's got Nate downstairs, I guess. I can patch you through."

"No," I say quickly. "It's nothing that can't wait. Over and out." I squeeze the ring, effectively hanging up. At the end of the alley, car horns blare, and a woman curses.

"What's the nothing?" the old actor asks.

I turn his way.

"The nothing that can't wait."

"The nothing is nothing," I say. "None of your business."

"All right by me. But I'll bet it's not nothing to Deb. If you can't talk about it, try roses. My Gloria always liked pink ones, before they bloomed, when the buds were all tight and waiting."

"Thanks," I say. "I'll think about it. I hope you find your star."

"Whatever," he says. "Hope and a dollar will get you four quarters and a broken heart."

I've had enough of this back-alley mystic, so I say, "Take care," and cruise into the night, cutting against traffic on 39th.

While I was getting ready for my shift tonight, Deb and I had another blowout, this time in front of Nate. I said things no four-year-old should have to hear. I want to apologize for the fight. I want to tell her how I rescued that family from the fire on South Holland and hear her say, "Good job." I want to tell my wife that everything will be OK.

But I know that these would be half-truths, and knowing this makes me feel the weight of that dying thing in my gut, and the pain in my skull spikes. I crave escape, even a temporary one. I head for the presidential district, to get away from the life I lead.

During my second year as a Guardian, before Ecklar joined the team, I charged ahead of Titan and the others into the underground lair of Professor Parallax. I hadn't yet learned that whoever goes first usually falls into the diabolical trap. I flew down a long hallway, dodging death rays and spinning metal disks, then burst into his laboratory, crashing headlong into a computer bank. When I recovered, I saw not one Professor Parallax but two dozen. Simultaneously, they all pointed my way and yelled, "Destroy him!"

They scattered for various control panels, there was a flash of white light, and I was gone. He hadn't killed me, of course. Despite what happened to Sparkplug, killing's always been against the rules. Instead, I'd been warped into an alternate dimension, Earth 1.2. In that reality, I was leader of the Guardians, Sheila and I never got divorced, and we had three girls. Deb was part of the team, and she and Sheila were best friends, like sisters. That Vincent Shepherd—who had a mustache—put me in contact with his reality's Brainbuster, who jury-rigged a device she thought would realign my molecules and shift me back to my rightful place in the infinite multiverse. But the gizmo wasn't entirely reliable, and it took me weeks of bouncing from Earth to Earth until I finally homed in on the world I'd left behind. Sometimes it feels like I never got it right.

The taxis flow beneath me on 39th, and I have the sense that I'm swimming upstream. If I were merely out to stop a crime, I could have my choice now on any block. Prostitutes gather on the corner at Hoover. Three hoodlums linger in the shadows by an ATM. But I'm on the prowl now for a very particular kind of criminal. Over on Eisenhower Avenue, just past a row of strip clubs, I see a sedan pull up to the curb in front of a boarded-up bookstore. The make and model—too nice for this ratty neighborhood—draw my interest. I settle on the fire escape of a pulsing nightclub across the street. A man with a wool cap emerges from the alcove of the bookstore. Through the rolled-down window there is a brief conversation, and an exchange is made. The sedan pulls away, and the man returns to the darkness.

Over the next half-hour, a few cars make use of the curb service. Like the sedan, the vehicles are consistently high-end, which suggests something about the quality of the product I'm dealing with here. Technically, what I'm doing could be considered a stakeout, and I am now in violation of the union's agreement with Kingdom Town's PD. They can write me a goddamn ticket.

While waiting, I try not to think about why I'm here. Instead, my mind goes somewhere else I'd rather avoid. It rolls back to that fire on South Holland, the part of the story I'll never tell Debbie. From atop a water tower, I smelled the first wisps of smoke. The house was just below me, and I floated down into the fenced yard right away. The first flames were licking low on the clapboard at the front corner of the house. I could've blown the fire out right then with a blast of my ultrabreath. Hell, I could've grabbed the damn garden hose and extinguished it like any ordinary citizen. But I found myself hesitating. I backed away into the shadows, through the chains of a rusting swing set. I let the fire burn. Nobody inside was in danger. Not really, not with me around. I haven't lost a civilian since Peru, and that was three years ago and under extraordinary circumstances. Gripping the swing chains, I waited till the smoke detector shrieked, and I heard the kids crying—a surprise. Then I stormed into action, and, yeah, I saved the day. This won't make the news or anything, but nobody can deny it. When I stepped back and allowed the flames to rise up the side of that house, I didn't know there were kids inside. If I did, I would've stopped it right away. I'm sure I would have.

And even though I'm so sure I'm a good guy, when the man in the wool cap leaves his alcove and climbs into one of those nice cars, I follow it without a second thought, my intentions far from pure. The car heads all the way down Eisenhower, past the Lucky Star hotel and casino, and into the warehouses by the rail yard. The car bounces through potholes still filled with this afternoon's rain, then pulls over by a parked Hummer and a motorcycle. The man in the wool cap steps out along with the driver, and the two of them casually scan the abandoned street—this time of night, everyone with a legitimate job is home with family. Satisfied that they are alone, they step up to a steel door and slip inside the brick warehouse.

At the door, I listen carefully and hear multiple voices, laughter, and a strange electronic clatter I can't place. I study the steel door and wonder if my foot would simply go through it if I tried to kick it in. There's also the wall itself. I could cover my face and run through the bricks. But I remind myself I'm not a young bull and decide to be creative.

The Harley is heavier than it looks, enough to strain my back. I doubt I could fly with it. But with my feet planted, I can carry the thing just fine.

I whirl a few times, like a hammer thrower, then pitch the motorcycle through the brick wall. It makes a hell of a racket and a nice hole, which I charge through into the chaos. I find myself in the middle of what looks a whole lot like somebody's basement.

Three guys sit around a card table in the corner, smoking. A bearded lard ass cuddles with a topless girl on a couch, and a boy stands baffled at an ancient Donkey Kong machine. I bolt to the card table, flip it over, and crack two heads together. The third guy, linebacker thick, sits in his chair and holds his hands up. He hasn't dropped his cards, and I see he's got three queens. The half-naked girl is screaming now, scrambling into the arms of the fat guy with the beard, who seems unfazed. He's not even blinking, just playing the role of calm kingpin, and I'm about to speak to him when Donkey Kong kid pulls a pistol and aims it at my face. The chubby wannabe godfather pushes the girl off him and lifts a hand, then speaks with a Central European accent. "Not the gun, Schullo. Only if you want to be pissing him off."

I turn to the obese leader and say, "You're smarter than you look."

"I was dumb shithead like this one when I was a boy. But now I know better. Where are police and sirens? I wonder. Do you have warrant for searching?"

The cardplayers gather now in a little huddle. On the other side of me, the kid hasn't lowered the gun. Stupidly, I've lost the momentum. All the advantage of my shock-and-awe entry has faded. I tell the guy in charge, "Where's your shit? I'm shutting you down."

"The fuck you are," the linebacker says as he charges. I step into his attack and smack an open palm into his face. It's the same kind of energy a normal man might use for a high five, but there's a satisfying crunch at the nose. The linebacker goes weak in his knees but doesn't fall. Blood dribbles from a nostril. His eyes roll, and everybody sees he's defenseless. But you don't get to assault a cape like me without paying a price. I poke my fist into his gut, doubling him over so I can baby-tap a knee into his falling face. He ricochets back up and collapses into a heap.

I turn back to Mr. European Union. He says, "Perhaps we can apply reason to situation."

After leading me down a slim hallway, the fat man fishes a key from his pocket and opens a door. Inside are a bare mattress, a wooden desk, and a metal cabinet. He opens it, exposing a mini pharmacy of bottled pills, tiny packets loaded with white dust, brown paper bricks. I scan the inventory. "What about the rest?"

"You are overestimating me. This is all the goods that I have."

"The Zone," I say.

He rubs at his beard and studies my face. "Xonopexal is high demand, low supply. This is economics."

I grab him by the shirt and pull him into me. "In ten seconds I'm going to fly straight up. I'll keep going until the air is too frozen and thin for you to breathe. Think you'll be cracking wise then?"

As he listens to my threat, which I truly wish I could execute, a grin spreads across his flabby face. "Mens like you I know when I was a boy. You like the smashing and hitting. The wars for you is always in your blood."

We look hard at each other, and it occurs to me that this guy's a veteran of one of those conflicts that involved ethnic cleansing. He's seen evil up close. And now he's staring me down. I let go of him, and he smooths his shirt, then goes on. "But the mask does not cover your eyes. And your eyes tell me there will be no arresting tonight. My strong new friend, I cannot offer you a thing I do not have. But I can find this thing for you." Slowly he slides a hand into his pocket and eases out a cellphone. "Then perhaps you can leave me to my capitalism." He tilts his head forward and raises an eyebrow, waiting for a response to his offer.

I wish I'd never come here. This asshole sees me for who I am and who I'm capable of becoming. I reach for his cell, yank it away, and crush it into glittery metal dust. His expression barely changes. So I turn and grab the cabinet by both sides. Though it's bolted to the floor, it comes up easy. I spill the contents out and then pound the cabinet onto the pile a few times.

Judging by the bearded guy's face, he's still unimpressed, unperturbed by the loss of inventory. But then his eyes flash behind me, and there's a bang. Something bites into my head, a bitch of a sting, and I turn to see Donkey Kong kid standing in the doorway with that gun aimed my way. On the wall next to the door is a hole from where his bullet bounced.

I reach back and feel my hair sprouting from a tiny tear in the mask. When I bring my hand around, blood spots the tips of two fingers.

The chubby crime lord begins to speak—"Schullo"—but in the breath before his next word, I flash across the room, snap that gun from the kid's trembling hand. Only when the boy starts screaming do I realize I got his trigger finger too.

He cups his good hand over his bleeding one and drops to a knee. His boss shoves past me, ripping off his shirt and balling it up to help stem the bleeding. The other two guys and the girl show up. One guy trains a shotgun on me, and the girl, ridiculously, has a knife. They all gather around the bleeding boy and face me, prepared to fight, ready to defend the weak and the wounded.

I know I could just fly away from this, but that's not what's going to happen. I'm only waiting to see which one will be first and reminding myself that each of them is a criminal, involved in illegal and immoral activity. Any justice I mete out is entirely warranted. This is what I'm telling myself when the bearded leader says to them, "Stop. We must think now of Schullo." He holds an open hand up to me, and it takes me a second to realize he's asking for the boy's severed finger.

Before I can decide whether to give it to him or start breaking heads, my Danger Ring starts blinking. They all wait to see if I'll answer, and I raise it to my face. "Invincible here."

Ecklar's voice crackles through. "The Chili's in Little Germany. Code 26. All-Star's on-site."

My friend is hard to rattle, but something in his voice sounds peculiar. Not nervous but weird. "Screw Clyde's secret codes. What's the deal?"

"Time is of the essence. Haul ass, Vince." Then he's gone.

I could take out everyone in this room in ten seconds, but that urge has somehow vanished. This wouldn't be worth even the minimal effort. "Back off," I say, and they slink to the other side of the doorway, clearing me a path to the hall. The guy with the shotgun keeps it trained at my face. I turn my back on him and take two steps, some part of me hoping he'll shoot and ignite the fight. Then the bearded boss says, "Mr. Vince," and I look back. He's holding out that open hand again. "For the boy. I am asking you please."

I toss the kid's finger onto the floor, snap his pistol in two ragged pieces and let them fall from my hands. Then I walk past the linebacker I knocked cold and step through the opening made by the motorcycle. The night air is cool and feels good in my lungs. I stretch a hand toward the sky and fly away from what's behind me, trying to put it all out of my mind. I want to be pure of heart for whatever's ahead, and I think about the situation that awaits me. It's something urgent and dangerous. And it might not be like in my heyday, when I battled at the bottom of the ocean or on the dark side of the moon. Evil has reared its ugly head now in a strip mall joint that serves jalapeño poppers and has fake astronaut helmets on the wall. But surely, lives are in peril. I streak up into the clouds hoping that some horrible crisis is unfolding, something that can only be stopped by a hero like me.

# TWO

*Positive Outcomes and Minimal Exposure. The Practice of Active Listening. Fight the Good Fight. Doing the Lord's Work. An Object of Pity.*

---

As I head toward Little Germany, I try to clear my mind in anticipation of the emergency. But I can't shake what happened in the warehouse, the things I did and the things I was about to do. And strangely, something still bothers me about King Lear and his lost star. Like me, that guy is clearly past his prime. Assuming his story is true, though, at least he had his season in the sun. This is one of the things keeping me awake lately, one of the reasons I only feel at home on rooftops, one of the things I can't explain to Debbie or Ecklar or even Sheila. It's not like I'm upset about being a has-been. I'm not a has-been. I'm a never-was. At twenty, twenty-five, everybody knew I was destined to be one of the greats, a Titan or a Paragon or a Sergeant Superior. Even Gypsy would emerge from her room in those doped-up prophetic trances and give me one of her deep, knowing looks. Lately, though, with my fortieth birthday bearing down on me, I've been wondering more and more just what she saw in that goddamn crystal ball.

I descend through the clouds near the Chili's, and nothing seems out of order. Clyde steps out from behind a minivan in the parking lot. I'm thankful he's dressed as a normal citizen, not in that gaudy All-Star costume, a bright yellow bodysuit that makes him look like a freaking figure skater. Subtle as always, he waves an arm over his head to get my attention. I land back behind the kitchen, and he joins me.

"What's the situation?" I ask.

He tosses me a backpack. "Get changed, quick as you can. The Mad Mongol's in the bar, doing shots and making threats. We want to take him out quietly."

Mongol's a bona fide bad guy, one strong enough that I can unload on him without holding back, so this news makes me a bit giddy. A good fight is just the medicine I need. But when I scan around for a little privacy, there's just a thin line of trees between us and an adjoining mall parking lot. So I back in close to the building by the grease dumpster and start stripping. Clyde says, "We go in as civilians, get close as we can, then I'll start an argument, and you take him out. I'll maintain the perimeter. You think you can handle him?"

I'm bent over, just stepping out of my leggings. "It's Mad Mongol, not King Chaos."

"Don't get all defensive. I'm just asking."

The door next to me opens and spills out light and the clatter of dishes. A thin waiter steps out, sees Clyde, checks out my boxers, and says, "Sorry, guys. Just getting my smoke break." He closes the door.

Clyde shakes his head like it's my fault. From the backpack, I pull out a flannel shirt, something with black and red squares. "Is my cover a lumberjack? Where the hell did you find this?"

"Just come on," he says. "The situation could be deteriorating."

I follow Clyde, who I've never gotten used to taking orders from. He's not a terrible guy, just part of the new guard. He joined the Guardians with Bigfoot and Ice Queen at the same time Debbie came on board, during a big shake-up about five years ago. Titan had retired, Menagerie had checked out, and Gypsy just couldn't hold it together anymore. On top of all that, Sparkplug's seat at the Guardian power table had remained empty for almost a decade. So the team needed some new blood. And

I'm OK with that. Change is inevitable. It's just that this younger generation has their own way of doing things. Like this. Way back when, Titan and I would've dropped through the ceiling, scooped up the Mongol, and dumped his drunk ass in the river. Case closed. Now, between lawsuits, federal regulations, insurance liability, and bad PR, everything's got to be low-key. On the rare occasions when we find a lingering, washed-up supervillain, it's all about Positive Outcomes and Minimal Exposure. We're licensed, and our union has oversight, even a mission statement we need to follow. Real heroes don't need mission statements.

All this bullshit is even thicker lately because of the Tucker Commission, a Senate committee that's studying the financial benefits of merging some of what they call Paranormal Action Units. In Texas, they cut the Rogue Rangers' funding in half, and the West Coast Super Squadron was totally disbanded. The rumor is the Feds want to make a lesson of the Guardians, cut us off too and show everyone how the public can get along fine without masks.

Clyde leads us through the front door of Chili's and past the crowd waiting to be seated, past the hostess at her stand. We cut through the dining area and round the bar, where drinkers sit atop stools watching baseball. I don't see the Mongol or any sign of trouble. "Clyde?" I whisper, but he keeps moving, determined.

"This way," he insists, dodging a waitress with a full tray of hot wings.

The thin waiter from out back emerges from the double swinging doors of the kitchen and avoids eye contact. Clyde is now ten feet in front of me. "Here," he says, and disappears around a corner into what looks like a private room. This is hardly a serious situation, but we shouldn't be separated. He knows that. So I power ahead quick, duck my head, and turn with my shoulders low, ready for anything, eager for a brawl.

The first thing my eyes register is Debbie, whose face is as stunning now as it was at our wedding. She's beautiful and young, and to this day I don't know what she saw in me. Lately, I think she's begun asking the same question. For now, though, she's beaming that model's smile and standing on those long legs at the front of a crowd of two dozen. Clyde turns to join the group, and in perfect unison they yell, "Surprise!" Balloons bounce along the ceiling, and streamers line the wall, and above them a banner reads, "Lordy, Lordy, Look Who's Forty!!" Clyde points a glowing fingertip at my flannel shirt, and a black dot smolders. "Gotcha," he mouths. Debbie shrugs apologetically and crosses the space between us with her arms out. She hugs me and whispers, "I'm so sorry."

I can't tell if this apology is for her part in the fight we had earlier or for being complicit in this cheery ambush, but I don't care. I embrace my wife, and her body feels good and warm in my arms. I don't attribute the heat to her ability to burst into flame.

Everyone's still clapping, and I begin to recognize familiar maskless faces. Some are ex-heroes from the old school, and a few are representatives from other lingering teams like the Renegades and the Southern Gents. Off to the side are Clyde's handpicked junior varsity team, his so-called Guardian Deputies. Young punks like Kid Cyclone and Jersey Devil and the Scarlet Speedstress, they hang around the HALO and take part in simulated battles under Clyde's tutelage. But completely unexpected is a singular gentleman rising from a corner booth. On fragile legs, Magus rises and tips his magician's top hat.

I pull back from my embrace with Debbie and scan the floor. "Where's Nate?"

After pausing for a moment, my wife says, "With Ecklar." My alien best friend has a way with both my sons, who seem to prefer his company to mine. Back on Andromeda, all his horde of kids must miss him terribly. As a cake is wheeled out (the thin waiter, of course), the assembled well-wishers break into a sloppy rendition of the birthday song. Debbie looks embarrassed for me, and Clyde sweeps his hands like a conductor. Just as the burning candles are presented to me, I see Billy along the back wall, behind everyone. Twelve years, and the prick hasn't aged a single day—same boyish face, same flaming hair. When the Guardians formed, because we were close in age, we quickly became inseparable. As always when he comes to me now, he's wearing his Sparkplug costume. A red lightning bolt crackles across the blue of his chest. This is the bright background for the lethal wound inflicted by King Chaos, leader of the Insidious Six. The charred black stain is right over Billy's heart, which I know is heavy and troubled still. He raises a red-gloved hand and nods. When I don't acknowledge his salute, my former teammate and best friend lowers his face, then turns and walks through the wall.

"Blow out the candles!" somebody shouts, and I realize the room has gone silent. I lean in and blow, and the forty flames flicker out, then they reignite, and everyone laughs.

"What the . . . ?" the waiter says, and Clyde turns to my wife, who is both a level-two telekinetic and a fire-starter. Our fearless leader assumes his principal voice. "Deborah."

The candles stay extinguished after my second attempt, and people crowd around, pat my back, and rattle off wisecracks. "How's it feel to officially be old?" asks the Jersey Devil, one of Clyde's prized Deputies. With thin, dark-skinned fingers, J.D. pinches at his satanic goatee and grins. The Devil, who used to run with a team of ethnically diverse heroes called the Spectrum. Among his powers is the rather nasty ability to cause others to experience waking nightmares. Part of me thinks I'm in one of his hallucinations now.

"Ain't it past your bedtime?" asks Robert "Bigfoot" Pembroke III, cracking a smile at J.D.'s side. Though he's a rich kid from Oregon, he insists on going by Bubba, part of his country-hick shtick. At will, he can make his body grow, and his strength increases proportionally, so at fifty feet he can yank a pine tree up by its roots. Unfortunately, as his muscle mass increases, his intellect declines. He elbows J.D. and says something about my eligibility for Medicaid.

While the thin waiter starts passing out pieces of cake, Debbie leads me by the elbow, away from the others. She hugs me again and says, "Clyde swore me to secrecy."

"This party was his idea?"

She nods. "I think he's trying to patch things up."

He and I had another throwdown a few weeks back after an unauthorized action I took in Biloxi. There was a hurricane, and people were in danger. I wasn't about to wait for a governor's signature on an Interstate Intervention Form. I say to Debbie, "Did you see Magus is here? I haven't seen him in five years." Her hand slides along my bicep, and I pause.

She says, "This isn't a big deal. And I don't want to spoil your party. But we promised each other . . ."

I turn to my wife and block her from the others. "Go ahead," I say. "I'm eager to hear what you have to tell me." This is the exact line Dr. Janet told me to use. My wife and I rehearsed this very scene in our therapist's office to enhance our flawed communication style.

"Maybe I'm still a little raw from our fight before, but when I heard you ask where Nate was, I felt like you were questioning me as a mother. In front of all these people."

"That's crazy," I snap. "I just was curious, and it came out. Can't I even ask where my own son—"

My wife's softening eyes tell me I am failing her, invalidating her essential emotional response, and I stop to recall Dr. Janet's script. I breathe in and out and practice my active listening. "I'm glad you're telling me this. I understand how you feel. I don't want you to feel bad. I am sorry. I cherish you and love you." Some of these statements have the added attraction of actually being true.

"Thanks," she says. She steps into me and presses her cheek into my chest, and her arms wrap around me and squeeze. My wife feels good in my arms. This is the kind of hug that once suggested a preamble to lovemaking. It's been five months since the night of white wine and tears, the last time we made a real attempt. The hairs on my arm begin to tingle as the air around us heats up. The two of us, still embracing, lift off the ground just an inch or so. My young wife's abilities are sometimes triggered by strong emotional states. "Deb," I whisper. When she opens her eyes, we come back to earth, and the air around us cools.

She lets go of me and wrings her hands together. "I should go call Ecklar. I don't want Nate staying up late watching westerns."

"Right," I say. Last week, Deb reprimanded me for letting Nate sit through half of *Guardians United II,* an old R-rated film version of the original team's battle with a race of rock people.

My wife is flustered now, perhaps by the emotions she's feeling, perhaps by their effect on her powers, but she scoots around the corner and is gone. The moment Deb disappears, Vivian zips to my side. As the Scarlet

Speedstress, she's been clocked at over one hundred miles an hour. She runs one hand through my hair and another along my hip. "How about a kiss from the birthday boy?"

"Don't," I say. Her breath smells of gin. When she snakes her hand around to my ass, I step back. "Enough." We're off to the side of the party but in plain view of anyone who wants to look.

The Scarlet Speedstress's eyes flicker, and I know she's remembering our encounter at a conference a few months back. We were riding the elevator up to our adjoining rooms. She was loopy on margaritas, and I was feeling pretty loose thanks to a double dose of the Xonopexal Dr. Hippocrates prescribed after my back surgery. She was unsteady on her feet, leaning into the faux-wood grain paneling of the elevator wall, one hand on the rail, one touching the ruby pendant just above her ample cleavage. Maybe Vivian noticed where my eyes had wandered and let herself slump into me. And yes, I put an arm around her slim hips, and yes, her red lips looked beautiful, and yes, I smiled when our eyes came together. But five seconds later, after she'd hit the emergency stop and stripped off all her clothes and mine too, I looked away from her naked body and said, "Get dressed. This isn't going to happen."

She reached an open hand for that part of me, and I'm only a man, so the natural thing happened. She said something about her hyper-metabolism and the depth of her needs. "C'mon," she whispered as she pressed up against me. "Say the word, and I guarantee you the best seven seconds of your life."

I pushed her away and reached for the pile of my clothes. "The word is no," I said. When I stepped off, she stayed on the elevator, I guess to go back to the bar and tend to her hyper-metabolism. But when I got to my room, I checked our adjoining door and found it unlocked. To my shame, I left it that way.

In the party room at Chili's, Clyde appears behind Vivian. "No fair hogging the guest of honor," he says. Lowering his voice, he says, "And Viv, lay off the booze. I need you sharp for the morning." Clyde has scheduled some kind of major war game for 9 a.m. "Most importantly," he says, "no powers in public, OK?" She rolls her eyes and walks away, deliberately dragging her feet in slow motion. She heads for Ice Queen, who is watching all this while sipping on a frozen daiquiri.

Clyde offers me a piece of cake and a mug of beer, something else that surprises me. He discourages any drinking, let alone while on duty. I accept both suspiciously, and he leads me to a long table, where my place of honor is waiting.

The party gathers its own momentum, fueled by alcohol and strained camaraderie. A couple of the old-timers, Vanguard 7 and Silver Centurion (whose name now seems to apply to his hair, not the armor he once wore), start trading stories about the Glory Days—the atomic shark-beast that crawled up on the Jersey Shore, the time the Guardians were tricked into fighting the American Champions. The younger generation feigns interest and pretends to show some respect, laughing when appropriate, showing genuine envy at the kind of real threats we once faced. The Deputies are taking their cues from Clyde, sucking up like they always do, and something about all this feels wrong. In the pauses between stories, I feel the weight of memory's balance. Nostalgia, in its essence, is a pleasant way to deal with the fact that the present sucks.

I glance over to see what my wife thinks of these stories of the days when I was young and strong. At the end of the table, she's chatting with Bubba, who had his thumbs hitched inside the straps of his denim overalls. The way he's eyeing up my wife, I'm thinking of challenging him to an arm wrestling contest.

The last time Debbie and I tried to make love, things fell apart when I paused and reached for the nightstand drawer. As I fumbled with the condom, her fingers found my hand in the darkness, and she said, "We don't need that, do we?"

The walls of this restaurant are decorated with memorabilia—reproduced movie posters, retouched black-and-white photos, a wagon wheel—the kind of stuff you'd shove in your garage if you had one. Somehow putting this crap on the wall makes it art, and no one minds it's all fake. It's supposed to be old but shines bright with its newness. The older something gets, the less it shines. This is a thing I'm learning.

The Pixie Princess, whose tightened forehead suggests a recent round of Botox, eases through the crowd pushing a high-tech wheelchair holding Boss Thunder. Not long after retiring, Thunder had some kind of seizure on the thirteenth green at Augusta. Pixie, nearly three decades his junior, quit the Fairy Force to "help tend to his needs." Rumors about her interests in his fortunes abound. Ecklar and Brainbuster helped design the chair, which has a computer equipped with a voice synthesizer. Pixie guides the chair alongside me and leans in. "Ned's had a great time, but we have to be heading home. All the excitement, it's a little too much for him."

She pats his sweatered shoulder. His eyes show no recognition, no awareness he's at a party. His right hand, strapped to a touchpad on the wheelchair's arm, twitches as he scrolls through letters. From a speaker mounted on the headrest comes a voice I can only think of as robotic. "Fight the good fight!"

Everyone at the table falls silent out of respect, and a few folks lift their glasses. Thunder taps his pad, and the refrain repeats. "Fight the good fight!" Once, this man could clap his hands and reduce buildings to dust. He's nodding now, spastically, and Pixie wipes a bit of drool from the corner of his mouth. He jerks his head away and slaps the pad with his hand. "Fight the good fight!"

Somewhere inside this shell, his soul is intact. This strikes me as marvelous and bitterly sad. Pixie wheels him away, almost against his will. And I wonder what the second half of my life will bring.

On Earth 1.3, I died at twenty-five in battle with Maelstrom. Apparently, his Apocalypse Machine was parked over Kingdom Town, destabilizing molecules and threatening the very fabric of reality. That Vincent Shepherd flew into the radiation storm, and even as it shredded his skin, he flew on, making his body a living missile driven into the heart of Maelstrom's reactor. In that reality's Center Circle, a grateful city erected a marble statue of me with my hands on my hips. Carved in the base were the words "Gone but Undefeated."

At the party, rumors spread about the trouble in Washington Park. Some say it's a turf war between rival drug gangs. Others speculate it could be a troop of homegrown terrorists, ready to wave the flag and strike down immigrant invasion. All matters the cops can deal with, unfortunately. Debbie starts working the crowd, chatting here and there with everybody, it seems. Now and then she moves behind me, and her fingertips drift across the back of my neck, something that feels so good it gives me chills. I just stay in my chair, nodding at the small talk around me. Every now and then I check out that wall Billy walked through, just to be sure he hasn't returned.

At one point, when there are no civilians present, Clyde stands and clanks on his glass. He offers a toast I can tell someone wrote for him—probably Ecklar, who's got a way with words despite his ESL. In the middle of the toast, with his glass raised, he says, "Vincent has fought the forces of evil for two decades, and his career will be remembered as one of the most impressive, certainly the longest. Everybody here knows we're sitting with a future Hall of Famer." The Deputies clap with unexpected enthusiasm, but they keep their eyes on Clyde, like they're applauding his speech more than my accomplishments. Standing behind me, Debbie rubs my shoulders, leans over and pecks my cheek. I can't help but wonder if perhaps she'll want to try again tonight.

With dramatic flair, Clyde pulls an envelope from his back pocket and starts reading a telegram from Arthur—"Good to be reminded I'm not the only old hero. If you think forty's rough, try fifty! Sorry I couldn't make it, but evil never sleeps." Titan's famous tagline draws great applause. Even these heroes are impressed that the most popular superhuman of the previous generation would spend his valuable time composing a message for me, a guy who started off as his teen sidekick. Once upon a time, Titan was the one we all wanted to be. But unlike most of the folks in the room, I actually had the chance.

Bigfoot pulls a karaoke machine out from under a table, and things start getting messy. He and the Jersey Devil end up arguing about the opening lyrics of "Ebony and Ivory," and when they finally get going, their attempts at harmonizing are painful. For an encore, they shift to "Walk This Way," and Ice Queen and Scarlett Speedstress start close dancing. Vivian slides a hand down Rose's back, stops just short of her ass, and of course catches me watching. Debbie finally sits next to me but gets pulled into a conversation with Typhoon Man about the new rules of engagement being drafted by the union. Along with being second-in-command of the Guardians, Deb's our local rep. Not wanting to get dragged down into politics, I excuse myself and head for the john. The beer tasted good going down, and sure, it took some of the edge off that spike in my head, but now I've got some low-grade heartburn kicking in. I can't even get drunk anymore.

Halfway to the bathroom, I see Magus sitting alone in his booth, elbows planted on the table, palms facing each other. A single sugar packet floats in the air between them. He's wearing his top hat and tux, though it hangs loose on his aging frame.

When he sees me coming, the packet drops and he starts to rise. I hold up a hand to stop him and stand tableside, like a waiter. He smiles up at me, a knowing look, and says, "So good to see you, Vincent. You look well."

"I'm getting by," I say. "How are you?"

He shrugs and smiles. "I'm blessed."

Magus found Jesus during a fifteen-year stint upstate. From behind bars, he reached out to me, wrote a letter asking my forgiveness and seeing if I could contribute something to a charity auction benefiting inmate literacy. Long before I became a hero, Magus was a small-time illusionist hood with a few above-average sleight-of-hand tricks. Midway through his career, on a museum heist in London, he stumbled across a wand rumored to be Merlin's. Oddly enough, this magical talisman capable of warping reality looks like any old stick. These days, we've got it under lock and key inside the HALO's Vault, gathering dust with a ton of other nefarious accessories. But decades ago, when Magus began wielding it, his powers and aspirations grew. In my earliest days behind the mask, before the formation of the Guardians, Titan and I foiled his zany plot to blackmail the city by turning the mayor and the chief of police into toads. Once he cast a spell that made everyone speak in rhyming couplets. His crimes seemed more charming than evil. Though always a criminal, he never struck me as a bad guy. I slip in across from him. "Keeping out of trouble?" I ask.

"I'm doing a lot of charity these days." He pauses to pick something out of his teeth, which I'm pretty sure are dentures. "Hospitals. Shelters. The churches that don't take issue working with someone with a checkered past. It's important to feel useful."

I try to think of something encouraging. "You're lucky to be doing the Lord's work," I come up with.

"Everyone is doing the Lord's work, Vincent. Some people just aren't aware of it. You know, I could use you anytime. You'd be a big draw. Maybe we could raffle off a flight around town with you or something."

My eyes roll to my wife, who is resting one hand on Typhoon Man's forearm. She's making a point, of course, and I know the physical contact doesn't mean anything. I'm just thinking of our courtship, how once she loved our nighttime flights. "I'd be happy to help," I tell Magus.

Magus rolls his wrist, and a business card appears in his gnarled fingers. He hands it to me. *Magus: Christian Magician,* it reads. *A Sinner Reformed.* At the bottom are his phone number and his real name, Martin van Alkemade. I tuck the card in the flannel shirt's pocket. Martin sips at his black coffee, holds the cup with two hands. On the table is a plate with crumbs from my birthday cake. In the room's far corner, Bubba begins to belt out "Ring of Fire." I see Clyde staring our way, suspiciously. I say, "I can't believe All-Star had the class to invite you. Must've been Debbie's doing."

Martin's fingertips rest on the rim of the cup. "Oh, I wasn't invited."

"You crashed my surprise birthday party?"

He nods. "In a manner of speaking." He waves one hand over his open hat, then reaches inside. He pulls out a bottle of beer and offers it to me. When I shake it off, he shrugs and sets it on the table anyway.

"So what are you doing here?"

"I'm not altogether sure," he says. "Most nights, when everyone is settled and asleep at the center, I go for strolls, just to stretch my old legs. I'll end up on the subway or in a taxi, then I walk again, just following the Lord's voice. Usually when I stop walking, I find somebody who needs help."

"World's full of lost souls," I say. I scan the room. "So who's in crisis tonight?"

"I don't know," he says. "I kind of thought it might be you."

I shake my head. "Sorry," I tell him. "My life's pretty peachy."

Magus seems disappointed, slightly embarrassed, and worried that I don't believe him. Mostly to fill the silence, he asks, "How's the little one?"

Thinking of Nate brings up an image from last week: 3 a.m., me on the couch, him standing before me sleepy-eyed, asking, *Why did you call Mom ridiculous?* I smile at Magus and say, "Nate's the best. The other day he asked me if I knew the difference between inertia and friction."

"Quite a curiosity for a five-year-old."

Nate's just four and a half, but I don't correct him. Thanks to Ecklar, he's reading at a third-grade level.

"What about Thomas?"

I reach for the beer, twist the top free, and take a slow drag. "Things with Thomas could be better."

"Teenagers are tough," he says. "At least that's what I hear. That's probably my one regret, and such a strange one, that I won't leave behind any children."

"Not that you know of," I say, attempting something like bawdy humor.

Magus smiles. His veiny hand stretches across the table, and his fingers tap my forearm gently. "Dear sweet boy," he says, "you don't know me at all, do you?"

As I try to make sense of what he's telling me, he points toward the sugar packet. It rises into the air and sails itself back into its container. "Listen," I ask, "you know anything about the Majestic?"

He looks at me.

"It's an old movie house on the south side. I'm wondering if it used to be a theater, if maybe you ever did your magic act there."

His eyes turn upward. "Were there golden orbs hanging off the ceiling? A big chandelier under the balcony?"

"I don't know."

"Then I can't say for sure. Maybe. Sorry, but my memory's slipping. Frankly, everything's slipping."

I know how he feels. The beer is no longer giving me a buzz, isn't relaxing the pressure ratcheting up in my head. In fact, there's a familiar tightness forming in my throat, the bitter taste of my own stomach acid. I reach in my pocket for some Tums, but then remember that Clyde packed these clothes. Magus says, "So, tell me what you'd like for your birthday."

"Antacids would be great. Got any in that hat?"

"I'm entirely serious, Vincent. You were always respectful to me, always treated me with decency and kindness. And I haven't forgotten how you flew upstate to speak at my parole hearing—more than once. I've made amends with those I've wronged. So, if there's anything I can do, anything within what's left of my powers, all you need do is ask."

I consider asking for another burning house, maybe a tip on some bank robbers I could capture without risking my back. I glance around the room, take note of Clyde coming our way, and lower my voice. "It's maybe not such a good idea to talk about violating the terms of your probation."

"Bone my probation. I'm seventy-seven. I doubt I'll see eighty."

Clyde sidles up to the table. "Try clean living. You'll live to be a hundred."

Magus gives me a look of disgust, and I shrug. Clyde goes on. "Listen, Mr. Magic, I just learned who you are, and I'm going to have to ask you to leave the premises. This is an invitation-only affair."

"He's with me," I say.

"We can't consort with known felons. Even when we're dressed like civilians. It may suggest the appearance of impropriety."

"Clyde, give it a rest, eh?"

He turns to Magus. "How did you learn about this gathering? Did you tell any of your cohorts?"

"I live in a nursing home, young man. Most of my cohorts these days wear diapers and use walkers with tennis balls on the legs."

"What's the big deal, Clyde?"

"The big deal is that I orchestrated this event. It's to celebrate your birthday and the illustrious career you've had. I don't want it spoiled by some villainous plot. For all I know, you could be under his mind control right now."

"I don't do mind control," Magus says. "It's morally reprehensible."

They keep arguing, but something Clyde said starts looping in my head. I scan the room and realize again that quite a few folks don't keep eye contact with me, especially among the young crowd. Jersey Devil sees me looking and actually turns his back. "Hey Clyde," I say. "You're being a bit premature talking about the career I've *had,* aren't you?"

Clyde's face turns two shades of red, and he looks to his left and right. Now I notice Debbie watching. Next to Typhoon Man, she stands up but does not approach. Clyde tells me, "I didn't mean anything by it."

Magus thrums the table with his fingers. "Liar."

"Clyde," I say. "You got three seconds to level with me."

He puts his hands on the table and leans down. "There's no need to raise your voice. There are civilians close by. Now look, you're a big boy, and your feelings shouldn't get hurt by this. Hear me out. It's just that there's been a lot of talk, with the Tucker Commission and all, about maximizing the team's assets. Maybe changing up the roster."

Acid sours my throat, and I have to swallow hard to force it down. "You're looking to put me out to pasture?"

"Don't be crazy. No one is talking about firing you. That'd be a PR nightmare. But yes, there are those who have begun to discuss your graceful exit from the active team."

I rise up and stiff-arm Clyde square in the chest, hard enough to launch his body straight back about fifteen feet. He flips twice in the air and lands upright on an empty table, then leaps down and assumes one of his bullshit kung fu ninja poses. Both his hands glow a dull red, a sign that he could be ready to unleash one of his starburst blasts. I'm striding toward him, ready and spoiling for all this, when Debbie steps between us. "Maybe you two didn't notice we're in public?"

Bubba has grabbed Clyde from behind. I say, "You know Clyde here's decided I'm past my prime?"

Debbie blinks. Both her hands are palm down on my chest.

"That's right," I tell her. "He's had his first original idea—a surprise retirement party."

Her hand over my heart tightens. "It wasn't just his idea," she says softly.

These words suck the life from me. My anger dissipates, and my knees go weak. Rather than fall, I stumble backward and sit down in the booth. Magus says something. Debbie kneels and tries to look into my face. "Get him some water." Bubba and Clyde step up behind her. Quietly, she says, "We all want what's best for you, Vince. And I think that means getting you out now. I need you healthy, and Nate needs you healthy."

"Hurricane Juno was a Category 5," I say. "People were in trouble."

Clyde says, "There are other ways to serve the team. We could use you in tactical training or combat analysis. You could oversee—" He keeps talking, but I don't hear a word. I'm disgusted with myself, that instead of feeling rage or betrayal, all I can muster is a gathering nausea. I feel tired and old.

Clyde's speech sounds like it could go on forever, so I'm thankful when his cellphone rings. This is followed immediately by Debbie's, then Bubba's. There is an awkward pause, then Clyde reaches into his pocket. Just as he's answering, my Danger Ring glows.

Clyde says, "Got it. They're all right here with me." He snaps his cell shut. "Trouble in Washington Park. Cavemen on the loose, throwing spears at tourists. And get this—there's a saber-toothed tiger! Ecklar just got the official request for intervention and support. We need to go."

Somebody puts a glass of water on the table in front of me, and I ignore it. Debbie stands and places a hand on my shoulder, squeezes it to show something, I don't know what. Clyde, giddy with the rare possibility of a genuine threat, says, "Given the circumstances, Vince, you should sit this one out. We can pick up the conversation tomorrow. Tonight, you're in no condition to fly."

He's wrong. I know that even on my worst night now, even with a few drinks in me and a spine bolted together with screws and rods, I'm twice the hero he'll ever be. I decide I'll prove it to him, prove it to them all, and I lift my head to show my wife my new resolve, show her my power and confidence. She'll see this resurrection, and it will ignite her, and she will look on me again with desire and love and belief. But when my eyes find Debbie's, all that comes back to me is disappointment, something just a few degrees shy of shame. It's more than a man can stand. "Go," I say.

Debbie says, "We'll talk later," then kisses me, not on the lips like a lover, but on the top of my head. I watch them leave. The Deputies join them at the exit, and the tumblers fall into place. Clyde has been recruiting all night, looking for my replacement. The trouble at the park could turn into tryouts.

Magus asks if he can do anything for me, maybe share a cab. I think about his wish and wonder if he could make me young again, but I recognize this as an absurd idea born of a bad night gone worse. I tell him I'm fine and get to my feet. I'm a little wobbly on my way out. The remaining well-wishers clear a path for me. There are a few pats on the back, something that makes me feel even worse. I won't be an object of pity.

Outside the cool air feels good. A breeze makes the treetops rustle a bit. Autumn isn't far off. My plan was to catch my breath, then change into costume and join the others, regardless of whether they want me or not. I can think of worse ways to deal with the night's revelations than beating on some Neanderthal or going head to head with a prehistoric man-eater. But in the parking lot, my resolve seems to weaken, and then I realize that Clyde has my mask and cape.

I don't know where to go. I can't think of what I should be doing. But I know I don't want to be where I am. So, dressed like any civilian in jeans and a goofy flannel shirt, I lift my arms to my sides and rise up into the night, hoping to outrun the man I'm becoming.

# THREE

*Taking Refuge in a Tree House. Periodicals of Questionable Literary Value. Bobbling Headlights. Debts You Can't Pay Off. Moving Unfettered into the Future.*

Below me, the city's density gives way to suburbs and strip malls, then hotels and gas stations clustered around interstate exits. I leave the highways behind, cross high above the Allegheny Mountains, pass valleys with towns nestled between sloping giants. Before long I find myself over the patchwork quilt of farmland and rolling open spaces of central Pennsylvania. Maybe it's seeing the barns and silos that makes me think of my ex-wife, or maybe I was thinking of her all along, but realizing my destination comes as a kind of inspiration, and I accelerate through the clouds. Less than a half-hour after lifting off from Chili's, I settle gently into a tree house in the branches of a sycamore on Sheila's farm.

The main house is dark except for the blue glow of a television on the first floor. Maybe it's Sheila watching late-night cable news, silently critiquing the biased coverage, gathering notes for her next lecture. But there's an equal chance it might be Thomas. I'm not exactly sure what I'd say to either of them. Actually being here has made me question my motives.

It saddens me to see the tree house fallen into a state of such disrepair. Rain has gotten in through a shattered window, and some wood beneath the sill is rotting pretty bad. A two-legged telescope sits crippled in the corner. This was one of the only projects Thomas and I worked on together as father and son, a feeble attempt at being a good dad on the verge of the divorce. When Thomas and I helped Carl build this tree house eight years ago, my son didn't yet know that I wasn't moving with him and his mother. To help ease the transition, I stayed for a couple weeks, sleeping on the couch. One brilliant autumn morning, Carl and I loaded a pickup with lumber and he scratched out a basic design on a napkin at McDonald's. Carl's a great guy—told me at the wedding that he and I were a good match, seeing as he had no sons and I had no father. And he never blamed me for the divorce, something I greatly appreciated. He was foreman on the construction site, and Thomas and I did our best to follow his instructions. When we finished, Thomas insisted we call it HALO 2. Both of us slept in it that night, shivering in sleeping bags side by side. The next morning I woke to an aching back and my eight-year-old son gazing out the window at the sun rising over distant peaks. This was one of my life's finest moments, and even in the instant I was lucky enough to know how good it was. But I also knew the rest. I knew that soon he'd find out I was leaving. Gypsy has told me that being able to see the future isn't all it's cracked up to be.

It looks like the farmhouse has fared quite a bit better. Since I was here last, Sheila's closed in the screened porch and added a brick deck in the back. Probably Carl's doing. The rhododendron she planted on the side have grown in nicely. She made the right choice, leaving Kingdom Town to return to her family's farm. It's peaceful out here, and I'd be lying to myself if I didn't concede that part of me, maybe the best part, wishes we had made things work, that I too could be living in this place. Central Pennsylvania probably doesn't have much need for a superhero, and I doubt the university would let me teach criminal justice classes with a mask on. But maybe as a civilian, I could sign up as an assistant wrestling coach at the high school. Even junior varsity would be fine.

As my eyes adjust to the dark, I make out a tiny cooler tucked in one corner. It's the kind of thing construction workers and fishermen use for lunch, and it looks less beat-up than the rest of the tree house. My heart lifts as I imagine Thomas climbing up here for old times, enjoying his solitude and a meal and thinking perhaps of me. I reach for the cooler but stop. I worry now that my son, like any teenager, is prone to certain vices. I worry that opening it could reveal a warm six-pack of beer, a pouch of marijuana. In my prime, I could have seen through the cooler's plastic, but now I'm going to have to open it. When I pull back the lid and reach into the blackness, my fingers find slick paper. A thick stack of magazines nearly fills the cooler. For a moment I imagine them as Guardian comic books, a hidden stash he keeps from his mother so he can maintain his teenage hostility while secretly admiring me. But they are too heavy for comics. In the darkness, I hold one up to my face and squint, trying to confirm my second guess (*Sports Illustrated*?). Then the Danger Ring glows, and in its red illumination I find myself inches away from two unnaturally huge breasts. There are pert nipples, a beaming smile, and spread legs. I drop the porno and stumble back. I am stupid and old. Old and stupid.

I squeeze the ruby and say, "Yeah?"

Ecklar says, "Vince. We both know you shouldn't be where you are."

I think of the little green man's supercomputers, their tracking systems, and the locator chip I know damn well is part of the Danger Ring's design. "No shit," I say. "I should be in Washington Park kicking some caveman ass. But I wasn't invited."

"I heard about Chili's. I'm sorry you learned about the situation that way. Wish I'd been there."

Because of Ecklar's appearance, he tends to draw a crowd and isn't much good on undercover ops. I'll say in his defense, though, he's loyal to a fault. If he's representative of Andromeda, it's a far better planet than ours. Still, I can't repress my anger at the evening's revelations. "Did you know this was coming?"

He is quiet for a moment, then says, "No, no. Well, not tonight at least. But Clyde did discuss this with me, the notion of you stepping down."

"And why, precisely, did you not knock him on his ass?"

There is another pause, this one long enough for me to imagine Ecklar running a long-fingered hand over his hairless, bulging head. "Vincent, Clyde is a troglodyte. Put that issue to the side. Really, do you think you can do this forever?"

In the main house, the blue TV light goes out.

"I don't want to do it forever," I say, not even sure it's true. "I just want to do it until—" The different ways to end that sentence—until I get it right, until I prove myself, until I have a chance to die like a hero—flash through my mind. And each of them seems right, and none of them seems right. I leave the statement unfinished.

Ecklar says, "You sound like shit. Why not come on home? I'll open a bottle of something unhealthy."

"How's Nate?" I ask.

"Snoring. We watched *Montana Moon.* 1930. Classic western."

"Let me talk to him."

"He's asleep, Vincent."

"I didn't get to say good night. That matters a lot to a kid, don't you think? He'll fall back asleep. Now wake him up."

"I have a rational counterproposal: you return and carry him down to your quarters. That sounds like what a father would do."

I'm about to say, *I don't need your approval of my parenting skills,* but I realize how right he is. Instead, I say, "The situation in the park is contained?"

"Interesting plot twist there. Apparently, hostages have been taken, some sorority girls. Clyde's opened up negotiations."

"He's negotiating with cavemen," I say. I'm sure Clyde's got a bullhorn. Guys like him love bullhorns. "I should be there." I accidentally speak this thought out loud.

"Maybe so. But I know you shouldn't be where you are. I'm not trying to intrude. I know this night is painful. But don't forget—things can get worse." With three spouses of his own, Ecklar fancies himself a bit of a relationship expert. He goes on, "You know how Sheila feels."

Upstairs in the house, a small window lights up. She's brushing her teeth, taking out her contact lenses. All this I see in my imagination, though not long ago my ultravision could have pierced the walls and watched her prepare for bed. In a way, I'm glad I no longer have that option. "I don't need you to tell me how my wife feels."

"Vincent," Ecklar says, his voice heavy and sad. "She's not your wife anymore."

When I crush the ruby in my fist, it bursts into dust. The gold band left on my finger reminds me of that other ring, and I tug it past my knuckle and toss it through the broken tree house window.

I know that my alien friend is right, that the most prudent course of action is for me to fly back to the city. Debbie will be worried about me, and perhaps later she'll try to offer comfort, stretch across the cool space between us in our bed and waken me with a touch. The notion of consolation sex makes my stomach tighten. More likely than not, though, even if something got started, Nate would appear. A creaking door would still Debbie's hand, and just like that, I'd find myself escorting our son back to his bed, where I would threaten him to stay tucked in, poking a finger in his face and gritting my teeth. All this in the slim hope of climbing back in my bed and groping my young wife. This is the sort of man I am on the verge of forty.

I descend the sycamore using the two-by-four ladder Carl nailed into the trunk, crooked now with the passage of time but still functional, then march through the leaves, wondering why Thomas hasn't bagged or burned them. I am confused and tired and still don't know what I hope to accomplish, but I step up on the porch and approach the door like some broken-down traveler in need of help. I thumb the doorbell, and I wait.

After a minute a light ignites inside, and I hear muffled footfalls. A yellow bulb snaps on over my head, and then the door swings back. Sheila stands in sweatpants and an oversized Penn State T-shirt, one that looks like it belongs to a man. She squints through her glasses, studying me for a second, then says, "Christ Jesus. Who the hell dresses you these days?"

"I know it's late," I tell her.

"Just tell me you're not here to cancel the plans for Sunday," she says. "That's taken some major negotiation."

"Everything looks great for Sunday. I just . . . I need to talk."

We stare at each other for a moment, then she quietly steps out of the way. I accept the invitation and cross the threshold. She closes the door behind me, and after another second of strained silence, she leads us to the kitchen. I take a seat at the round table, and Sheila yanks the pot from the coffeemaker. At the faucet she turns to me. "Is this a half-pot crisis or a full-pot crisis?"

"I'm not sure it's a crisis. More of a situation."

She fills the pot. "Don't quibble with my word choice, Vince. You're in my home. That by itself qualifies this as a crisis. Nathan and Deborah all right?"

"Sure, sure," I say. "Nobody's hurt or anything."

The coffeemaker starts gurgling, and she settles across from me, covers her mouth to hide a yawn. On the fridge behind her I see photos of her nieces and nephews, who were once my nieces and nephews. I want to ask when Katie got braces, how her brother's band is doing, how Carl's rehab is coming along after the stroke. But all this pertains to the life I left. On Earth 1.4, we lived happily ever after. Really. Me and Sheila went the distance, had two daughters after Thomas, ended up running a garden center from this very farmhouse. In the reality I occupy, she listens to the coffeemaker and says, "So you going to tell me why you're here, or should we do this multiple choice?"

"I'm sorry. I just feel kind of strange being here."

"That's because you being here is kind of strange."

I want to tell her she looks good. I want to tell her that I know about the choices she made a dozen years ago, but I don't know why she made them. I want to ask her if she knows how exactly I failed her as a husband. I want her to tell me how to get my old life back, or at least how to stall the disintegration of my new one. Instead of all these things, I ask, "So isn't it about time you went up for tenure?"

She cocks one eyebrow. "Vince."

I look away from her and see my fingers folded together on the table. "They're trying to force me out of the game."

"All-Star?" she says.

I nod. "Debbie too. She thinks it would be better for me."

"She's thinking like a mother, putting her family first."

"Yeah," I say. "That's the thing. She wants to expand."

"Come again?"

"Another kid. Deb wants to have another baby."

"She should do it while she's still young, if she's going to," she says. "I take it you're not on board with the plan."

"Face it, my track record's not the greatest."

I wait for her to tell me that my problems with Thomas aren't that serious, that he's just going through a phase, that I'm a fine and capable father. But she shifts, awkwardly, in silence. The oil heater kicks on, and the basement furnace rumbles beneath my feet. A moment later, warm, dry air descends from the ceiling vents. "I am glad to see you," she says. "I've been worried."

Sheila holds eye contact like a reporter conducting a hostile interview and waits for a response. I say, "I take it you know about Biloxi."

"Just rumors. Hal's still at the network and heard a few things."

While I'm tempted to finesse the facts, Sheila's pretty good at detecting my lies. "The first responders were a coast guard unit out of New Orleans. They found me pinned between a warehouse and a casino barge."

Sheila shakes her head. "Jesus, Vince. It was a Category 5. What were you trying to prove?"

I stand up so quickly I almost upset my chair. For the second time in an hour, someone close to me has asked this question. I try to think of an answer, but what comes instead is an intense flash of memory—Sheila and I on the balcony of our quarters in the HALO, baby Thomas asleep inside, both of us whispering so he didn't hear. *I know you're trying,* Sheila said, and she was holding my hand. *I know you're doing your very best with all this. But it isn't enough.*

Sitting down would seem stupid, so I go to the cabinets, open one, and find plates and bowls. Sheila tells me the next one over, and I get down two mugs. I pour us both coffee and shake some sugar into mine. Sheila takes hers black. That night on the balcony, when it seemed clear our marriage—our family—was hanging in the balance, I thought for sure she would come clean and tell me what I'd already known for almost a year. I thought my wife would confess. But when she didn't, I knew she never would. And rather than tell her I knew all about Sparkplug and put one more thing between us, I decided I'd swallow one more secret. It would be silly and cruel to tell her now, here in her kitchen at midnight, that I know she was unfaithful. Plus, I'd have to explain how I know, and that one even I still have trouble believing.

The day after the balcony, I came home from night patrol and found empty cardboard boxes stacked in the living room. Boxes and packing tape.

Sheila leans back into the countertop and sips at her coffee. I linger by the fridge, looking at the photos. "How's Carl?" I ask.

She looks at the floor, shakes her head. "We moved him to assisted living, a place over in Altoona."

"Shit," I say. "You should have told me."

"Why?" she asks. But before I can react, she says, "That was mean. He does ask about you."

I wonder what my ex-wife tells my ex-father-in-law. I used to go fishing with the old man to humor him. He smoked a pipe and told stories about growing up in the Depression, using a flour bag stuffed with rags for a football, that kind of thing. After the divorce, I realized how much I missed his company. I'm still studying the picture—Carl bent forward, braced up by a walker, next to Thomas in a bright baseball uniform. I say, "I don't know what I'd do if I quit. I can't imagine what my life would be like."

"Just because you can't imagine it doesn't mean that it couldn't be good." Sheila moves behind me and puts one hand on my shoulder. "You're a good guy, Vince." She squeezes, and my knees go weak.

"Maybe I'm just not ready to be done. I know I've got more to give. I don't think I've ever really shown just how good I can be."

Now Sheila pats my shoulder, the same way she'd console Thomas when he had a nightmare or broke a toy. My ex-wife, who knows me better than any other human being, makes me wonder if perhaps Clyde and Debbie are right. My best days are surely behind me. I'm past my prime. It just wasn't as good as I'd hoped it would be, and that makes it hard to walk away.

When the phone rings, we both jump. She crosses the kitchen in two strides, yanks it from the wall, and says, "Tommy?"

But the concern melts from her face. "Oh. Sorry. No, no, it's not too late. I was awake. Yeah, I knew that." Now she's looking at me. "Yeah, he's actually right here. We're having coffee and talking." She listens, smiles, suppresses a laugh. "Really everything's just fine. It was sweet of you to call." She nods, listens, nods again. "Sounds like a plan." She hangs up.

"Ecklar?" I say.

She turns back to me. "Guess I shouldn't be surprised he found my unlisted number."

"He's an alien super genius, remember?"

Her smile looks wonderful. "So how much of this is a birthday thing?"

I consider her question, then ask, "Remember how we used to celebrate my birthday?"

She folds her arms, hugs her own elbows, swivels her hips a bit. "I haven't forgotten much of anything Vince. It's not for lack of trying, though."

"Youch," I say. "Medic!"

She laughs, a sound that gives me chills and makes me cocky. "Any chance I could maybe just crash on the couch? I'd be gone first thing." She stops laughing. The furnace quits, and the house feels suddenly still. I say, "My ass is beat, that's all, and the air over those mountains was freezing. I wouldn't—"

She holds a hand up. "I'm sorry," she says. "It's just not a good idea."

"Sure," I say. "You're right." I dump my coffee in the sink, rinse out the cup while she tells me not to worry about it.

She walks me to the door. I decide to make it a quick exit. "Thanks for the coffee," I tell her. "I'm looking forward to Sunday, I really am."

She pecks me on the cheek. "Be safe, Vinnie."

I want her to say more, but she pulls back the door, and together we step through the threshold into the cooler air outside. The sound of a rattling engine draws our attention to headlights bobbling down the rutted dirt road. Sheila settles a hand on my arm. "You should go," she says. "You'll see him soon enough."

I step away from her, onto the porch, and I watch my son pull up and park his truck. When he gets out, I'm struck by how big he's grown in the few months since I've seen him. He barely pauses when he sees me, and he mounts the stairs quickly, as if I'm not between him and the front door. Face to face, but with him looking down, I say the obvious. "You're taller than me."

"Aren't you like two days early?" he asks.

I nod and tell him, "I was just saying good-bye." But I stand exactly where I am. "Sunday we'll have some fun."

My son still hasn't made eye contact. His hands are shoved deep in his pockets. "It'll be good to see Nate."

To ease the awkwardness, Sheila asks how the game was. Thomas looks her way and answers. "McCarthy dropped a pass in the end zone. We lost 35–32."

"That's rough," I say. "Did you get in any good hits at least?"

Thomas shakes his head, and Sheila steps to his side, one hand finding his shoulder. She fixes me with a pained expression and says, "Thomas decided to focus on advanced calculus and physics this semester. He may do baseball in the spring."

"Sure," I say. "It's a good idea to make choices based on your priorities."

My line from *Father Knows Best* falls flat, and I consider simply flying away from all this. But even in the tension I find it feels good to be here, the three of us beneath this yellow light in the cool air. The paint along the porch rail is flaking, and I imagine Thomas and me in ratty sweatshirts, speckled jeans, sanding and dabbing paintbrushes along the spindle works. I remember being on this porch that last day with Thomas, before I left the family, looking away from his face, focusing on the sleek curve of these wooden spokes. Back then, they didn't need painting.

Sheila lifts her chin at Thomas. "How about that other thing?"

Thomas does not blush, but he glances at me then away again before answering. "Not great. But it could've been a whole lot worse. What you said was right."

"Of course it was. I'm your mother."

They smile at each other, and I smile too, though of course I have no idea what they're talking about. Feeling left out, I take a stab with, "So what's her name?"

My son cocks his head, and his eyes find mine. "As if you care."

"Thomas," Sheila says.

"What?" he snaps. His chin is raised, his jaw set. I recognize this as an aggressive posture, a possible prelude to violence.

"Go inside," she tells him.

"What? I'm supposed to pretend?" Here he looks at me again, and his eyes are hard. "Gee whiz, Dad, you're the best. I'm always so glad when you help me solve my life's problems."

I hold up a hand. "Hang on now. I've always been there for you."

"Yeah right, when some freakin' plant monster wasn't attacking."

"Give me a break," I say. "Every job has certain demands. With great power comes great re—"

"Stop!" he shouts. "If I have to hear that stupid saying one more time, I swear I'll throw up."

Sheila says, "Listen, guys."

But I go on. "That stupid saying is part of a code of dignity and honor, something that gives a life meaning."

"So that saying is the thing that gives your life meaning? Classic. A cheesy motto and a cape, and poof! You're fulfilled. You really do live in a fantasy world." He doesn't slam the door behind him, but I hear his feet banging up the stairs.

"It's a rough age for boys," my ex tells me. "Raging hormones."

I think of the magazines in the tree house.

"He'll come around," she says. "It's just your turn right now." For a couple years after the divorce, Thomas blamed Sheila. They fought all the time, and he begged constantly to come live in the HALO. Almost every weekend he slept over, hanging out with me and Ecklar. Then once, when I was out here dropping him off, we lingered together on the porch. He told me he'd figured out what the problem was between me and his mom, that he'd found a way to get everything back to the way it was before. *Stop being a hero,* he said, just that simply. *Be with us instead.* I guess on Earth 1.4, I did as he asked. But in this world, I stood stone silent for five minutes, while he looked into my face and tears gathered on the rims of his eyes. Then I shook my head and walked back to the hovercar. Thomas canceled our weekly visits. Later, when Deb became my wife, he refused to attend the wedding.

"Well," I say to Sheila. "Maybe we'll straighten a few things out on Sunday."

When I turn away, she takes my hand and stills me. "Tomorrow Thomas'll sleep in till nine or ten," she says. "If you promise to be gone before he comes down, you could take the couch. It's late."

I picture Sheila sneaking down the stairs in the dead of night, climbing on top of me. I shake the image from my head. "Nah. It's better I get back."

"If that's what you think." She's still holding my hand, but there's no romance in the touch. We're old friends now who share a fractured history and a child. Nothing more. Still, I do not want this scene to end. I remember her phone call. "Ecklar gave you a message for me?"

She thinks, and it comes to her. "He offered to come get us Sunday morning. Wanted a chance to visit with Tommy."

"Sure," I say. "Good old Uncle Ecklar." I look into the starlit sky, trying to pick a destination.

"Be safe," she tells me again. She squeezes my hand twice, a sign of reassurance or encouragement, then lets my fingers slip from hers.

I can't think of anything good to say, so after a time I step away from her, push off from the porch, and let the air take me upward. I float straight up, over the house and into the cold starry night. When I'm sure I'm out of sight, I hover and watch the house. She's already back inside, but I do see the lights go out downstairs, leaving only the white rectangle of Thomas's bedroom. I imagine her knocking gently on his door before going in, the two of them talking, she trying to explain to my son that I really do love him, that life is more complicated than he can realize at sixteen.

What I do now sickens me really, but I'm so damn tired, and it feels so wrong to leave this place. It's like walking away from a fire when you're cold. I relax my mind, and my body slides back down till I set down near the chimney. It's a few feet over to the dormer window, and I ease my ear up against the wall. Eavesdropping on my former family with what's left of my ultrahearing, I'm not sure what I hope to learn. Perhaps specifics about the girl Thomas is pursuing, perhaps some hidden tender feelings about his father. But the first thing that comes through the brick is my son saying, "He's just such a loser."

"Your father's not a loser," Sheila says, a knee-jerk response I'm not sure she believes.

"Why was he even here?"

"That's between us. He and I, we're still friends, you know."

"If you say so. Everybody makes choices."

"Don't be ugly, Tom. I know you're angry at him."

"I'm not angry. I'm just tired of pretending to care. It's not fair—you got to divorce him, make him not your husband. But me, he's my father no matter what. I wish he'd just go away and stay gone."

"You don't mean that."

There's a silence, and I picture my ex-wife giving our son a look. But rather than backing down, he pushes forward. "Why did you marry him in the first place?"

I press my head into the brick so hard I nearly crack it. Sheila's words are soft, slow. "He was a different man then," she tells him. "People change, Tom. That's something you'll have to learn. As you grow, you'll change too."

"Sure thing," he says. "Just so long as I don't turn into him."

"OK," she says. "Tell me more about halftime."

They keep talking, but I pull my head back. My son's words have weakened me, sucked out any vestige of hope for salvaging this night. I lift away from the house, away from this family that is clearly mine no more.

Surrounded by clouds, hidden, I fly in the general direction of Kingdom Town. My elder son, I have to concede, is lost to me. I could no more be the father he needs than I could be the husband Sheila once wanted. But I still have Nate. I can still try to do better with my second child. I decide that I will go home and bring him to his bed. I will sleep on his floor to be there when his nightmares return. Tomorrow I will skip Clyde's stupid war game drills and instead spend the day watching cartoons with Nate. We'll play with Legos, build a castle and spaceport. I'll read to him and have him read to me. Maybe I'll just quit the team to devote myself to him entirely.

But all this reeks of fantasy, and I know it. Despite what Dr. Janet has told me, recognizing one's delusions isn't helpful. It only makes you feel worse.

In Biloxi, I stood my ground on Highway 90 in sustained winds over 150 miles per hour, wind gusts up to 200. At that point, I'd stopped looking for stranded civilians and knew I was alone. The storm surge was up to my belly, and the waters were rising. In those conditions, flying would be tricky, but something I might manage. Still, I did not leave. Debris spun in the air, and I let the hurricane pelt me with rage. Something, an oil drum maybe, slammed into my face, and I nearly passed out. But then I heard the sounds of people crying for help, screaming loudly enough to be heard over the howling of those locomotive winds. Peering into the pelting rain, I saw the shape of what looked like Noah's ark, shifting in the rocking waves. It was some kind of casino hotel, built on a barge and loose from its dock. Half the size of a football field, it lumbered my way. And though I could see no people, and my brain told me there was no way anyone was inside, my heart heard their desperate cries, and I knew I had to save them. So, instead of swimming clear or trying to take flight, I tried to find some purchase beneath my feet and braced myself the best I could. For the sake of those people, I raised my hands and stood my ground.

I came to when the eye passed over. In water sloshing up to my waist, I was pinned between the sideways barge and the shell of a warehouse, and I could only see a sliver of bright blue sky above me. I was weak and couldn't move. Even breathing was hard. I knew the second half of the storm was bearing down on me, and I thought it quite likely I would die. And this seemed fine with me, perhaps even better than fine. Maybe because my head got whacked or maybe because I'd already gone a little bit batty—I heard people clapping. From the sideways casino, which I knew to be abandoned, I heard cheers and applause. I'd blunted the force of the barge just enough. I'd saved them all. And it was such a pleasant delusion, waiting for my end that way, that in the moment I truly wished it were real.

Maybe before I fly back to the HALO, I'll visit a middle-of-nowhere pharmacy, one that's not open all night. One that has no security cameras. The Zone helps me forget who I am, so I can pretend to be the man I'm supposed to be.

I start scanning the landscape below me, looking for a small town or a cluster of lights. Instead, though, incredibly, I pick up a flying figure. It's too small for a plane, too big for a bird, rising toward me. Even in the moonlight, without being able to see his bright red hair, I recognize Sparkplug. He floats alongside and says, "Thought maybe you could use some company."

I stare straight ahead, rub at the back of my neck, and wish this were a dream. "Please just fuck off, Billy."

"Why don't you let me help you? Look, I know you're having a doozy of a night."

"Can't you go haunt somebody else?"

He shakes his head. "You're the only living person I've spoken with since the accident."

I pretend I don't see him and consider his choice of words. Accident. At the World's Fair in Hamburg, King Chaos had just done the unthinkable, defeating Titan in hand-to-hand combat. The rest of us—Gypsy, Sparkplug, Menagerie shaped as a green-eyed rhino—surrounded him. Chaos, wearing the full red-and-black battle armor that covered even his face, knew that with Titan down, I was the next biggest threat. He turned toward me with that helmet crowned with three horns and unleashed a laser blast from one of his power gauntlets. The blue beam came right at me, but at that point in my life, I truly was impervious. I knew I could take it, and then I would move in, defeat the man who had defeated my mentor. I would take my place at history's table.

But that didn't happen. Instead, Sparkplug jumped in front of me, absorbing the blast and suffering a mortal wound. Chaos escaped from Gypsy and Menagerie. As for me, I held my friend as he died.

In the twelve years since Billy's passing, he and I have had maybe a half-dozen conversations. His appearances come in clusters, usually around some major event in my life. The last time was the birth of Nate. Billy showed up in the damn maternity ward. Looking at him now, flying beside me at high altitude, a strange question occurs that I can't help asking. "So you're saying you actually speak with dead people?"

"Don't sound so surprised. I'm in the club."

I laugh but catch myself. It's too easy to forget that we're not friends anymore. Though the wind is biting cold, I accelerate with the slim hope of leaving him behind, but he keeps pace easily, something he could never do when he was among the living.

"It's kind of against the rules," he tells me, "but I could get a message to somebody if you wanted. Really, anything I can do."

I picture my father, who died when his NASA rocket exploded on the launchpad. Then my mother, who loved to travel but despised maps. I remember the eyes of that woman who burned to death in my arms in the fire in Peru. What would I say to any of them? But then I come back to where I am and what Billy's trying to do. "Some debts you can't pay off," I tell him.

"That's what you think I'm doing? You think I'm haunting you all these years hoping you forgive me?"

I plow into a cloud bank, ripe with moisture and blessed with zero visibility. I don't need to see his face anymore. The truth is that I have forgiven Billy. In my heart, at least a dozen times, I've let this whole thing go and been at peace, focused on the good in my life. That's the value of confession as well as forgiveness. They free you from the past so you can move unfettered into the future. The only problem for me is that the forgiveness never sticks. The old bitterness worms its way back into my heart, and I am cast down. I emerge from the cumulonimbus, and he's still at my side. I pull up and hover in midair, lay a hand over my heart, and say, "I grant you absolution."

He frowns, not sure if I'm serious.

I try to look as sincere as I can. "I forgive you of any wrongdoing and free you from further obligation to me. I hereby forgo my vengeance. Now please, fuck off."

Billy shakes his head. "I'm worried about you," he says. "That's why I'm here. And I miss you. I miss how you used to be before everything turned. God, Vince, remember how you used to be? You weren't like this. You used to shine."

I know exactly what he's talking about, the glow of confidence and true invulnerability, and I barely catch myself from saying *I miss me too.* But his words have spurred another notion I can't shake. "I guess Sheila didn't feel that way."

"You can't believe that," he says. "She did what she did. But she never stopped loving you."

"Shut up," I say.

"Or what, you'll kill me? It's true and you know it. She told me once, before we'd done anything, she said—"

"Stop talking."

"I'm not going to deny that she and I, that we developed feelings for each other. But you're crazy if you think she didn't love you. We both loved you, Vince. And in all the ways that matter most, we both still do."

I reach for his throat but clutch only air. Though he knows I can't hurt him, he flinches at my attempt, and his eyes dim with disappointment. Then I say, "Understand me, Billy. There's nothing you have that I want, nothing you can say I want to hear."

These words wound my former best friend, the man I thought would fight by my side for decades, help me change the course of history and make the world a better place. When he closes his eyes it's reluctantly, and I can tell he's got the message. His image shimmers and fades until he's gone, and I'm floating alone in the clouds over central Pennsylvania. Some part of me I hate misses him.

Barely a month after his funeral, Billy first appeared to me and confessed about him and Sheila. I was so distraught—at the loss of my friend, at the loss of my wife's fidelity—that I went kind of nuts. People thought the three-day bender was some aftershock following Billy's horrible death. Titan gave me a long pep talk about fallen comrades and renewed his vow that we'd find Chaos and make him pay. Ecklar, who up to this point was only doing technical support for the team, was driven by guilt to find a way to get onto the field of combat despite his diminutive size. He went to work designing a battle suit of his own, one based on a version of Chaos's armor we'd confiscated from an abandoned hideout in Madagascar. I knew it was a bad idea, messing with technology we didn't fully understand, but against my better judgment I helped him test out the old armor, gave some suggestions for improvements to the weapons systems. Ecklar just wanted to make a difference, and how could I blame him?

As for Sheila, in the aftermath of Billy's death she tried to comfort me in the way she always found most successful, and one afternoon while Thomas was napping, we fell into the old flow. We were in our bed together rolling and naked, and it shouldn't have felt good, but it did. Then I found myself wondering if Billy had kissed this exact spot on her neck. If her hands now on me had caressed him in the exact same way.

I'd lost my wife, just as I'd lost my best friend. The same way I'd later lose Thomas. And now I'm losing Debbie, because I can't bring myself to give her what she wants. I'm nothing like the hero I once thought I was. I am not the man I wanted to be. And at forty, there seems little chance of turning all that around. Only Nate stills looks at me with admiration. It's wrong, I know, to place such a weight on a child, but he can still justify me, give my life meaning. Tonight, my boy can save me. I know he can.

I think of Nate and burst into high altitude, where I go to full burn. At this velocity, my body creates friction with the air, and I heat up, leaving a fiery wake. Once I hit top speed and streak over the countryside, I must look like a falling star.

# FOUR

*Matters of Great Import. The First Step in Being a Good Father.*
*Anomalous Radiation in the Upper Ionosphere.*
*Everything We Set Out to Do.*

As I approach the HALO, floating and spinning slowly a half-mile over Kingdom Town, the hangar doors split down the center and begin to recede. The column of bright light expands, and I see a solitary figure standing in the back of the landing bay. The planets are finally aligning. Somehow, Nate is waiting for me. He's always been a perceptive kid, and I shouldn't be surprised that he sensed his dad needed him tonight. Before I put him to bed, I'll make us some hot cocoa and we'll talk. We'll discuss his latest science project. I'll let him tell me about that western he watched with Ecklar. I'll ask what he wants to be when he grows up and hold my breath waiting for the answer.

Only, as I come through the doors, I see something's not right with my son's head. It's too big. It's not Nate who steps forward to greet me but Ecklar. His hands are behind his back. On his green-skinned face, his slit of a mouth forms an expression of deep disappointment. I know how he feels.

"What precisely were you thinking going to see Sheila?" he asks. He's wearing fuzzy yellow slippers and a dirty apron that reads DON'T SAY THANKS, JUST EAT. "Really, explain to me the optimum outcome."

“I needed a friend,” I say. “That list looks to be getting shorter all the time.”

“Abandon the martyr act and come with me. It’s cold out here, and we have important matters to discuss.”

“The park?” I say. “How are the hostages?”

“Drunk, as it turns out. Those cavemen were fraternity boys, and the ‘hostages’ were from a sorority. It was all some kind of massive prank gone awry.”

“And the sabertooth?”

“Stolen team mascot. Clyde insists that mind control is involved, but Deb sent me a text. The only mystery is what they were drinking.”

At the entrance, Ecklar’s thin fingers run along a control panel, and the hangar doors grind closed. As I follow him along the curved hallways, I tell myself that he’s almost the same size as my son, that mistaking him for Nate was just a manifestation of my desire, not a hallucination brought on by the Xonopexal I swallowed dry twenty minutes ago.

I found a closed CVS on the outskirts of Binghamton, went straight through the plate glass windows like a car with no brakes. There was a whole box, of course, half a shelf really, but I only took a single bottle. My back’s in real pain. My need for pharmaceutical relief is entirely biological. And the ache in my spine has indeed diminished, though the rise in spirits I also expected has yet to materialize. I feel hazy, not high. I may need to increase my dosage.

The elevator brings us to Ecklar’s quarters on the upper level. He opens the door, and as usual, I’m taken aback by the mess. A dining room table overflows with paperwork, reports from his experiments and unread fan mail. In his time on Earth, Ecklar, who does not sleep, has mastered a dozen professions: he’s composed two operas, earned a graduate degree in landscape architecture, learned Navajo, and advanced to the final table at the World Series of Poker. Just past a row of his abstract paintings, by the sliding glass door that goes to the balcony, his battle armor stands like a statue. Once, this technological wonder blew a hole the size of a tank in the Great Wall of China. Now, draped over one robotic arm is a wet bath towel.

Ecklar leads me into the kitchen, which seems a half-scale model of the real thing. As the HALO's architect, of course Ecklar customized his quarters. The miniature countertops, only two feet off the ground, are covered in white flour, and pots and pans pile up in the tiny sink. Despite his status as supergenius, Ecklar's efforts at cooking have consistently failed. He walks to the short oven and pulls down the door, releasing a smoky cloud and a burnt odor. As he fumbles with two lobster claw oven mitts, he says, "Foznar's beard! There goes my blueberry banana bread."

He dumps the pan on a counter, then gives me a disgusted look. He slips off the apron, folds it, and tosses it on the toylike countertop. Naked except for his fuzzy slippers, he crosses his apartment and enters his private lab. For a moment, I think he's just walked away from the whole situation and won't be coming out, but then he emerges, holding a white box in his stringy hands. He offers it to me, and when I open it, I find a new Danger Ring. "You think I'm going to need one of these?"

Ecklar gets a knife and starts digging out the bread. "Vincent, I know you had a rough night, but it's probably a good idea if you quit being such an unmitigated ass. Later, you will see my wisdom is sound. There are things we have to talk about now. Matters of great import." He deposits a crumbly piece on a napkin and hands it to me. "You should eat something."

I take a bite, and, no surprise, it's awful. He sees me struggling to chew and gets a glass of milk. He asks, "So what do you think?"

I put the bread down. "Don't quit your day job."

He says, "You will regret being unkind to me this day. I tell you this as your *naddeo.*"

The Andromedan term translates to something like "friend who stands at my side when all others have left me, though I am faced with a thousand fierce enemies, each with a sharpened spear." He doesn't use it except on occasions like this, when things are pretty serious. I try to read Ecklar's alien expression, guess at his agenda. When I fail, I simply ask, "How's Nate?"

"Passed out on the couch in my media room. He very much enjoyed the movie."

"I'll carry him to my quarters," I say.

"Perhaps that can wait until we've spoken."

"I think whatever it is can wait. He's my boy."

Ecklar finishes chewing a bite of the bread. "You are being unreasonable and obstinate."

My friend heads for the sliding glass doors beyond the living room, and, after a moment, I follow. We pass his man-sized battle suit, standing like antique armor in the corner, its golden luster covered in a fine layer of dust. Except for its color, it really does look like a replica of King Chaos's. All across the chest plate, Ecklar has papers held up by thick magnets. Some are shopping lists and coupons; others seem to be diagrams for the interstellar vortex generator he's been working on for nearly two decades. Like anybody, my friend wants to get home. I wonder, though, why he's kept the armor here in his living room. Why keep this constant reminder of his best days in a public place? I consider asking Ecklar if he wants me to store it down in the Vault, but then it occurs to me that I might not be the only one clinging to the past.

Ecklar pulls on the door handle, and a gush of wind sweeps in, making me think of flying. The crammed patio has one miniature seat, a gas grill, and a dying ficus. All around us, patches of wispy clouds drift and float, pull apart and come together. The hum of the HALO's antigravity engines fills the air. Like everything else in this place, the technology is pure Andromedan. In his old life, Ecklar designed command stations like this for his planet's war with the Malkovians, a ruthless race of fifteen-foot-tall lizard people. Together, he and I move to the railing, which only goes up to my knee. Almost three thousand feet below us, Kingdom Town stretches out like a map.

Ecklar sets his hands on top of the railing, right at my knees, and gazes out on the skyscape. "You and I, we've done lots of good, don't you think, Vincent?"

Ecklar usually only waxes philosophical late night and post-vodka. But something in his voice is intensely sober. "I guess," I say. "What's your point?"

"I'm not sure. We've been allies for coming up on twenty years. I have fought beside you in countless battles. And I refuse to think it's all been in vain. This world is better for our efforts. I know it is."

He sounds like he's trying to convince himself. "We've done a lot," I say.

"Certainly more than we expected when we began. Remember those gaudy costumes? Titan's ridiculous battle cry?"

"Go! Go! Guardians!" I say.

Ecklar says, "Hee hee hee," which is the sound he makes when he finds something funny. Andromedans apparently don't laugh naturally.

"Look, I know Deb wants me to quit, be some kind of stay-at-home dad and sit on my ass waiting to collect my pension. But I'm not ready to talk about my career in the past tense."

He releases the railing and looks up at me. His eyes tell me I'm misreading him, and again I realize that he's the exact same height as Nate. "I know, *naddeo,*" he says. "But I am."

I gape at him. "You've completed your generator?"

He shakes his green head, then explains. "For six weeks I've been detecting a buildup of anomalous radiation in the ionosphere. I'm virtually certain now that it's an Andromedan transport signature."

"Speak English."

"Someone's been working on the interstellar vortex from the other end, constructing a tunnel through space from Andromeda to Earth. They're coming to get me, Vincent. My people are coming to bring me home."

I feel dizzy, almost like I might drop over the railing, a sensation I blame in part on the Zone. "That's great news," I hear myself saying. "That's wonderful. How long?"

"My calculations suggest it will be fully formed in the next few days. A week at most."

"And then you'll be gone?"

He nods.

A plane floats across the star field above us. I back into the sliding glass door and wish I could sit down.

"You're the only person I've told. And I'm telling you now because I feel bad about leaving you. I don't want you to be the last one."

"You think I should quit?"

"Our time is done, Vincent. The kind of thing we used to do—it's obsolete. There aren't any more villains."

"There will always be villains."

"You know what I mean. The world changed around you. It's time for you to accept that."

"I hate change."

"I know you do. But Debbie and Clyde came to me on the very day I was coming to my conclusions about that radiation. It's a kind of galactic harmony. The last two original Guardians. We could go out together. Really Vincent, that business in Biloxi. You can't think you're making good decisions."

"It was a Category 5," I say.

"There's nothing left for us. We did everything we set out to do."

Not everything, I think. I picture the Guardians, all of us standing over Sparkplug's grave on a day with a perfect blue sky. It was Titan who said it, but he spoke for us all. *We'll make Chaos pay.*

Just then, a rapid series of beeps sounds from a speaker on the outer wall. The HALO's computerized voice says, "Incoming heat signatures. Recognized and affirmed as non-hostiles."

Rising up from below us, I see a dozen shadowy figures and a hovercar. The triumphant heroes are returning. My wife is surely among them, and right now I have no words for her. Ecklar says, "I'd better go help debrief these guys."

"Sure," I say. Even though it was all a hoax, there's a ton of paperwork. By the time Debbie gets out of that meeting, I'll either be passed out or pretending I am.

"There's more to this, Vince, a silver lining. Clyde has put together a little something to send you off in style."

"Clyde wouldn't know style if it bit him in the ass."

My friend makes his laughing sound, but I can tell it is more forced than usual. He didn't think it was funny. He pats me on the leg, then shuffles off.

Once he's gone, I remain on the balcony alone for a little bit, trying to get a grip on just what I'm feeling. The wave of anxiety at Ecklar leaving, the deep desire to smash Clyde's skull, the consuming regret at a life that isn't what it was supposed to be: all this swirls in my head. I can't quite be sure how much of it is compounded by the Xonopexal, which is supposed to take the edge off things like anxiety.

Finally, I decide to gather my son and return to our quarters. The first step in being a good father is acting like a good father. Debbie will return to find all has been put in order. I stumble into Ecklar's back room and find Nate sprawled on the couch, snoring softly. Ecklar is right. I scoop one arm beneath his legs, one under his back, and hoist him. His head lolls back for a few steps, then his dead weight stirs, and his eyes come open. Without smiling he says, "It doesn't feel like morning."

"No," I tell him. "It's still night."

"Is Momma home?"

"I'm here," I say. "I'll bring you to your bed."

"I want to walk."

I set him down, and he knuckles his eyes. I say, "Ecklar told me you guys watched a cool movie. About cowboys."

"It was all right. I liked the black-and-white. Did you like movies without color?"

"Cowboys are heroes," I say. "Same as your daddy."

"These cowboys were singing," he tells me. "Do you ever sing?"

"Well, I sang to you when you were little."

"I'm still little. Are you talking about lullabies?"

"Yeah," I say. "Lots of lullabies."

Perhaps Nate can tell I'm not being entirely truthful, but he holds a silence before changing the subject. "Are you gonna come to Grandy's tomorrow?"

I didn't know my wife had plans to visit her parents. "We'll see," I say. "Daddy saved a family tonight. Their house caught on fire, and I saved them."

"Ecklar let me eat popcorn."

I stop and take a knee, face my sleepy son. "Popcorn? Did you hear what I said? There was a house on fire, and I flew into it. I pulled people out and saved their lives. If not for me, right now those people would be—" I manage to stop.

Nate blinks a couple times, unfazed by my sharp tone. He says, "Awesome."

I grin, and we stare at each other for a few awkward moments. Then I ask if he wants to be a cowboy when he grows up.

"I want to be a book teacher like Grandma," he says. "Either that or I want to train dolphins to help sick children get better."

These are the kinds of answers he always gives. And usually I can shake it off, focus on the fact that he's just a boy and boys change. Still, I remember being not much older than him and determined already to follow my dad into space, be an astronaut just like him though it cost him his life. "Maybe you'll be a hero," I say.

Nate smirks, like I'm telling a joke. "I'm too little to be a hero."

"Size has got nothing to do with it. It's your heart that matters. That's the most important muscle."

Nate yawns, and I picture his bed downstairs. The longer I keep him awake, the harder it will be for him to settle down. I know this. "If you could have any superpower, which one would you pick?"

He shrugs. "I dunno. Maybe be invisible?"

"Invisible?" I say. "That's good for sneaking around and hiding. But you want something better than that, don't you?"

"OK," he says. "How about flying?"

"Now you're talking. You could be Captain Speed or Mister Torpedo."

Nate looks away. "I might be scared of being up in the air by myself."

"No," I tell him. "You wouldn't be scared. You'd get used to it, and it would be great fun." I've flown with my son before, of course, brief flights like balloon rides, never far from the ground. I consider taking him out right now to show him there's nothing to fear, but I realize this is a bad impulse, quite possibly influenced by certain chemicals coursing through my bloodstream. Nate's face is still downcast, and I look away. My eyes fall on inspiration just a few feet away, and I slide my hands under his arms, swing him into the air. Before he can ask what I'm doing, I take three strides over to Ecklar's battle armor, dormant and dusty. With one hand I swipe off the magnets, mostly goofy souvenirs from amusement parks and tourist traps. A few are thick, heavy black squares of metal. I pull open the chest door, and the mask above it lifts like the plate protecting a knight's face. There before me is Ecklar's tiny control chair. I roll Nate off my forearm into the seat and beam. He glances around at the computer screens and control panels. The helmet covers both sides of his head. "This feels funny," he says.

"You're a hero," I tell him. "The world is counting on you. Be brave."

"I don't want to be brave," he says. "I'm too little to be brave."

"Don't be silly," I insist. "I told you it isn't a question of size."

"I'm not silly," he says, and he fidgets as if he's going to slide down.

I set an open hand on his tiny chest. I hold my son where he is, against his will. "You can't really pretend with this thing open. Here." I secure the five-point safety harness, the same as the seatbelt in the hovercar, then swing the chest hatch shut. It snaps into place. Now only his face is exposed, with the metal plate flipped up like a welder's mask. Nate's eyes scan left and right quickly now, and he's squirming. "I don't like this," he says. "Get me out."

"You're OK," I tell him. "This is fun." I reach up and tap the faceplate down. When it clicks shut, three bulbs on the armor's chest flash red. The whole contraption hums like a computer booting up. I say, "Shit."

"Dad?" I hear from inside.

"Hang on." I try prying up the faceplate, thinking this might deactivate the startup sequence, but the helmet is sealed tight. "Don't touch anything. I'll call—"

"Dad!"

Beams of light ignite from the massive boots, and a high whine rises to earsplitting volume. With a whoosh the suit bolts straight up, punching through the ceiling. Above me, a ragged circle shows the stars. I bolt up into the night sky, pouring on the speed and trying not to choke on the exhaust from the flaming rocket boots.

The damn thing's got a decent head start on me, and it takes maximum burn to stay even close. That suit's got collision dampeners and automated evasive programs, along with enough firepower to raze a small city. Ecklar controlled it mostly through a brain-scanning device in the helmet, technology he pirated from that old set of King Chaos's armor. But there are all kinds of manual overrides inside, plenty of shiny buttons Nate could push that would send him soaring into space or corkscrewing into the earth. So I keep screaming, "Slow down!" in hopes that Nate hears me and thinks these thoughts, perhaps triggering that action. Above the racket of the armor's engines and the wind in my ear, I pick up the sound of my son crying. This could be my ultrahearing, but I tell myself instead it's just my imagination, and I will myself to go faster. We're traveling together straight up, toward the stratosphere. I feel panic trying to get hold of me, but in a crisis, you need to stay calm.

The thin air gets difficult to breathe, and ice crystals start forming on my cheeks, but I've gained some ground. I inch up alongside the suit. Flying parallel and in close proximity, I can hear his weeping clearly now. "Hang on!" I yell, and I open my arms wide then wrap them around the big barrel chest in a bear hug. It's so thick that I can't grab my own hands, and the streamlined shell gives me nothing to take hold of. I strain to the side, hoping to tilt us, veer us away from the stars at least. But the armor's boosters are too powerful, and I find that I'm basically a passenger riding a missile. Along the horizon, I can make out the curve of the darkened planet. I find myself sucking just to draw breath. I squeeze harder, hoping to break something nonessential and shut down the flight program. If I squeeze too hard, I will crush my son. I picture the boy's fragile ribcage.

The suit's automated defenses finally interpret my actions rightly as an attack. Blue lightning crackles around the armor, and electricity floods my brain with white pain. I try to hang on, but the shock is too much. The rocketing armor rips free of my grip, and I tumble backward. Above me, like a shuttle launch, I can see the thin trail of his flame, fading as he escapes Earth. The madness of this, that I'm about to lose my son to space the same way I lost my father, is more than I can take. So I gather what strength I have and blast up in hopeless pursuit, determined to die in a vacuum rather than bear witness.

Only, as I rise up, the distant tail of white flame seems to curve, loop back around. And then I see the armor facing me and growing larger, heading my way, back to the planet. I inhale and let the breath escape, then fall in formation beside it. I yell Nate's name but hear no response. As we descend together, I wonder if he's simply picturing his home, his bed, his mother, and the cerebral scanner is magically interpreting his wish. But as we zoom in on the HALO, I see this is not the case at all. On a rooftop helipad, a cluster of heroes has gathered. There are Clyde and Debbie and Bigfoot and the Jersey Devil and Ice Queen. At the center, Ecklar wears what looks like a flight helmet, complete with lowered eye screen. In his stringy hands, he holds a joystick with a massive antenna.

He guides his armor down for a perfect landing, and I'm next to it in an instant. As Deb pushes me out of the way, a series of beeps sounds, two streams of steam burst from the shoulders, and the face and chest plates spring open. Inside, my son is trembling, huddled into a fetal tuck. His eyes are locked closed. Debbie unstraps him and takes him into her arms. She brushes back his hair, looks into his eyes, then settles his head onto her shoulder. "What the hell happened?" she asks.

Ecklar pulls off his helmet, and his huge eyes fix on me. Clyde, Bigfoot, most of all Debbie, they all stare my way and wait for an explanation. "He crawled up into the armor when I wasn't looking," I say. "This damn thing was sitting around active all this time?"

Ecklar holds up a hand. "There's a weight sensor in the control chair. Twenty years ago, who else would I expect to sit in it? Besides, I had servo magnets locked on the exterior. They're pretty heavy."

"Well, install a freakin' safety lock, would you? Christ."

Nate stirs at my outburst, and Deb shushes him. She says to no one in particular, "He's pretty rattled. I'm calling Dr. H."

We all start walking in, and Ecklar falls in beside me. He's got one hand on the joystick, and the armor marches obediently behind us. "It's a good thing you slowed him down when you did." There's something in my friend's tone, a hint of accusation. Nobody else seems to notice.

"Yeah," Clyde says. "Guess you saved the day after all."

Bubba pats my back, and Deb turns her head just enough so I know she heard this. I know that she's imagining the unthinkable. And she's got it in her head that only my fast action prevented a tragedy beyond description. But this thought—that she views me as a hero—warms me for only a moment. Then Nate lifts his face from his mother's gentle shoulder. His eyes seek mine out. I can't stop walking, and I can't turn away. In silence, my son bears witness to the truth of what I've become.

# FIVE

*The Threat of Nazi Domination. Erecting Barriers to Absolute Honesty. A Chance to Finish on Top. Provisions in the Bylaws. Engaging the Enemy.*

During the glory days of WWII, when the fate of the free world hung in the balance, the USS *Endeavor* was recognized as a singular vessel. An Atlanta Class antiaircraft cruiser, the *Endeavor* played a crucial role in the Battle of the Komandorski Islands west of the Aleutian Islands in the Pacific theater. During the invasion of Normandy, she protected the Mulberry Harbour off the coast of France. Though she was among the smaller cruisers, her sixteen .38 caliber dual-purpose guns, twin-mounted, could rain down a veritable shitstorm upon the heads of her foolish enemies. In battle, she was never defeated.

I learn all this from the man at the lectern set up beneath a trio of those five-inch barrels. The man is not the captain, who died after a battle with leukemia back in the '70s, but the *Endeavor*'s first mate. He is frail, bent, but speaks with a proud voice. Even though the sky is overcast, his uniform shines white. Serving aboard the *Endeavor,* he tells the audience, was the most meaningful experience of his life. His aged compatriots, the half-dozen they've managed to drag from nursing homes and hospitals, struggle to their weary feet and applaud. I clap too, of course, and a young lady escorts him back to his folded chair.

Then a long-haired thirtysomething wearing jeans and a green T-shirt steps to the mike. With the glee of a game show host, he announces that the *Endeavor's* service isn't done yet. She can still defend freedom, he insists, just "the freedom of eco-diversity." Since it was saved by a junior senator from Virginia during the Eisenhower administration, the *Endeavor's* been a floating museum docked just south of Newport News. They thought it would draw tourists and money to a disadvantaged area. Instead, things kept getting worse over the decades, so much so that by the time Hurricane Edwina trashed the dock they'd built around the *Endeavor,* town officials decided it was no longer worth supporting. So now she's been towed eight miles off the coast. In an effort to promote ecotourism, which apparently has something to do with reef development and scuba divers, today she's to be sunk. This is where the Guardians come in.

After the environmentalist finishes his lame-ass speech, there's a scattering of applause. But compared to beating back the threat of Nazi domination, fostering sea life just isn't sexy. The reluctant octogenarians are escorted respectfully toward a waiting helicopter. They wear oversized jackets and caps. Two have walkers, and a handful more are bent into canes. One man has a hold of Clyde's arm. Bubba and J.D. help load the folding chairs and lectern on board. Behind them, toward the stern, is an anachronistic rocket with red wings and a skull painted on the side.

An oval-shaped door to my left swings open, and Debbie strides through, speaking on a cellphone. She's dressed in her Venus outfit, a spandex bodysuit covered in red and orange flames that is, ironically, inflammable. As she nears me, she snaps the cell closed. "Mom says Nate ate seven pancakes."

I nod. "You could've stayed with him if you wanted."

She fixes me with a look. "Last night was scary as hell, but he's fine," she says. "I'm second in command of this team, and this is a major event for us." She's starting to sound more like Clyde every day.

Both my hands go up in surrender. "I didn't mean to suggest you weren't being a good mother—or a good Guardian."

"OK," she says. "But it did kind of sound that way."

I turn from her and lean into the rail. A half-mile away, a small flotilla of observation ships bobs like ducks on a pond. Unexpectedly, Deb comes to my side and wraps both hands around my bicep. It's her way, perhaps, of apologizing for being defensive. Dr. Janet says this is the key flaw in how we communicate, that each of us is constantly erecting barriers to genuine intimacy. She knows we're in the superhero business, and she uses analogies she thinks are clever. "These barriers are like force fields," she says. "They prevent your love beams from getting through." I've been told that the only way to save my second marriage is to destroy my own force field, to be brutally honest in all things. So in theory, I should be looking for a chance to tell my wife that I put our son in harm's way, that I nearly killed him while making him pretend to be something he's not interested in. And of course there's the bit about the stolen drugs. I have no intention of telling Debbie anything.

Even with all the trouble between me and my wife, or maybe because of it, it feels fine and good to be out here on the sea, both of us in our costumes, with the sun above us trying to break through the clouds. She squeezes and says, "Later on, you should come up to Pop's. I think me and Nate may spend the night."

"Maybe I will," I say. "That might be nice." Her family is full of strange but genuinely kind people. Though we've been married nearly six years, I still feel like an interloper among them. "Everyone would be happy to see you."

"I haven't forgotten your date with the boys. When the time is right, I'll shift from wine to coffee and drive us home. We'll sleep in our beds. "

The helicopter's blades begin whirring, and we turn together to watch it lift off. Clyde moves over to the camera crew, which films the copter as it ferries the veterans to what looks like a military yacht in the center of that flotilla. From there, they'll watch our little war game, witness the destruction of this monument to their youth. The cameraman lowers his rig, and the film crew heads for a second copter.

"I'm glad you're on my team today," Debbie says.

"I'm always on your team," I tell her.

My corny line brings about an "Aw shucks" look, and a kiss feels imminent until Clyde approaches. Debbie releases my arm. He says, "They need a few minutes to get in prime location, then we'll light this candle."

"Sounds good."

Thanks to a coin toss, I'm on Deb's team of faux villains, trying to defend our battleship headquarters. Clyde, of course, has taken lead of the good guys, who will ultimately sink our ship after we've jumped through a few hoops. Naval experts have rigged explosives throughout the ship, linked the detonator to the fake rocket's control. Rumor has it that members of the Tucker Commission are on one of those boats, that any flaws in our performance may be used as rationale against our continued funding. Clyde shared this information at the mission briefing. He's the brainchild behind today's media circus. When he got the request for a single hero to come help sink the *Endeavor,* he immediately saw the opportunity to combine the task with a training session. The fact that we're about to broadcast our battle tactics to the entire world, including potential enemies, never occurred to him.

Behind Clyde, on the now-empty deck, the Jersey Devil shrugs off his overcoat and starts flapping his tiny bat wings. Kid Cyclone stretches his long legs, capped in cowboy boots, and does a few lasso tricks. The Ice Queen and Scarlet Speedstress lean into a rusting wall on either side of a porthole, chattering like high school girls. Vivian flashes me a look, and I add that elevator scene to the list of things I'll never tell Debbie.

Clyde says, "Deborah, give me and Vince a moment, will you?"

My wife nods and steps away, but her eyes linger on me, as if she knows what is about to be discussed. Once she's joined the others, Clyde sets one hand on my shoulder. "Vince, look, last night was a total mess. That business at Chili's, that was my fault, and I'm man enough to admit it. It came across like we're trying to force you out of a place you've worked hard to earn. What we've really done is prepared a pearl of a last chapter in the grand story that is Commander Invincible. One last gem for your crown."

"I'm listening."

"Two words, big man: Bone Crusher."

I imagine a bald head, bulging shoulders, thick biceps. "Bone?" I say.

Clyde goes on. "We'd had him under surveillance for almost a week. How would you like to be the guy who brings in King Chaos's strong man?"

"Where is he?"

"Don't worry about that. He's not a flight risk, and we have containment on the intelligence. We have time to plan this properly and get maximum exposure. Ecklar, Deborah, and me, we've all talked this through. It would be your operation from start to finish. You'd get full credit, right up through the official announcement."

Bone's capture would make the papers, maybe even the front page, but it wouldn't get the headline. At the press conference after the arrest, a dozen bored reporters would scribble in their notepads. KQEP would show up, and surely the other local networks. Debbie would stand behind me in her Venus costume, doing her best impersonation of a proud wife. No doubt, though, good footage from a live capture would be in heavy rotation for a solid news cycle. Thomas and Nate would see me on TV.

"OK, Clyde. Say I play along. Then what?"

"You stay a full-fledged Guardian, just on reserve status. After Ecklar talked with you about this vortex thing, he debriefed me. With him leaving, I need someone who can operate the HALO, coordinate our combat actions in the field. You've got to believe in synchronicity. Everything happens for a reason, see?"

The station practically runs itself. Technically, it's nearly sentient. "Sounds exciting." I spit into the ocean.

"Be realistic, Vince. Not many men get a chance to finish on top. It'll be like retiring after winning the Super Bowl. What more could you want?"

Clyde's question prompts me to recall Magus's wish offer, and I wonder how I'd like to go out, if I could write the script myself for my final heroic adventure. Defeating impossible odds to save a crashing jetliner? Heroic death stopping an asteroid?

"You think this through, talk it out with Debbie. We can go into specifics later. But trust me, this is better for everyone. Our charter's bylaws address this issue, and there are legal means to accomplish the same result. But it'd be a terrible shame if things had to get ugly."

The tone in Clyde's voice tightens my hands into fists. He sees my anger rising and says, "Save it for the war game." Then he turns his back and walks away, toward the waiting hovercar. He climbs in with Speedstress and Bubba, who activates the rotating jet rockets and pilots it into the sky. The Jersey Devil and Kid Cyclone fly alongside. The hero team has officially left the *Endeavor.* Even though we haven't begun the drill yet, today I am a villain, and when the hell did they ever play by rules? I'm thinking hard about bolting up, snatching the Devil's pitchfork, and piercing the hovercar's engine block. See what the freakin' bylaws have to say on that issue.

Instead, though, I work my way up a flight of winding metal steps and find Debbie and the Ice Queen in the control tower. When I enter, my wife is quiet for a minute. Then she says, "It's not a bad deal, you know, Vince?"

The Ice Queen puts on a confused look, pretending she doesn't know what's going on. I take in the panoramic view afforded by the bridge's many windows. "It's a lot to think about. For now, let's focus on why we're here."

"Right," Deb says. She claps and says, "OK, so we're the Terrible Trio, and we've supposedly stolen this cruiser and are now blackmailing the U.S. government. Unless we get a billion dollars and six of our compatriots freed from Megajail, we're going to launch our death-skull rocket at Washington, D.C. It's loaded with nerve gas, toxins, something like that. Odds are on the Guardians to come in under radar to avoid detection and try to take us out."

Ice Queen pulls out a file and starts working on her white nails.

I say, "And there's a 100 percent chance this piece-of-shit ship will get sunk in the process."

Deb shrugs. "Well, yes. Clyde is going to override the launch codes and detonate the rocket. That's the story—but all he's really got to do is hit a big red button."

"Guess we're not too terrible," Queen says. When she speaks, puffs of cloudy breath float from her mouth as if we were at the North Pole.

"Look, guys," Deb says. "This is my command, and we've got to put on a good show for everyone. Even though Clyde wants everybody going three-quarter speed, we need to run the other Guardians through their paces.

That's our role here. We don't want anyone hurt, but the camera footage we gather will be used for training purposes. It's also streaming live on the Internet."

Deb confirms that our rings are in sync, then dispatches me to the bow and the Queen to the stern. I scan the horizon, pretend not to notice the observation vessels, and wait.

I'm distracted from surveying the empty sky by a stray thought—how has Bone managed to stay off the radar for so long by himself? The kid, just a teen back in Hamburg, could crush a cannonball in the palm of his hand, but he's never seemed liked the brightest star in the sky. Once Menagerie tricked him into lowering his guard by turning into a puppy. He was more gullible than malicious, quick to follow the lead of a strong personality. If he would have come across a different kind of mentor, he could just as likely have been fighting on our side. A guy like that, he'd never be able to stay underground all these years without outside assistance.

"Contact to the northwest," Deb says through my ring. A waterspout rises from the ocean.

"That's the kid," I say. "No reason for a show like that except a diversion." Clyde loves reading books about combat tactics, so of course he's got a diversion.

Deb's way ahead of me. "Queen, give me an ice sheet to the southeast, now!"

I turn in time to see the surface of the ocean shimmer and freeze solid. An instant later, twin sprays of water in the distance tells me the Speedstress is pulling one of her favorite stunts, running so fast she won't sink. In the next instant, though, she hits the Queen's ice sheet, and her feet fly out from under her. Still traveling at highway speed, her body skids along the surface like a spinning torpedo, and she slams into the side of the *Endeavor.* There's a dull *whump!* that makes me hope she's wearing her safety helmet.

"So much for the sneak attack," Queen says.

"Stay sharp," Deb says. "They'll come in force now. Vince, get airborne, take cover in the clouds."

I zip up, admiring my wife's battle tactics. One eye is on that waterspout, approaching fast now, so I'm surprised when I break through the clouds and find the hovercar a quarter-mile above me. "Engaging the enemy," I say into my ring, and I fly straight up. Exploding light bursts like flak all around me, making me cover my eyes but not slowing me down. One of All-Star's starbursts sizzles into my chest, causing me to veer left. My momentum carries me high around the car in a swooping arc. I glance back to see Bubba steering, Clyde standing in the back with both hands out. Brilliant beams of energy flow from his fingers. Staying out of range, I put myself a half-mile directly above them and then plummet straight down in a hell-bent nosedive. At full speed like this, with gravity helping, I can't breathe, but it's worth the look on Clyde's face. He scatters starbursts into the air, but his aim is random, fearful. Just before my impact, Clyde ceases fire, and Bubba activates the hovercar's proton shield. The translucent blue bubble shimmers in the sunlight. Ecklar designed it to withstand a thousand pounds of pressure per square inch, so there's no way I'll penetrate it. But I know a bit about physics, and I've been in a few pool halls in my time. I turn my face and drive my shoulder into the shield. At impact I bounce off, ricocheting into the sky. But the hovercar, safe inside its bubble shield, plunges down like a well-struck eight ball. "Yo, Deb," I say into the ring. "Incoming."

By the time I regain my equilibrium and make it through the clouds, the hovercar has crashed on the Queen's ice sheet. Bubba and Clyde are trying to double-time it to the *Endeavor,* but they keep slipping. They have hero boots with crappy traction. On the bow, Deb and the Queen take shots at a twenty-foot-tall tornado, one with fire and one with ice.

Clyde sees me coming and shouts something at Bubba, who goes Bigfoot and shoots up to fifteen feet tall. As I buzz past him, he snatches my leg and drives me onto the ice. My body cracks the surface, but I don't break through. He's following the rules, going three-quarters. Flat on my back, I look up into his gigantic bearded face. With a shit-eating grin he recites, "I'm an authorized agent of the federal government. Cease your hostile acts, and you won't be harmed no more."

I get my breath back, shake off the pain, and reach for his hand around my shin. I get a grip on some fingers, say, "Blow me," and snap them backward.

Bigfoot wails and withdraws his wounded hand, tucks it under his other arm. "Damn it, Vince! Now you done pissed me off." At this size, Bubba's already not thinking clearly, fuzziness compounded by the adrenaline of fake battle and the pain endorphins flooding his brain. So I'm not surprised when he closes his eyes and causes his body to inflate. He grows to twenty-five feet, then thirty. As he passes forty, I lift off from the ice, float up to his face level. When he opens his eyes, I can tell he has the IQ of a child, but his anger still registers. He's about to say something when a sharp crackling sound brings his eyes downward. Like I figured, the ice gives way beneath him, and he crashes into the Atlantic, flailing in panic. At the *Endeavor,* Clyde is climbing over the rail.

As I fly across the ice, Clyde sprints along a gangway, heading for the battle. Now only Deb attacks the cyclone, which moves along the hardtop toward Clyde. Just as I reach them, he ducks behind the storm and slips past the control tower, surely on his way to blow up our rocket and sink our ship. I fight through the winds and land by Deb, kneeling over the Ice Queen trussed up tight in the Kid's lassos. She looks pretty ticked. Deb keeps shooting volcano blasts into the whirling storm, but each one extinguishes on impact. She's frazzled and can't catch her breath. I drape my arms over her, shielding her from the wind, and say, "That little shit's got to breathe too!"

She nods and focuses. I glance over my shoulder to see the show as the air around Kid Cyclone ignites. He's suddenly at the center of a fiery tornado, one that consumes all the oxygen it can. Almost immediately, the winds die down, and through the dying flames I can see his lanky frame suspended in the air, gasping. He drops to the deck, clinging to his lasso, wearing those goofy boots with spurs. Deb, exhausted from this effort, inhales sharply, touches her chest, and says, "Clyde." We start for the stern together.

But we haven't taken more than a few steps before a high-pitched howl takes out our legs. The sonic pain drives me to my knees, but far worse are the mental images suddenly flooding my mind. My mother on her deathbed staring at the purple Jell-O. The empty sky, ridiculously blue, that my father's rocket disappeared into. The moment Sheila let go of my hand on the bench in Washington Park and said, "I'm going to go ahead and file that paperwork." This psychic assault is the work of the Jersey Devil, who can also turn invisible. He's somewhere behind us, probably in the air.

I get to my feet and help Deb stand. "Try to block it out!" I shout. "I'll cover you." She's crying, and I can only imagine the horrors he's making her relive. "Go!" I say. The farther she gets away from the Devil, the less intense the nightmare effect will be.

On the deck, the Queen is writhing in the hogtie and screaming, "No! I promise I won't! No!" I make myself ignore her and focus on my own terror. I realize that as I turn my head, the feeling of terror grows more and less severe, like a sound fading and rising. Looking over the port bow causes me to visualize last night, shoving my son into a piece of weaponry and nearly causing his death. I imagine what could have happened, the armor crashing to the Earth, and it's like inhabiting a living dream, scrambling into that smoking crater and peeling back the steel. But I don't turn away from the vision, despite the anguish it brings. Instead, I walk into it, past my bound teammate. And I find my beautiful boy with his head crushed in. I see the white bone of his skull and the meat of his brain.

"Queen!" I yell, and I look down at her, and her teary eyes come into mine, and I try to keep her here in this reality. I hold my open hand out to her. "It's all J.D!" And in the next instant the flesh of my hand grows bitter cold, and an ice ball, hard as brick, takes shape. I turn back into the fear, see Nate disfigured and still dead but speaking somehow, saying, "Daddy, why did you—" and I pitch the ball with all my might into the center of the howl. The piercing wail ceases, and the nightmare vanishes from my mind. Fifty feet above us, the Devil, now visible, drops from the sky. He slams into the pad where the helicopter was earlier, but I don't run to check if he's bleeding or injured. Instead, I snap Cyclone's lasso off the Queen, choking back sobs, and take off in pursuit of Clyde. He planned the Devil's little sneak attack, and that was nothing like three-quarter speed.

As I tromp past the control tower, still bathed in the terror of those nightmare visions, I'm not feeling like a hero at all. All I feel is anger, the desire for vengeance, the need to inflict pain. And it's cleansing, really. It's a feeling just as pure as the desire to do good, even simpler in a way. After I kick Clyde's ass, I'll go back and pummel the Devil, even if he hasn't come around yet. This is my absolute intention, and it fills me with delight and purpose. I know exactly what to do. Being a villain, it seems, provides a certain amount of indisputable clarity.

And even as I'm running, I can't help but think, *Is this why King Chaos was always cheery and laughing? Is this what it's like to be evil?*

Flashes of light ahead tell me I'm nearing the fight. I hear Clyde shout, "Villainess, the American people are under the protection of the Guardians!"

I charge past a nest of antiaircraft guns and immediately see the camera set up on a tripod just past the fake rocket and the detonator for the real explosives. Clyde is standing in a perfect hero stance before the lens, his hands glowing yellow. And at my feet is my wife, acting defeated though her eyes are clear and bright. She turns to face the deck and whispers, "It's over, Vince. Let him take you out." All this is being beamed out live to the world.

Clyde says, "Evil can never defeat good."

This is such a horseshit line that just for a second, I really wish I were a villain. I wish I had an excuse to kick the shiny teeth from his skull. And I'm not even that surprised when I find my body granting my wish. I hurl myself at Clyde, my arms stretched out to tackle him, but he cartwheels to the left, leaving me to smash into the camera. I get to my feet amid the shattered pieces. Deb yells something, but I ignore her.

Clyde steps toward me, drops his hero smile, and says, "Now look what you've done."

I drive a right into his gut, and his body careens back into the rocket. He's flat-backed on it when I grab both his arms and spin him around, fling him hard into the railing. He nearly goes over. When he recovers and gets his feet beneath him, he makes the mistake of looking at me, just in time to catch my left fist on his jaw. He collapses to the deck, and I feel it swelling in my heart, the glee of malice. I stand over my vanquished foe, a hero bested, and I find myself searching for the words King Chaos might say at a time like this. And just like that, when I realize who I'm imagining for a model, the tumblers turn in my head, and my question about Bone gets answered. I know how he's stayed hidden all these years. And this, this changes everything.

I don't know yet just what to do with this revelation, but with the leverage it might give me, I know enough to stop beating on Clyde. I step away and say, "That was for the bullshit with J.D." My heart rate is calming. "And that regretting-things-getting-ugly crack."

Deb helps him sit up. "Jesus, Vince."

Clyde spits blood and says, "You're through. I'll have your license revoked for this."

"Right," I say. "Like you're going to announce to the world that I kicked your ass, and that proves I'm incapable of being a hero. Interesting argument."

We're all quiet for a few seconds, and Deb asks, "What's that beeping?"

"I'll find a way," Clyde says. "I swear it. You'll never wear a mask again."

Deb rises and walks over to the death-skull missile. I say to Clyde, "Save your speech. I'll tell everybody you single-handedly defeated us both. And I'll take your lame-ass deal."

My wife turns, her mouth just a little bit open. Clyde stands up, and I go on. "That's right. I'm retiring. I'll handle this business with Bone, and then I'll hang up my cape. You'll both get everything you want."

Deb studies my face, not quite sure whether to believe me. This just shows that my wife knows me as well as anyone, but that nobody knows you entirely. Her eyes brighten, and she crosses over to me, wraps her arms around my neck, and gives me a kiss on the cheek. "Oh, Vince," she says.

That beeping accelerates, and now Clyde goes over to the fake rocket. When he looks up from the control panel, his eyes flash wide, and he snaps his ring up to his mouth. "This is All-Star. Detonation sequence has been triggered. Imminent explosion. Evacuate the *Endeavor.*"

He looks at us. "We've got to go."

"Come here," I say, and I wrap one arm around Clyde, pull him into my chest. Deb slides inside my other arm, and when I reach around her, I feel that she's already engaged her telekinetics, making herself and Clyde essentially weightless.

We're in the air then, silent and in flight. At the thundercrack behind me, I don't turn, and the shockwave from the explosion comes up like a tailwind. It shoves me a bit, but I maintain control.

I land on the nearest observation vessel, and Clyde and Deb run off to attend to the other Guardians. The Ice Queen rubs at rope burns on her wrists, giving Kid Cyclone dirty looks. Bubba, back to his normal size, is shivering inside a towel. The Jersey Devil has a nasty black eye—eggplant purple blooming on dark brown skin—and the Speedstress is bleeding from an ugly split lip. No doubt, we're a stellar bunch of heroes.

Content that she's not needed in a command capacity, Deb comes back to me and quietly asks, "You meant it, what you said back there?"

I nod.

Clyde steps over, and clearly he's about to start some kind of argument about all this, probably try to fire me on the spot, when an audible gasp from the crowd turns all of us toward the ship.

The mighty *Endeavor* has cracked clean in two. The nose rises slightly, and then that whole section slips beneath the waves. Strangely, the back end floats on just fine, as if it hasn't noticed the water rushing in. Or maybe it's just sinking more evenly, lowering itself into the ocean. It's still on fire, and as the flames reach the sea, they hiss and extinguish. Soon the deck is swallowed, and now only the observation tower remains visible. It looks like a submarine submerging, ready to begin a crucial mission. But this comparison, of course, is only my mind at work. Everybody here knows the truth. We'll never see this ship again.

One by one the octogenarian marines begin to stiffen. They release their grips on their walkers and their canes and stand as best they can at attention. With trembling fingers, some wipe tears from their cheeks. A few reach for handkerchiefs. But every one of them raises a tight hand to forehead in a sharp salute. If it were my place, I would join them. Because right now, especially with the plan taking shape in my mind, I feel as if I am their brother. I know they are not honoring the metal that's sinking to the bottom of the ocean. They weep for fallen comrades, the glory of the past, the men they used to be.

# SIX

*Passing over the Great Wall of China. Evading Explosive Projectiles.*
*The Revenge of Gigantus. Logic and Desire.*
*A Job Offer Refused. A Plan Revealed.*
*A Vow Recalled.*

A few miles ahead, a white glistening castle that looks disturbingly like a cathedral rises from the swampland of south Jersey. Titan Spire. The two-lane highway below me, which I've been following since I left the turnpike, is crowded with minivans and SUVs packed with children and traveling at unsafe speeds. The digital billboards on either side form a kind of neon corridor. They advertise discount hotels, restaurants, an outlet mall. Not quite a decade ago, when Arthur showed me this land and announced his intentions, there was nothing here but pine forests, marsh, and mosquitoes. On the road below, the caravan of families begin to honk their horns, and when I squint I see why—a huge sign that arches over the highway with blinking letters: WELCOME TO TITANLAND.

While the civilians begin jockeying for a prime parking spot, I peel high and to the right, toward the top of the Spire, where Arthur lives and from which he oversees his tiny empire. From my airborne vantage point, I can make out rollercoasters rising above the trees like serpents from the ocean, a monorail looping around the compound, a slow-churning Ferris wheel, and a pyramid painted the colors of Titan's costume: silver and red.

The perimeter of the park is a replica of the Great Wall of China, and when I pass overhead, two warriors aim spears my way.

I hang in the air for a second, trying to take it all in. It's an entire city, really. There must be five thousand people down there right now, happy families making memories together. I suppose I envy Arthur his success. Not only was he his generation's finest hero; he also had enough marketing savvy to cash in on his name. Some nights on patrol I've found myself wondering if he felt it coming, the end of the way things were, or if his leaving brought it on.

He's made a lot of changes since I was here last—the outer wall, a waterpark, something that looks like a high school football stadium. Beyond them all, I see the ocean, out past the spires. Sheila and I brought Thomas here on opening day, and everything went wrong. The automated rides malfunctioned; the toilets backed up; people were dropping from heatstroke. We bailed out, jumped the rear fence with the help of my superpowers, and found we had the shore to ourselves. The three of us spent the afternoon beachcombing barefoot and making sandcastles. It was a simple, easy few hours, the kind I once took for granted.

A high-pitched whine interrupts my reverie, and I see a smoky trail snaking through the sky. A tiny rocket zips over the park, flame flickering from its tail. At first I take it for some kind of amusement, but then I see it's a heat-seeker, hot on the trail of a caped figure in silver and red. I reach forward with my fist, and just that fast I'm in pursuit, looking left, right, up, down, for other threats. It's been years since I've seen Titan in action, but the old man hasn't lost a step. With blazing speed he dodges and spins, rolling like a fighter jet to evade the missile. I was never as fast as him, and I have a hard time closing the gap as he buzzes past the Ferris wheel, dips straight through the curve of a loop-the-loop rollercoaster, drops down and skims the water of a fountained lake surrounding the Spires. Since I'm following, I see all the park goers turning their heads, screaming and pointing. I'm reaching for the Danger Ring, ready to call in backup, when I see my chance to save the day. Arthur's looped around one of the turrets of his home and is coming back now, leading the rocket right at me. It's true I'm not as invulnerable as I once was, but I figure a small rocket can't do more than shake me up, so with both fists leading the way, I fly straight at my one-time mentor. For an instant it seems like we're playing chicken, and for the first time he sees that he's not the only cape in the sky. His eyes go wide, and he shakes his head madly, even saying "no-no-no" I think, trying to cut off my sacrifice, but I'm committed. I fix my gaze on the target behind him and pour on what speed I have, double fists aimed ahead, and he has no choice but to bank up to avoid a collision. The rocket's nose begins to curve after him, but I have the angle now, and with skill I thought I'd lost long ago, I snatch the goddamn thing like a lofted ball.

Only I didn't count on the rocket to keep burning, and though I'm strangling it, it propels us both in a dizzy, looping, spinning roll. We're like two birds locked in combat, each unable to fly, and we're dropping fast, heading for civilians with all-day passes and cotton candy. I could let it go and hope for the best, but instead I rely on old instincts. When in doubt, break things. So I squeeze with all my might and feel the metal giving way, and I wonder what happens when a bomb breaks in two.

A battering ram slams my chest, black and red flash across my face, and I'm tumbling sideways, seeing the fountains, the sky, the Spires. I can feel myself starting to black out, and I try to gain control, but it's no good. I'm too groggy, arcing like a man shot from a cannon. Then the spinning stops, and the world around me stills. I'm at rest, in the air, and Titan's maskless face is a foot from mine. He's wearing a headset of some kind, with a tiny mike hanging before his mouth. Arthur says, "You've put on a few pounds," and I feel his arms cradling me.

He lowers us to the ground in the center of a food court, one with white cobblestones. Even before I set my feet down, we are surrounded. Arthur holds up a hand, a gesture that creates a small perimeter, and announces in a booming baritone, "That's just a sampling of the thrills you'll see at *The Revenge of Gigantus,* showing again today at four and then the nighttime show at six in Hero Amphitheater. The best action's in the air, so every ticket's a front row seat."

Children rush forward holding tiny notebooks shaped like Titan's silhouette, and he bends down and begins signing autographs. Between beaming smiles, he touches the headset at his ear and says, "Big Red. Sector Seventeen. Priority Extraction."

The spinning has left me feeling a bit nauseated, and if I were smarter, I'd take a seat. But not in front of the fans. Instead, I post my hands on my knees, take a few deep breaths, and shake my head to clear the cobwebs. My stomach hasn't calmed, but I can't look weak, so I straighten. And my eyes spread over the kids, over the parents waiting behind them taking pictures, to the back of the crowd, where Sparkplug stares my way. My dead friend is standing beside a wagon loaded with popcorn, not twenty feet from me, and his expression is a mixture of sadness and pity. I decide that as soon as I get my wits, I'll push through the civilians and make a go of pummeling a ghost. But then, just next to him, I see Mr. Squid, a tentacled villain who once tried to melt the polar ice caps. This makes no sense because he can't breathe air, and he's also absently holding one of those autograph books. I look around and see more: a girl with her hair dyed white dressed as Gypsy, a soft cuddly version of Ecklar, something like a college mascot. There's got to be a dwarf in there. And worst of all, of course, is my own doppelganger. He's two inches taller than me, and his shoulders have a muscular curve mine lost years ago. I tell myself it's probably stuffing. Three kids are asking for his autograph, which makes me feel good.

Arthur leans into my ear. "Help is on the way. We'll be out of here in sixty seconds."

A guy in his thirties steps up to me holding a corndog on a stick and hands me his notebook. "Would you mind?" he asks. I reach for the pen he's offering, but when the smell of that corndog hits me, I can't be held responsible.

The vomit splatters the white cobblestones between me and the fanboy, and Arthur drops an arm down to safeguard the kids waiting for his signature. A half-dozen men in red jackets and sunglasses jog into the courtyard, and one announces, "Titan! There's trouble in the stadium!" The others jackets extend their arms and cordon us off.

Arthur signs a last autograph, stands tall, and says, "That's all the time we have here now, folks. Evil never sleeps!" They applaud like maniacs. Under his breath, he asks me, "Can you fly?"

I nod, though I'm worried about it. Still, I won't be carried.

After he lifts off, I follow. My stomach is empty and tight, and when I see the loop-the-loop rollercoaster, I look away. Titan slows, and we float side by side. He glances over and says, "So who the hell taught you to fight?"

"I take it you weren't worried about that rocket on your ass."

"Not when my effects boys had the self-destruct button queued up. On weekends, that rocket chases me three times a day. Only we're supposed to save the firework display for the folks who paid extra. Come on, I've got a story to finish."

With that we angle down into the stadium, where indeed about five hundred people are gazing upward. In the middle of the field stands a forty-foot-tall replica of Gigantus, a robotic creation of General Mayhem that siphoned radiation from nuclear power plants. Arthur clears his throat, then reaches up to his headset. "It'll take more than a rocket to deter me, Gigantus! And now you've really got trouble! Commander Invincible fights by my side!" This booms through unseen speakers.

The robot's head tilts back, and it faces us. Its headlight eyes fix on me. Even though I know the threat is phony, my stomach calms, and I feel battle ready.

Arthur takes his hand from the headset. "Care to have the honors?"

"You bet," I say. And it's true, I remember the day in the desert when we toppled the real thing. It was marching for the spent fuel rods stored outside Yuma and had just walked through a truck stop. I lured it into the shade of a building-sized balancing rock, and Arthur pushed it over, crushing its titanium shell.

"Be gentle," Arthur tells me. "Just tap the chin. The whole head is rigged, and my guys are watching." He glances over at what looks to me like a press box.

I make a fist and swoop down, fly over the heads of the roaring crowd, and soak up the energy of their cheers, then I flip on my back, scoot through the giant's legs, and launch straight up. Even up close this thing looks pretty real. It must have cost a fortune and a half. So I keep Arthur's advice in mind and barely slap the metal cheek. On cue the head springs back, sparks fly out, and the whole monstrosity drops backward with a satisfying whump. The fans applaud and whistle. I take a quick victory lap, bathing in their admiration. Then I land on the riveted chest of the vanquished foe. Titan sets down beside me, and the crowd goes wild. They are wide-eyed and clapping madly, as if we just saved them from some genuine menace. I wish I could say it doesn't feel great, that this rising in my head is only the rush of adrenaline.

Ten minutes later, we're landing on the balcony at the apex of the highest white spire. I'm waiting for Arthur to ask what I'm doing here. It's been six months since I've seen him last, at a cancer benefit in Albany, I think. But he's always been a patient man. He reaches for an iron loop on the wooden door. "Sorry I couldn't make the party last night," he says, then steps inside his penthouse.

I've been in his home before, but it always sets me back. Hardwood floors, a fireplace, paintings lining the walls. It feels like a mansion in the sky. "Yeah," I say. "I got your note."

"How'd things go?"

"Gangbusters," I say. "Turned out to be a surprise and then some."

He unfolds the mike from his head and says into it, "Big Red. In the bird's nest." He drops it on a table, drapes his cape over a chair, and turns his attention back to me. "You don't sound very festive."

I'm about to start in when three ladies, girls really, appear suddenly. They are dressed in silver skirts and red jackets, each one size too small. It's impossible not to notice their exposed midriffs and how their breasts are pressed together. A tall blonde, likely Scandinavian, holds a bottled water, and a bouncy redhead with ponytails carries a bowl stacked high with apples, oranges, and pears. Bringing up the rear is the tiniest of the trio, and I can't be sure of her ethnicity, but I'd guess it's somewhere close to India. I'm bothered by the fact that they remind me of females from the comic book version of the Guardians, all thick chested and thin hipped. I wonder about Arthur's selection process, if he's deliberately populated his private world with cartoon caricatures. "Sylvia has drawn your bath, sir," the shortest one tells him. "What does your guest require?"

Arthur twists the top off the bottled water and takes a slug. "I need to get cleaned up," he says. He looks over the fruit before choosing an apple. "See anything that looks good?" He snaps a bite and chews.

The redhead offers the basket, and the blonde clutches her hands behind her back, tilts her chin at me, and smiles. The three of them wait for my answer.

"I'm good," I say, breaking eye contact. "Maybe just some of that water."

"As you wish," the Indian says, and she leads them away. Arthur brings up the rear. I hear him say, "Bring my friend an Alka-Seltzer too."

What my body needs isn't anything so over the counter. The stolen brown bottle of Xonopexal is in our bathroom in the HALO, just behind my shaving cream. After last night's excitement, and knowing the war game bullshit was ahead of me, I decided to pop one this morning. If I hadn't, my back would be killing me right now. Instead, I feel only a persistent low ache.

Once I'm alone, I consider calling Deb. By now she's joined Nate at her parents'. Back on the observation ship, she again invited me to come along to Connecticut, but I told her I felt obliged to find Arthur and speak to him. I told her that if the original Guardians were coming to an end, he had a right to be told in person. "Maybe you can come by later," she said. I nodded and said, "Maybe." She looked away then, and I knew she could tell I was holding something back, that I had erected my intimacy force field and deflected her love beams. There was no way my wife could guess my real agenda in coming here.

In Titan's empty study, I sip at my water and browse the bookcases, look at some of the commemorative plaques and framed photos. One displays the front page of the *New York Times* from the day he diverted a plummeting North Korean communication satellite into the Bay of Bengal. One is from when a dam burst in Tennessee and the Yalobusha River threatened to drown the entire town of Danville. Titan knocked off the top of a mountain to stem the flow.

The one that really gets me is an eight-by-ten of the original six Guardians. It's on the fireplace mantel. It's a staged PR shot, from early on. Sparkplug, up on his tiptoes, has his hand behind Menagerie's back, giving her rabbit ears with split fingers. Even in the faded photo, her green eyes, a rarity among Chinese I'm told, are stunning. Billy was always playing practical jokes on Huan, like the time he replaced her bed with a doghouse or gave her a hundred cat toys for her birthday. He teased her like a big sister.

In the picture, we all look so young. Grace's hair hadn't started to turn white, and her smile, something I haven't seen in a decade, is radiant. In those days, she hadn't even heard of twelve step. Couldn't she see her own future? Ecklar, sitting cross-legged in the front, looks more like a kid than a warrior, but a few years later, after Hamburg, he'd been deep in the gears of his battle suit, ready to inflict violence all his own. Arthur and I are side by side, dead center in the back, each trying to out-flex the other. It's clear, though, he's bigger than me, and at that time, his blood was as pure as his intentions. I wonder what I would say to them, to me, if I could whisper back through history.

From a row of books I pull out Titan's autobiography, *With Great Power.* I skimmed through it when it was originally published but never got around to really reading it. So I settle on the couch and open to the first page: "When I was five years old, my father taught me that there is no duty more sacred than helping one's fellow man." The opening chapter explores the lessons of his childhood one incident at a time. I'm reading about a bully in eighth grade when Arthur appears at my side, wearing a red bathrobe and smelling of minty soap. "You've got great taste in books," he says.

"Yeah, but I know how this one ends."

A freckled girl, Sylvia I presume, comes out wearing a robe that matches Arthur's. On bare feet she crosses to the kitchen area, where she begins dropping fruit into a blender. Arthur introduces us, and with a southern accent she asks if I'd care for "the best smoothie on the planet." I feel like a kid is asking me if I want a glass of lemonade, so I accept.

Arthur and I sit on facing armchairs before the fire. "Feel free to lose the mask," Arthur says. "All my aides have signed iron-clad confidentiality agreements. Plus, I trust Sylvia."

I consider this briefly, but it feels unnatural, so I change the subject. "Business seems good," I say.

"Revenues across the company are up 7 percent this quarter, which barely covers my new capital outlay. The board is squeamish about my expansion plans, but I keep telling them we'll only reap what we sow."

"They say the economy's in the crapper. How the hell do you keep making money?"

"People will always find ways to pay for what they need, Vince. That's food, shelter, and dreams. Thanks to human nature, I'm recession proof."

The blender churns, and Sylvia pours two tall glasses of something peach colored. She says, "Arty, will your friend be indulging?"

I turn to see her unscrewing the cap off a blue jar. She scoops out a white dust and stirs it into one of the glasses. "No," Arthur says. "Just me."

His pecs bulge through the split in his robe, two mounds of muscles that belong on a twenty-year-old. His blond hair seems to shine. By now he must be sixty, but he looks impossibly younger. I'm pretty sure he's dyeing that hair, and I imagine myself poking around his bathroom, finding a bottle of Clairol for Men. I'm not sure what else I might find, and I decided long ago I didn't want to know. The innuendos about Titan's steroid use started on talk radio, but once the parents' groups got on board, those rumors grew teeth. He retired before anything came of it, but nowadays the union enforces pretty strict testing for muscle enhancement. We're recipients of federal funds, role models, et cetera. Xonopexal hasn't yet been added to the screening list, but it seems inevitable. At some point, I could be asked to pee in a cup.

As Sylvia brings us our drinks, I notice she's dropped a straw in mine to be sure to keep them straight. I feel guilty, but I wonder about the extra kick in Arthur's concoction. She gives us our drinks and stands behind Arthur, lets a hand settle on his bare shoulder, just inside the robe. "We're going to skip your muscle treatment?"

He takes a sip and tells me, "Sylvia's a certified physical therapist. She's also had training in Portuguese massage."

"Those Portuguese," I say. "They know their muscles."

He pats her tiny hand. "I'll come find you. Vince here isn't the type to pay social calls unannounced. He's got business to discuss."

Sylvia leaves us by ourselves. I try my drink, and it seems bitter, pulpy.

Arthur sees me wince and says, "It's not supposed to taste great. It's good for you. And before you even start in on me, I've got legal documents on all my special assistants verifying their age. Last year I had one opening for Sylvia's spot—chief special assistant—and I got three hundred applications. That's just from in-house."

"What happened to the former chief special assistant—she needed to finish high school?"

"Andrea's taken a position as a graphic designer with our Prague team. She left on great terms."

"No doubt."

"Would you please take off the mask? Nobody cares who you are."

Though undeniably true, this statement stings. It's been decades since I had a secret civilian identity, since I was just Vincent Shepherd. Now, I feel more like myself under the mask. Still, I realize this is silly and unhealthy, so I peel the spandex hood over my head. "I've got a situation, Arthur. Clyde is pushing me out."

He finishes the last gulp of his power drink. "Perfect. I'll take you on. You can do weekday shows at the theater. I'll double your salary and guarantee you better benefits. How do you feel about working holidays?"

"I didn't come here looking for a job."

"Doesn't matter what you came here for. That's what you should do. You can't be a hero forever."

I don't think Arthur ever doubted a single notion that came to him. But when has he been wrong? "I came here to tell you about something I have in mind. I want to do something before I hang up my cape, take care of some unfinished business."

"Now you're making me nervous."

Between us the fire crackles, and a log drops down. Glowing embers float up the flue. "Arthur, I'm going to find him. I'm going to track down the son of a bitch and kill him."

His mouth sets in a grimace, and he eyes me hard, trying to gauge just how serious I am. When he gets his answer, he rises, crosses to the hallway door, and closes it. So much for absolute confidence. He walks past the fire and says, "Let's get some air."

Outside, I feel cold just looking at him with his wet hair and his bare chest, but he doesn't seem bothered by the chill autumn wind. We stand side by side, and he sets his hands on the railing. Together we survey his kingdom. The Ferris wheel spins. Riders scream on a plunging rollercoaster. A single red balloon floats in the air before us, surely leaving behind some crying child. Arthur watches it ascend and finally speaks. "All of us, we looked like hell for Chaos twelve years ago and couldn't find him. Back then the trail was fresh. Now, you'll never find him."

I let him finish, then lay it out. "Bone Crusher's shown up on the radar. Somewhere in the city. Clyde has him under surveillance and is offering him to me as a going-away present. But think about it. Any chance that guy's stayed underground all this time on his own?"

Arthur furrows his brow, knowing I'm right. "No," he says. "This is all a bad idea. Like taking a stick to a hornet's next. Chaos is quiet somewhere, and you should leave him wherever the hell he is."

I turn to him, but he keeps his face aimed at his park. "Arthur. I didn't come here to ask for permission. It's a courtesy. I thought you might want to help."

He looks right at me for an instant, eyes narrowed as if he's about to activate his laser vision, then he steps away. Hands clasped behind his back, he walks to the far side of the balcony. I follow, waiting for my answer. But he's silent for a time, looking down on huge blue slides curving down into dirty ponds. A moat encircles the whole thing. "The waterpark is closed for the season. But next year we may look into heating that water, might keep us open into October, as least on weekends." Now he points beyond it, to scrub forests that dwindle away as they approach the ocean. "If I can convince the board, I'm going to put in a casino in that parcel to the south. My architect has drawn up plans for a three hundred–room hotel. I've had Fazio stop by twice to talk about designs for a golf course. Men will drop off their wives and kids at the park, then play eighteen before hitting the craps tables."

I take a breath to be sure he's done. Then I say, "I don't know why you're telling me this."

"Titan Enterprises employs almost twenty thousand people worldwide. Last year we donated over eight million dollars to worthy causes. My profits are feeding entire villages in Istanbul, cutting the malaria rate in Africa, doubling the literacy rate of children in Appalachia. My scientists, trying to find a way to run this park more effectively, are closing in on technology that may make solar-powered cars commonplace."

He looks at me to see if I understand. All I can give him is a blank stare.

"I'm doing more good now than ever before in my life. I'm entirely happy with who I am and have nothing to prove. Why would I want to risk this?"

"Maybe because your friend got murdered."

"Billy was a warrior. He knew the risks. I honor his death."

"By having some joker walk around your park signing autographs in a Sparkplug costume?"

"Have you lost your mind?" he says. "We've never had a Sparkplug character."

After a few seconds, I say, "Must've been some kid I saw." Of course I know better.

Arthur shakes his head. "What happened in Hamburg wasn't my fault. All wars have casualties. Don't put his death on my doorstep."

Till this moment, I never gave much thought to Arthur's guilt. It makes sense, of course, since at the time of Sparkplug's death, he was lying defeated on the ground. I'd somehow thought him above petty sentiments like regret. But with him glaring at me and feeling cornered, I need to say something I really didn't want to. "You took a vow."

He nods, grim faced. "So that's what we've come to now, old chum? It's your job to remind me of my promises?"

"Somebody needs to."

He seems to be considering the possibility but then shakes his head. "I'm saying no. At least that will keep you out of trouble. You're not fool enough to try this alone."

I shrug. "You're not the only one who took that vow."

"Get serious. Ecklar's too smart to waste his time on this. As for the others—"

"What about the others?"

He turns from the waterpark and aims a finger into my chest. "I doubt you can reach Menagerie, but I really don't care. But Grace, you leave her alone. She's free of all this."

I ignore his hand. "She can make her own decisions."

"What—you didn't get that letter?"

I remember the glitter twinkling to the floor when I unfolded her note, mailed from New Horizons. "That was early in her treatment," I say.

"You might feel differently if you read her latest doctors' reports."

My eyebrows rise.

"Who do you think has paid for therapy all these years? Insurance won't foot the bill for more than one of those clinics. She's in, what, number seven right now?"

An image from the KQEP story flashes in my mind: Gypsy's sunken cheeks, her eyes hidden behind huge sunglasses like those worn by the blind. She looked like the Soul Stealer had sucked out half her life essence. Arthur has a point, but I say, "Maybe what she needs most is to be out of those places, back in action. Maybe it was a mistake for any of you to stop."

He smirks, posts his hands on his hips. "Well, I'm convinced. Logic has always been your strong suit. I made a mistake by leaving to found a billion-dollar-a-month global corporation that does more good than Gandhi, and you made the right choice by staying behind to help fight the occasional third-rate bad guy—when the Feds give you permission. You've got me there. Don't forget how this has helped your personal life. I keep tabs on things at the HALO. I know how things are with you and Debbie. And I've been too polite to mention that clusterfuck in Mississippi last month. You're embarrassing everyone associated with the Guardians. But you're going to stand here—here in my home—and suggest that you're better off than I am? You should take Clyde's good advice, pick up Bone Crusher and get out of the game. Before something bad happens."

He's standing huge and powerful, and his empire stretches behind him. I know he's right, like he's always been. The rational part of me knows that I should leave Gypsy alone, that I'm likely fighting a failed cause. But logic has nothing to do with desire. I'm tired of Arthur's self-righteous expression, and I find myself saying, "You know who I am, Arthur. I'll grant you that. But let's not pretend I don't know you. You're charging nine dollars for cotton candy, pumping God knows what into your veins, and banging teenagers for kicks."

His arms extend to his sides, and his hands form into loose fists. I take one step back and feel my body ease into a combat stance. Then he smirks. "So we're both assholes, and now we're going to fight? We both know how that would turn out. I think it's time for you to leave, Vince. I've really enjoyed our little chat. It's always good to catch up with you."

I give him the finger and say, "Go go Guardians," then I drift up and away from him, not turning my back just yet. I leave him standing on the highest balcony of his private castle, king of a fantasyland he made in his own image. Then I turn to the west and fly back to the real world.

# SEVEN

*Victories of the Past. A Family Tradition. The Aphrodisiac of Surrender. Going into Overtime. Meteors and Comets.*

Three hours after I float away from Titanland, I finally locate a landmark to verify that I've arrived in Suffolk County: the big iron bridge below crosses the river a few miles from my in-laws'. Not that I was ever lost, not really. Had I stayed over the interstate, I would've arrived an hour ago, but the reek of exhaust and the whine of tires on macadam got to be too much. So I let myself wander off into the countryside, thinking I'd just rely on my own internal compass. Before she died, this was one of my mother's great strange joys, taking roads she'd never been on, just to see where they led. And she always managed to pop out closer to the place she wanted to be. Or she found somewhere that felt that way. On my seventeenth birthday, the last before she passed and left me without parents altogether, we wound country roads for two hours, me driving, her directing. *Take that turn,* she'd say. *Now let's head toward those mountains.* And when we came across a sleepy town with a country inn, one with the best steak sandwich I've ever eaten to this day, it was like she'd planned every twist and turn. It was probably just the perception of a child, a devoted only son, but her navigating seemed perfect, predestined. She just seemed to know which way to go. I wish I'd inherited that gift.

Titan's response to my plan has gotten under my skin, made me second-guess the whole silly scheme. I've been wondering how I'd really feel if I walked away from the Guardians altogether. The hero business is all I've known for so long, but maybe a change would do me good. Those fans back in Titan's stadium, people who in the city might barely glance in my direction, were rabid with excitement. And even though I knew it was all pretend, I still got a buzz when I knocked off Gigantus's blocky head. Would it really be so bad, spending a couple hours a day feigning mortal combat? We could relive our greatest adventures, bask in the glory of past victories. I could sneak out into the park sometimes, dressed in my costume, pretending to be me. I could sign autographs and chat with the faithful, let them think I was really just an average Joe. Part of me can't help but cringe at this image, and I think of all those gray-haired rock-and-roll stars, strumming the songs that made them popular thirty, forty years ago. It's pathetic in a way, but surely it's better than not playing at all.

Even my own indecision should be a sign. I don't have the resolve for battle anymore. But maybe the only way to get that back is to get into a good fight, something I haven't had in years. I wish my mother were alive so I could seek her advice. I recall Billy's tree house offer to commune with the dead, but I'll never be that desperate.

While she was alive, my mother did teach me enough to appreciate whatever was in front of me, and with the leaves changing color now and the October sun bright in the afternoon sky, it's been a pleasant diversion to drift over the mountains and valleys trying to find my way. From five hundred feet, the autumn tones of yellow and gold, the flaming reds and brilliant oranges, don't seem to suggest dying at all. They seem vibrant and alive. Of course, I know the truth.

Ahead to the east I see Monroe's water tower, with the letters curving across its round blue belly. I pass by and veer to the north, and sure enough, there's the pond where I've fed geese with Nate. Gloria and Woodrow Sullivan's house is nearby, and I ease down to treetop level so I can follow the winding street. There are only a half-dozen houses out here, spread between open fields and forest. I skim the tops of the sycamores and oaks, and the crisp air feels fine in my lungs. I feel so glad that I've come here. Although they're a bit richer than most, the Sullivans are everyday, normal people, the kind I've always admired and even envied. At these gatherings, you get the craziest sense that each one of them wants nothing more than to be with you, just share your company. Being among them will help clear my mind.

I smell the fire just before I see the column of black smoke rising from the canopy of trees. Picturing their home ablaze, I accelerate, imagining trying to blow my ultrabreath across the flames, or racing through town to find the fire company. Carrying an entire ladder truck isn't something I could do anymore, but I'm willing to give it a go. I would worry about Nate, but with Debbie at his side, there is no need. Before anything else—superheroine, daughter, wife—she is a mother. As soon as I come into the clearing that marks the Sullivans' property, though, I see no rescue is required. Below me on the great lawn, two piles of leaves smolder and crackle. My brothers-in-law stand over the small pyres holding bottles of beer, leaning on their rakes like spears. Closer to the house, Debbie and her sisters sit in Adirondack chairs holding long-stemmed glasses, while the kids splash in other leaf piles. And then everyone turns to me, a masked man in a cape hovering in the fall sky.

Because they are just beneath me, I land by my brothers-in-law. Henry, married to Debbie's oldest sister, Liz, says, "Nice timing. We're almost done."

I look at the field of green grass, raked clean and neat, and I speak the truth. "I'd rather have been here helping you. Trust me."

Sober Gary, Debbie's twentysomething kid brother, jacks a thumb toward the house and smiles. "You can always clean out the gutters."

"No, no," Henry says. "Jeremy's old enough to get up on the roof. I'll send him up, make him feel like a man."

"I wouldn't mind," I offer. The idea of climbing a ladder, balancing on the edge and being a part of this day, appeals to me deeply.

But Sober Gary shakes his head. "It's a Sullivan rite of passage," he says. "Pop sent me up when I was eight."

"Yeah, yeah, in the snow, without shoes, clutching a broken broomstick between your teeth. Every time you tell that damn story, it gets worse. Jeremy will be fine."

I glance at the angled roof and picture my skinny nephew (is he ten? twelve?) tumbling to the earth. Scooping out the wet leaves and pine needles that clog the gutter would take me less than a minute, but Debbie and I have a simple rule in this place: no powers. If not, she could have telekinetically swept the leaves into a geometric array, torched them, and extinguished the flame herself. She's standing now, along with her three sisters and Sober Gary's girlfriend, Kelly, watching my niece Marissa charge toward me down the sloping yard. She yells my name and waves something, a paper plate. The three of us step around, blocking her from the burning piles.

I bend over, and she crashes into my outstretched arms. She pulls back from the hug and asks, "Do you want a hot dog or a hamburger?" She holds a crayon and a paper plate with two columns, lines etched beneath each.

"What are you going to have?"

"One of each."

"Me too," I say. "Did you see me flying?"

She holds up a five-star oak leaf. "These don't have any more chlorophyll."

"No," I say. "Where's your cousin Nate?"

"Inside helping Grandy. She's making snacks."

I smile at her. "I could use a snack."

"Feel free to raid my closet," Henry says. I realize then that I'm still wearing the mask, and I take Marissa's hand and head up the hill.

Debbie meets us halfway up the incline, greets me with a hug of unexpected warmth. "I didn't think we'd see you," she says.

"Sorry to disappoint."

"Hardly." She kisses me, on the lips, then wraps her arms around me and squeezes.

I hate to question the embrace, but this public display is unusual, especially here. Her sisters—Liz, Julie, and Sondra—are staring. Even the dozen kids have stopped upsetting the last of the leaf piles to watch us.

Her chin settles on my shoulder, and she says quietly, "I've been thinking about it all day. I know walking away is a sacrifice for you. But you're doing the right thing. I'm so proud of you."

It's cruel, really, how this pains me. Because even though these are some of the exact words I've yearned to hear, I didn't expect to earn them by quitting.

"What's going on with Nate?"

She pulls back and says, "He's OK. A little on the sensitive side. Still doesn't want to talk about last night at all. Mostly, though, I think he's just embarrassed."

"Sure," I say. "That's probably it."

Ten minutes later, I descend the stairs dressed in a pair of Sober Gary's jeans and a Boston College sweatshirt. I head for the kitchen, from which I can hear my son's voice. "Sarah and Kevin say Pluto's a planet. But it's not. It's used to be, but the scientists changed their mind."

I step in to see Mrs. Sullivan listening intently as she cuts up a ring bologna. Nate sits on a stool, arranging crackers in the center of a silver tray. "Maybe it's a matter of interpretation, then," she says. "Maybe you're all right."

"We can't all be right," my son insists. "Something is a planet or it isn't a planet."

She slides him the plate of sliced bologna and is reaching for a hunk of cheese when I stride in. Mrs. Sullivan wipes her hands on her apron and wraps me in a huge hug, one of her trademarks. "Hello, Vincent. Can I get you a drink?"

I pass, then say, "Hey, Buddy. How was your trip up this morning?"

Nate doesn't turn from the tray. "Fine."

"Did you see any dragons?"

He sets the round pieces of meat down around the outside of the rows of crackers. "Dragons are make-believe."

"You used to see them all the time."

Mrs. Sullivan holds a hand up to tell me to ease off. "Nathan told me that tonight there are favorable conditions to observe shooting stars. Did you know that?"

"Nope."

"How does the boy even know these things? And why is he sounding more and more like a college professor?"

I shrug and feel just a little guilty for not giving Ecklar credit.

She slices the cheese, and I watch her and Nate finish the arrangement. My presence has killed their good conversation, and I wonder if Nate has told anyone the truth of what happened last night. Once they're done, I reach for the completed tray. "Can I take this outside for you?"

She shakes her head. "Woody's up front. Can't get him off that new flat-screen."

"Want to come along, little man?" I ask my son, though I know he hates sports.

He shakes his head.

My mother-in-law tries to warm me with a smile, ignorant of the true reason for my son's mood. She tells me as I leave, "If Notre Dame's losing bad, just leave it and go."

Woodrow Sullivan's temper, and his obsession with Notre Dame, are the stuff of legend. That I'm fifteen years older than his daughter didn't seem to bother him when she first brought me here, and he never mentioned my previous marriage. But he was deeply unimpressed that I had no college degree, nor any preferred team in the SEC. When I asked, in this very den, for his blessing to marry his daughter, he folded the sports page on his lap and said, "Debbie's a big girl. She's always made her own decisions." Over time our relationship has warmed, but he's never cared for me like Carl did. Maybe because Carl didn't have any sons.

A fire crackles in the hearth, but Woody and my nephew Jeremy, who is even taller and skinnier than I remember, focus on the game. Julie's husband, Dan, waves at me from the floor, and Drunk Gary, Sondra's notorious husband, is passed out next to Jeremy on the couch. When I bend to set the tray on the footrest in front of Woody, he tilts his head to keep watching. "Great to see you," he says. "Fourth quarter just started. All tied up. Sit sit."

Though I should go rejoin my wife or try to patch things up with Nate, I'm not upset to be summoned to less awkward duty. I plop onto the couch next to Drunk Gary. I lean over him and tell Jeremy, "You'd better not go outside. Your dad's got plans for you and those gutters."

Jeremy reaches for a hunk of ring bologna and gives me an appreciative nod.

I take a wedge myself and lean back into the cushions, feel the weight of the day slipping off me. The warmth from the fire feels good. One consequence of being raised fatherless is that I never played much organized sports. By the time I developed a sincere interest during high school, my powers had begun to emerge in fits and starts. In the middle of a wrestling drill my sophomore year, I broke Jeff Czerwinski's wrist. There was a popping sound, and a shard of bone broke through the skin. Czerwinski wore a cast for six weeks. I quit the team. It wasn't just because I'd hurt Jeff. It was because, deep down, while he was writhing in pain and cradling that arm, the other boys looked at me in shock and something like admiration. I felt then the temptation of raw power.

Every now and then, Woody explains something to Jeremy or offers commentary. "Linemen can't go downfield before a forward pass." "In the pros you need two feet in bounds. In college it's just one." I envy Jeremy for the education he's getting, and I wonder what questions Nate will have for me later. I try to remember Woody's answers.

Not long after the game goes into overtime, Debbie appears, cradling a baby. "That's where you got to," she says. She walks in, kicks Drunk Gary in the shin, and tells him to sleep it off upstairs. "Just resting my eyes," he says groggily. He locates his gin and tonic on the coffee table, recovers it, and wanders into the hallway. Debbie slides in between me and Jeremy. I do not ask who the sleeping child belongs to. Every time I visit, there seems to be a steady supply of newborns. It's like these people are trying to repopulate the planet. Debbie glances at the game. "What happened to Canipe?"

"Hamstring in the third," Woody says. "Lowe's a junior. Redshirt."

Debbie's arm is pressed up against mine, something that may be due in part to the cramped couch. But there's an empty rocking chair she could have chosen, and she smiles at me when I peek down at the baby's round, puffy face. After a Navy player drops a ball in the end zone, she leans into me and says, "Let's not go back into the city tonight."

"Sure," I say.

"Ecklar's not even going to pick them up till eleven. We could just leave first thing in the morning, be back in plenty of time."

"Sounds great."

My wife's eyes stay on my lips, and I believe that if her father were not in the room, she would kiss me like she did on the lawn. There is a brightness radiating off her, and it isn't just because we are here in her childhood home surrounded by those who love her. It's as if she has found me again, remembered why she chose me in the first place. In her eyes, last night I helped save our son from certain death, and this morning I bested our team leader in personal combat. On top of this, by agreeing to quit, I have finally followed Dr. Janet's advice and taken definitive action that demonstrates my willingness to change, my commitment to the family, and my openness to free communication. With the way my wife's looking at me now, I know that later, after dinner and more wine and perhaps a sloppy game of Scrabble, while our son sleeps with his cousins in the basement, my wife will lead me upstairs to her old bedroom. We will scrunch onto the slim mattress that makes it impossible for our bodies not to touch. We will huddle together under a ragged quilt. And there will come a point—she'll turn to her side and slide a leg over mine, her lips will barely brush my bare neck—when I'll be certain she is looking for more than body heat. With the condoms in my nightstand a hundred miles away, we will make love like fumbling teenagers, as happened about five years ago in that very room. That is how we got Nathan, and tonight we will conceive again. Later, as passion and alcohol twine us together, I do not know if I'll feel wrong, like we're making love under false pretenses. I do not know if I'll be able to ignore my guilt and screw, or if I'll be a better man, set a calm hand on her shoulder and bring everything to a halt and tell her the truth about my retirement plans and everything else.

After Notre Dame wins, an event met with joy by the whole house, we are ushered into the dining room to pick from pyramids of cheeseburgers, hot dogs, huge vats of macaroni casserole. Deb loads Nate's plate with CHEETOS and puts a stripe of ketchup down one side of his hot dog, mustard down the other. He sits with his cousins around a circular table in the kitchen, while the adults sit in the dining room. Talk at the grownup table floats from Monroe's plans for a new elementary school to Jeremy's choices of college to Liz's decision to return to graduate school for a second master's, this one in art education. Drunk Gary flirts with Kelly until Sondra whacks him in the arm with the salad tongs. At the head of the table presides Woody, smiling and chewing, content with the state of his kingdom. I am quiet and a bit bewildered, as I typically am among this thriving tribe. Since I was an only child, I often wondered about being part of a big family like this, and the many benefits are hard to ignore. It's not that I envy Woody—I have no desire to be a respected patriarch. What I'm jealous of, the thing I wish I could possess, is the sense of ease each of these people seems to have in this place. Even Drunk Gary seems at peace with who he is, and even he is clearly accepted. Despite everything, they accept me too, but I never get the feeling that I really belong here. I feel like an interloper, like I have taken over someone else's life. I don't quite know what my part is. Everyone else knows their role. So for them, everything makes sense.

Still, it feels good to smile and listen to the stories and be on the edge of this warmth. During one of the rare lulls, Mrs. Sullivan notices I've been quiet and asks how my hamburger is. This is clearly a token question meant to draw me into the conversation. I finish chewing what's in my mouth—the silence in the room escalates—and I say, "Good. Great. I'm glad you didn't have me take over the grill this time."

I grin at my line, recalling an episode from years ago when the grill ran out of gas. I tried to use my heat vision to finish cooking the meat. The result looked like hockey pucks and didn't taste any better. Could be that's when my powers first began to fade.

Mrs. Sullivan looks confused, and Henry, who always seems to do the grilling, glares down at me, looking a bit betrayed. Even Debbie looks baffled. "Come on," I say. "We ended up having to order from Domino's."

"Domino's won't deliver out here," Jeremy says. "But Pizza Hut will."

And this is when I realize that I've misplaced a memory, that I was with Sheila's family on a long ago Fourth of July when I burned those burgers. I ate that pizza with Thomas and Carl, not these people. The expressions from everyone at the table suggest they may be worried about my sanity, and it occurs to me that no one has mentioned Biloxi. Woody reaches for his rum and Coke. Dan clears his throat. Debbie's hand settles on my leg, and she squeezes. Mercifully, the little kids in the kitchen begin chanting, "We want dessert."

Liz, Debbie, Sondra, and Julie all rise to help Mrs. Sullivan, and before long everyone has a plate with a brownie and a scoop of vanilla ice cream. Everyone but me. I'm not about to call attention to the oversight. The kids, who couldn't have finished yet, come piling into the dining room with mischievous grins. Nate stands at Debbie's side, and he is smiling at me. After they all settle, Liz hits the lights, and Mrs. Sullivan appears with my plate—the same scoop and brownie—only a single lit candle has been staked into the chocolate. I am again serenaded with the Happy Birthday song, but this version buries the one from last night. Those folks at Chili's, they sang with the mocking tone of sarcasm. These kids, they want me to have a happy birthday with every ounce of their being. As Mrs. Sullivan lowers the plate to the table, the tiny flame illuminates my son's beaming face, and he is thrilled for me. "Don't forget the wish," he reminds me.

Behind him, Debbie smiles.

Eyes on her, I say, "I wish for something special tonight."

Nate turns from the candle. "It's supposed to be a secret."

I tell him to help me, and together we blow out the candle. Everyone applauds, and the lights come up.

Afterward I'm told it's a Sullivan tradition that the birthday boy does the dishes, something I suspect is a lie and part of my never-ending hazing. As Drunk Gary adds plates to a teetering stack on the counter, I let the hot water rush over my sudsy hands. And I think about how, back in my bachelor days, I would always do such tasks with superspeed. Vacuuming, laundry, the chores that burden the day, all passed through my world in mere moments. But more and more lately, and especially here among the Sullivans, I enjoy doing simple tasks that show accomplishment. Loading the dishwasher while others clear the table makes me feel like perhaps I do have a place among these people. The kids are bathed, and the basement is transformed into a huge dormitory—quilts and mismatched pillows, unrolled egg crates and old yoga mats. They are corralled to watch a Disney double feature, and the grownups divide into groups; some go outside to start a campfire, some catch the night game on ESPN, and the rest settle around the cleared table for a game of Scrabble.

Debbie and I are placed on the same team, and we rearrange the tiles on our rack, spelling out different suggestions. As the games goes on, I keep hoping for some overtly playful message from my wife, something like DO ME or O YES, but the closest I get is GRIP. Every now and then, Sondra comes back in with an update on the fire, or one of the guys watching football steps out for a cigarette. The cold air rushes in. It's probably dropping into the forties out there, but crazy Aunt Sondra is determined that the kids will have roasted s'mores. Sober Gary and Kelly play TACO, which Mrs. Sullivan—who always gets a dictionary before the game and who prefers to play without a teammate—considers challenging as a foreign word. Then she realizes it's opened up something for her. She plays OOZE for twenty-eight points. Without consultation, Debbie plays ZIP, which gets us out of third place.

Midway through our second game, Nate appears, padding up from the basement in footed pajamas. Debbie asks how the movies are going, and he says, "Not so good. Something sad always happens in those movies."

He pushes a chair over next to Mrs. Sullivan and climbs up. "Aren't you lonely without anybody on your team?"

She pats his back sweetly and smiles, but when he starts rearranging her tiles, she says, "No, no, honey, you mustn't touch."

"How about *quest?*" he asks. "Is that a good word?"

She glances at the board, plays it into an *S.* "Twenty-six points," she says, beaming. "Sullivan genes."

We finish dead last in the second game, but Nate's having such fun we begin a third. Aunt Sondra gets mad because the kids started another movie without going outside to make those s'mores. The house begins to fill with the smell of Mr. Sullivan's cigar, though the cigarette smokers still go outside. Vanderbilt upsets Texas Tech. Debbie works on her wine one sip at a time, but as soon as her glass is empty, she refills it.

We actually have the lead in the third game, perhaps because Mrs.

Sullivan is now letting Nate make all decisions for their team. This despite the fact that he's resting his heavy head on his hands. After Kelly and Sober Gary add an s to zoo, Nate straightens and says, "Hey Grandy, we forgot about the meteors."

"Buddy," I tell him, "it's freezing outside. And it's really late."

"I'll get a coat," Mrs. Sullivan says. "We won't be but five minutes. After that, straight to bed, though, right?"

Nate's eyes are bright, and he nods in eager agreement.

I turn to Debbie, but she's already standing, and I realize that the game is at an end. Nate suddenly stills and looks up at Deb. "A big poop is coming."

My wife glances my way, and I say, "Come on, Little Man."

Nate hesitates, then reaches for my hand. He's been potty-trained for a while, but when it comes to number two, the boy still requires a cleanup inspection.

As Nate sits on the toilet, his feet dangle. I am tired and ease down on the edge of the tub, emptied of water but still loaded with rubber letters, ducks, and various shipwrecks. Nate picks up a battered *Reader's Digest* from the sink and starts flipping.

I look at the cover and wonder if he's reading "Ten Ways to Make Money in a Bad Economy" or "Drama in Real Life: Trapped in Sutter's Canyon." Finally I say, "I'm glad you're having a good time tonight. This is a terrific birthday for me."

"Today isn't your birthday," he says. His eyes stay on the page. "It's your birthday celebration. Your real birthday isn't until Monday."

"You're right."

He closes the magazine and considers me. "I didn't want to go in Uncle Ecklar's flying suit."

"I know that."

"I didn't like it."

"I know. I'm sorry. I thought you would have fun."

"I didn't have any fun at all. It was just scary."

Footsteps shuffle past the door, and I worry about who might be overhearing. I lower my voice and say, "It was an accident. When I put you in there, I didn't think it would take off. I thought it would just be pretend. But I made a mistake, and I'm really sorry for it."

He shrugs and says, "Everybody has accidents sometimes. It's OK." The sincerity in his face makes me marvel. I've been witness to spectacles few men have seen—stars going supernova, a silver city at the center of the moon—but nothing compares to the easy absolution of a child. As I'm thinking this, trying to be appreciative, my son's face freezes, and his eyes fix. His skin turns red, and a vein emerges on his neck. Ten seconds later there's a splash, and he says, "A plopper."

"Sounded like a huge one."

"Enormous."

He climbs down, and together we gaze into the bowl. He says, "Ultimate gigantic." Bursting with pride, he reaches for the roll of toilet paper.

With minimal instruction, Nate cleans himself just fine, and we wash our hands in the sink. When we're done drying off, he stands in front of me at the door but doesn't open it. Instead, he turns and says, "How come you said I got in Uncle Ecklar's robot by myself?"

I look into the tub, then back at Nate. "That was wrong. I shouldn't have done that."

"That was an accident too?"

"I suppose so. Yes."

"Why did you do it?"

I rub at my chin. "That's a hard question. I don't know."

"How can you not know why you did something?"

"I'm not sure, Buddy. You know I love you, right?"

"You're my dad. Of course you love me. I just want to know why you told a lie when telling a lie is a bad thing and you're not supposed to do bad things."

"Like I said, I'm really not sure."

"Well, will you think it over?" This is one of Deb's lines, a question she poses when he breaks the arms off action figures or crayons the wall.

"Sure," I tell my son. "I will think it over."

"And you'll tell me if you figure it out?"

"You bet," I say.

Satisfied, my son reaches for the bathroom door. I think about what I just agreed to and realize it's a promise I'll likely never keep.

Outside, Drunk Gary is passed out in one of the Adirondacks on the edge of the campfire's glow. The only way we're sure he's not dead is the great clouds of breath blooming from his open mouth. Aunt Sondra is puffing on a cigarette. She's thrilled to see a child and tries to shove a stick in Nate's hand. "Ready for s'mores?"

Nate looks behind her at Mrs. Sullivan, who says, "We have to find some shooting stars first."

Debbie takes the stick from Sondra as a kind of consolation prize and impales a marshmallow, steps toward the fire. My wife could use her thermal powers to make it a bit more comfortable, take the chill out of the air. But I know she won't, and not just because of her rule. Here, she isn't Venus. She's just Debbie.

Mrs. Sullivan and Nate settle into the other Adirondack, and she tosses one of her husband's big coats over them like a blanket. They ease back and gaze up. Thin clouds spread across half the sky, but beyond them the stars blink and twinkle. Nate's arm emerges from beneath the coat, and he points. "The Orionids get their name from the constellation Orion."

"Do you know the story of Orion the hunter?" Mrs. Sullivan asks.

"Yeah," Nate says. "But you can tell me again."

I slide over by Sondra and Deb, hold my palms up to the fire. Drunk Gary begins to snore. "I could carry him inside," I offer.

The sisters exchange a look. Sondra says, "He's fine. I'll get him a blanket before I go in."

"Just don't leave him out here with this thing still burning," Deb says. "Liz would never let him hear the end of it if he caught on fire."

My wife smiles at her joke and hands me a perfectly toasted marshmallow. I take a bite and say, "Nice technique."

"You get no credit for noting the obvious." She reaches for my hand, and our cold fingers interlock. She squeezes, and together we scan the sky.

"It's too early, isn't it?" Sondra asks. "They don't really start till after midnight."

"We might see some," Deb says.

"The clouds don't help," I say. "It's a bad night for this."

Deb lifts her chin toward our son. "Tell me how miserable he looks."

Nate has melted back completely into Mrs. Sullivan, still talking about Orion. His face is sunk onto her shoulder, and his eyes are at half-mast. In ten minutes, he'll be as gone as Gary. My wife turns to her sister. "Hey, Sondra, why don't you go tell the kids we're stargazing? Maybe they'll come out if they know Grandy's out here."

"Tell you the truth, I'm about done with freezing my tush off. Little ingrates had their chance. I'm finishing this cigarette and calling it a night."

She takes a puff. Then Deb, without explanation, leads me by the hand away from the warmth, out into the dark, open field. Once we leave the fire's light, I can't even see the grass beneath my feet. Behind us, either Mrs. Sullivan has stopped talking or I can't hear her anymore.

Deb takes us most of the way down the sloping yard, almost to where the men were burning leaves this afternoon. When she stops walking, we face the dark tree line side by side, holding hands. For a minute, we're just quiet there.

"I know you've been worried about me," I finally say.

"I've been worried about us. All of us."

"I know," I say. "And I'm sorry."

"You have so much. Your health. Your powers. Nate. I don't understand why you aren't happy."

"I am happy," I say, and in the moment it feels entirely true.

"Right now you are," she says.

I step around in front, face my wife, then fold my arms around her body. "Things will be different soon," I tell her. "Better. You'll see."

"That's what I want," she says. "I want us all to be happy."

Up by the house, the screen door slams. Three kids come out along with Mr. Sullivan, who is trying to unfold the tripod legs of a telescope.

Debbie takes a deep breath and says, "You'd tell me if you still loved her, wouldn't you, Vince?"

"I don't love her," I say.

"Just a little?"

"No," I say. "Maybe like a sister, but not in the way you mean. I only love you like that."

"Good," she says.

"I'm glad I got divorced," I say, and the statement startles me. "If I hadn't, I wouldn't have you. And we wouldn't have Nate."

"Don't make me think about things like that. It's too terrible."

She plants her face in my chest and sniffles twice. It could be my superpowered wife is weeping. I want to tell her that I feel the same way, that our son is the one thing that really does make me feel good about myself. And out here in this field, the idea of another child, another person who would need me and accept my love and give it back tenfold, it seems like a grand one. I should tell her this, tell her I've decided I want another child. But I do not trust this impulse. I worry that I've lost the ability to separate our desires and can no longer untwine what I want from what I think my wife wants. So, instead of seeing if my wife would like to have another baby, I make a different offer. "Tomorrow night, come with me?"

"Where?"

"My last patrol," I tell her. "It would be nice to do it together."

She looks up at me and, indeed, wipes some tears, then smiles and says, "That would be great. I'd like that."

When she first joined the Guardians, we always patrolled together. Her telekinetic powers aren't strong enough that she can actually fly, but she can make herself weightless, so towing her around took no effort, like pulling a balloon. I remember the first time we did that, her hair streaming out behind her. *Just keep going,* she said. *I don't want this to stop.*

Up at the house, Sondra, maybe Liz, yells Debbie's name.

"That's got to be Nate," she says. "I should get him inside."

"You'll bring him downstairs?" I ask. I want us to have that bed to ourselves.

She nods. "He'll drop like a rock." She leans up and kisses under my ear, and her cold lips send a shiver through my body. "I like talking with you like this."

"I'll stay here," I say. "Come back and find me."

Our code talk feels intimate, close, and I feel certain that, like me, she's thinking of that too-small mattress. Maybe part of her desire is the creation of a sibling for Nate, or maybe it's just lust. My wife disappears into the darkness, and I stare into the night sky. Were I a better man, I'd wait upstairs for my wife with the lights on. And when she came in, I'd tell her about the Zone I stole from CVS, what really happened with Nate and Ecklar's battle armor, even that elevator encounter with the Speedstress. I'd come clean and seek her forgiveness. And then the way would be clear for me to tell her about the deadness growing in my chest, and my plan for Chaos. But at forty, I know myself. I know that if my wife turns to me in that bed, I'll quickly forget such noble thoughts. My rough hands will roam along her body, over her shoulder, and up the behind her ear. In the darkness, I'll tug her hair and expose her tender neck.

# EIGHT

*Navigating a Descent. A Change in Plans. Everyday Crimes.*
*Okapi Mystery and the Humor of Skunks.*
*Threat of the Techno-Horde.*
*Battle in the Food Court.*

"Trust me," I tell Thomas, as we stand on the helipad atop the western rim of the HALO. Behind my teenage son, a red windsock flaps madly, the tail of a desperate fish. Nate sits snugly on my right forearm, his chubby arms locked in a death grip around my neck, and I beckon Thomas with my free hand. "Come on already," I say. "It's not like I'm not going to drop you." When I hear it out loud, the possibility briefly enters my mind, but I keep the smile plastered on my face. Good fathers have confidence in themselves.

Arms crossed, Thomas peers over the side at the city a half-mile below. "Why can't Ecklar just fly us down in the hovercar?"

"He's maneuvering the HALO for us. Besides, the hovercar draws too much attention. Look, this is just easier. You and me, we used to do this all the time."

"I was, like, fifty pounds lighter then," he says. "And you were—" Rather than finish the sentence and embarrass me, my son falls silent. I'm sure of it now, by the expression on his face: he's seen those photos of me in Biloxi.

"Tommy's right. Let's just take the hovercar," Nate whines. "It's cold. I don't want to do this." With his hood up and his face planted in my leather jacket, his voice is muffled.

"Enough," I say. It's true that Ecklar could give us a ride, but today's primary mission objective is family unity—a father and his sons together. Flying down as a group should show Thomas that, despite our troubled history and his perception that I'm the next worst thing to a deadbeat dad, I can, literally, carry the weight. I walk over, loop my free arm around Thomas's waist, and say, "Hang on."

When we lift off, it's true, that shoulder aches, and we even tilt a bit like a boat with too many passengers on one side. I should've saved my strong arm for Thomas. But I right us pretty quickly, and it's just over a thousand feet to our destination. I drift us out over the HALO's sloping side and begin the descent. Nate squeezes my neck to the point where some air is being cut off. He may be weeping. I glance at Thomas only to find his eyes shut tight.

My target is a bank building's helipad, one of a dozen landing spots where we've made arrangements for situations like this. Ecklar piloted the HALO close so I wouldn't have far to fly, and as my shoulders begin to burn, I'm glad that all this requires is basically controlled falling. I doubt I could accelerate upward or navigate with both boys in my arms. Thomas is heavier than I expected, the crosswinds are a bit stronger, and we've floated off course. I strain to give us some lift, put us back on target. We corkscrew upward maybe fifty feet, and my lower back flares. I see flashes of white and feel dizzy, but I don't pass out. I remember the brown bottle of Zone. This morning I considered taking one just to help the day go more smoothly, but I decided against it. With all that's at stake, today I need to be sharp.

As we start drifting down again, it's clear Nate is crying.

Thomas says, "It'll be over soon, buddy. Just close your eyes."

I shake off the vertigo and reacquire the circular landing pad. It's closer than it should be, and a hundred feet to my right. Thankfully, the winds have shifted and are working with me now, so without too much effort I manage a rough touchdown on the outer rim of the bull's-eye. I stretch a foot back to touch the line so that, technically, I can tell myself I landed on the target. The instant we hit, before we even stop moving, Thomas pries himself out of my arms. I set Nate down, and he runs to his brother, who holds him and says, "It's OK. I'll call Ecklar to pick us up later."

I make the choice not to engage this argument till later and take Nate's hand. The winds up here are biting and still strong. We walk to the door, and I punch the code into the keypad. But when I grab the knob and twist, it doesn't budge. I try it a second time, then a third, before looking around in exasperation and seeing a similar building just two blocks to our east. I may have landed on the wrong roof, or my scrambled brain has lost the correct combination. Either way, I've screwed up. Thomas is three feet behind me. With one hand I grip the knob, and with the other I point into the clouds at the perfect **O** shape of the HALO floating above. "See how far we came," I say. When my sons glance up, I gently tug the door, popping the lock. I'm impressed that I kept the damn thing on its hinges, but Thomas clearly heard. As he and Nate step through, his fingers brush across the fractured housing. "Nice," he says. "We gonna have to fight our way through security guards now?"

I concentrate and indeed hear a subsonic alarm in the distance, perhaps several floors below. But when no one comes bursting into the hallway to prevent us from boarding the elevator, I decide it's just ringing in my ears.

Thankfully, the building's front door isn't locked, and we step out onto the sidewalk like normal people. "Stay close," I tell Nate, though he's holding Thomas's hand and the streets are far from crowded. Sunday morning. Folks are hung over or at church. I step off the curb and lift an arm at an approaching taxi.

"What are you doing?" Thomas asks. "It's like three blocks."

"Change in plans," I say.

"We're not going to the museum?" Nate says.

"Maybe later," I say. "First, Daddy has a surprise. It's a better place."

"Better than a museum?" Nate asks Thomas. "Does it have dinosaur bones?"

The cab pulls up, and I open the back door. "Way better," I say. "Bones are dead. Climb in."

I could fit in the back, but instead I ride shotgun. The cabbie is a heavy-set woman with olive skin and unruly eyebrows. She gives me a look, asking why I invaded her space instead of sitting with my kids. "Metro zoo," I tell her.

"The zoo?" Thomas says. "I think Nate would really rather go to the museum."

Nate looks out the window, but he's smiling, I'm sure of it. He's absolutely smiling.

"After lunch maybe," I say. "This is my birthday present. You loved the zoo when you were a kid. On a chilly day like today, we'll have it to ourselves. Plus, there's a new butterfly exhibit I read about it. It sounds great. Nate, don't you like butterflies?"

"Uh-huh," he says, and his enthusiasm is not entirely manufactured. He says to Thomas, "Butterflies come from caterpillars. They go through a metamorphosis."

"That's right," Thomas says. He points out his window. "Look at that guy's beard. Birds could be living in there."

My sons quickly fall into an easy chatter, and I relax. All morning they've been inseparable, laughing at dumb jokes, wrestling like puppies, working as a team to annoy me or Debbie or Sheila. Thomas showed Nate a crawl-space behind the levitation generator where he used to make forts. It did me good to see them playing, and though I'm not a part of the laughter they share in the taxi's backseat, it lifts my spirit. I only feel a little dirty for not telling Thomas the whole truth, that I've got a separate agenda for this trip to the zoo.

So far today, not much has gone according to plan. Thanks to a sleepless evening—Nate came upstairs with Debbie and spent the night tumbling between us on that narrow mattress—we had a late start from the Sullivans'. But I drove the hovercar on the way home, and I floored it a bit, as much as Deb would allow. Even so, by the time we landed, Ecklar had already returned with Sheila and Thomas. We found them down in

Ecklar's quarters, picking at a brunch he'd set up: fresh strawberries, melons, cheese, and mimosas. The boys disappeared into Ecklar's lab, and Debbie and Sheila, as always, acted like long-lost sisters. They hugged and laughed, and Debbie started in trying to convince Sheila to give up her day of research and go shopping in town. I feel nervous when they are alone together, like somehow they'll compare notes about me and realize that, hey, they both agree I'm kind of lacking certain essential qualities.

Ecklar took orders for omelets from the ladies. I followed him into the kitchen because it seemed everyone was breaking into twosomes and I didn't want to be the last man standing. Ecklar started beating eggs and said, "You had an interesting call from Arthur last night."

On the couch, Sheila and Debbie stopped talking and turned to listen.

I said, "Let me guess. I'm banned for life from Titanland?"

"No. He said to tell you he's in."

Debbie stood up. "Wonderful."

Sheila stayed in her seat and cocked her reporter's eyebrow. "What exactly is Arthur in on?"

Debbie outlined All-Star's plan about Bone Crusher, how Titan might come out of retirement to help me enter it. Sheila kept her eyes on me. She seemed skeptical, but in the end she still congratulated me. "You'll tell Thomas about this?"

I nodded, and there was a loud crash from the lab. "Anything back there they can break?"

"Plenty," Ecklar said. "But nothing I can't repair."

"The end of the original Guardians," Sheila said, and I realized Ecklar had told her about his impending departure on the ride out. "That's a big story."

"Clyde is hoping for front page," Ecklar said. "With any luck, Bone Crusher will put up a fight."

"We can hope," Debbie said. "Though he doesn't look real feisty." So she knew where Crusher is hiding—a fact no one had yet shared with me. With this realization, my face snapped to my wife's, but thankfully she didn't notice. I dropped my gaze and felt another surge of guilt: If I'm going to make this work, I'll need to exploit her knowledge, one way or another.

Ecklar went back to work on the eggs, beating them with more ferocity than the task required. I wondered about that phone call my friend had with Arthur.

"I'm not sure how Thomas will take this," I said, to no one in particular.

"I'll tell him if you want," Sheila said. "You don't give him enough credit."

Ecklar stopped scrambling. "Indeed," he said, and he turned those big black eyes up at me.

"What's that supposed to mean?"

"Only that the boy cares for you, and you should tell him everything now. The whole story, the entire truth. It's wrong not to be honest with people who care for you, Vincent."

From the sarcastic tone, it was clear I'd guessed right. Arthur had filled Ecklar in on my plans for King Chaos. I'd wounded my alien comrade's pride, only days before he leaves my world forever. I wanted to apologize, explain that I had every intention of telling him, that indeed I will need his help too. But with Sheila and Debbie watching, all I could say was, "No argument from me. You're right."

He nodded, and I nodded back, and those big eyes blinked, and his lipless green mouth formed its tiny smile.

When we take on King Chaos, raw power won't be enough. Our last encounter in Hamburg proved that. The weapons array in Ecklar's battle suit will no doubt come in handy. But I'm assuming Chaos has kept tabs on us, which means he'll be anticipating Ecklar. So, from a strategic standpoint, I knew victory might depend on another element of surprise. It was this need, and a sense of obligation, that led me to bring my boys to the zoo for my birthday.

After the taxi drops us off, my sons and I work our way through the turnstile opening, and I try to come up with a game plan. People mill around us—other families renting strollers, couples holding hands, and two dozen wheelchaired old folks, each pushed by a teenager with a red hat—but it's far from crowded. Thomas gets upset when I unfold the map and begin plotting the most efficient route. He hoists his half-brother onto his shoulder and glances up. "Yo, Nate," he says. "Which way?"

Nate, who studies the crisscrossing arrow signs, seems fixed on a simple image of a train, but finally points toward EMUS AND OSTRICHES.

"Perfect," Thomas declares and marches off without checking for my approval. And I feel a bit like a stalker, really, hands in my pockets, pursuing my two sons. I'd never leave them alone in a public place, knowing what I know about the world and human nature, but I stay ten feet behind, not wanting to spoil their bonding. As we're plodding along, Thomas laughs loudly and looks back at me, shakes his head in disbelief. I wonder if his brother is telling him about the other night.

In this loose group we move quickly from one exhibit to the next. The ostriches and emus strut slowly around the perimeter of their cyclone-fenced pens. The rhino sits, unmoving, his horn aimed at the back wall of its faux-rocky enclosure. I clap my hands to get its attention, but it's probably asleep. Plus, it's the only animal in there, so it couldn't be Huan. In the next pen, a lone camel curls in on itself beneath a tiny shed, chewing its tail. I make eye contact and wish I were telepathic. I realize I'm doing things in the wrong order. I should've tracked down Gypsy first and brought her along to help.

We find ourselves on an elevated viewing platform, scanning an empty enclosure below us in search of something called an "okapi."

"Maybe okapis can turn invisible," I say.

Neither boy laughs. Thomas studies a drawing on the sign. "Maybe it escaped, tried to get back to Africa where it belongs."

Holding his brother's head, Nate asks, "Are the animals happy?"

"They have it made," I say. "Out in the wild, they'd have to hunt for food, and they'd be in constant danger from predators. This is like a vacation for them."

"Not all animals have predators," Thomas says. "What hunts a camel? I'll bet every one of these suckers would rather be back where it came from."

"Something must hunt a camel," I offer. "Otherwise, they'd overrun the desert. That's how evolution works."

Thomas shrugs. "Maybe when you learned it."

Nate wiggles, and Thomas lowers him to the ground, where he bends to pick up a coin. He walks down the ramp, against the flow of a small parade of old folks. I want to tell them the okapi's a no-show.

We follow Nate to a fountain, where he contemplates tossing the coin. Thomas crosses his arms, and I say, "Can we please just have fun today? I'll send a check to PETA when we're through."

Now Thomas rolls his eyes, a move he inherited from his mother. Nate points his hand at a sign and says, "Hey! Big Cats!"

I ask Nate if he wants to ride on my shoulders, but instead he just grabs my hand and starts walking. Up that ramp on the observation platform, the rest homers and their teenage escorts point and smile. We must have missed something in that pen.

We cross a small wooden bridge spanning stagnant water and pass beneath an arched sign that reads CAT TOWN. Just inside, the panther paces behind bars, glaring. On the other side of a twenty-foot concrete pit, a sleeping tiger grips a white plastic bucket between its massive paws. It reminds me of the way Thomas clung to his stuffed panda bear, a nostalgic connection I know better than to share with him. For the lions they've built a savannah the size of two basketball courts. Rocks surround a wading pool, and a real tree spreads its branches, providing cover. But instead of playing in their water, which has got to be close to freezing, or hiding in the tree, or even taking their royal position atop the rock mountain, both animals lie placidly by the see-through wall. The lioness is collapsed on her side, a few gnats congregating in the crusty corners of her closed eye. The male sits nearby, looking away from her as if he can't bear another minute of seeing his wife like this. His mane is flat and tangled. A brown growth the size of a lime sprouts from one of his paws.

I wonder where he came from and pray it was a circus, or that he was saved from a barbaric roadside attraction in Nevada, something. I don't want to acknowledge the truth, that deep in his memory are images of open plains, the blackness of night, the sweet comfort of tall grass, the whiff of a gazelle lifting on the breeze. I have no doubt that the beast before me is grateful for the food he receives every day, that he eats greedily to sustain his body. But I also don't doubt what Thomas said earlier, that even if it meant his life, he would return to Africa for one more hunt.

"Why's the tiger so sleepy?" a little girl asks. I turn to find her between my two sons. She has a ponytail and glasses. A man says, "Gwen, that's not a tiger."

He and I share a look, both of us clearly understanding the other's predicament. We are dads without custody, trying to be good fathers by doing a fatherly act.

On Earth 1.5, I had no children. I lived alone in a studio apartment on the lower south side of Kingdom Town. My mediocre career as a superhero had been replaced with a mediocre career as a pitchman. My image was plastered on billboards in Center Circle, hawking shaving cream, light beer. I followed myself into Big Shanghai, where I paid an anonymous hooker to put on a cape and invite me into her bed.

Nate tells Gwen, "It's a lion."

The king of the jungle yawns and struggles to his feet. As he moves away, he favors that bad paw, limping just a bit. Thomas slides next to me and gets ready to unleash the wiseass remark I know he's working on. "Come on," I say. "Let's check out those butterflies."

In the darkened chambers of the insectarium, Nate and Thomas scurry from dung beetle to dragonfly to water strider. Since we're in a building, I let them wander together out of my eyesight. I begin to doubt that I'll have any success today. I'm not even sure Huan's still here, and if she is, she probably doesn't want to be found. She could be a Brazilian Leaping Spider, in the case right before me, or one of the dozen monkeys we passed, or a squirrel harassing passersby in the food court. Of all the original Guardians, Huan was probably the most powerful, though she never played it that way. Here was a woman who could turn into a mosquito, buzz up to an enemy, and—poof—transform into a Tyrannosaurus rex. She wasn't gung ho like the rest of us, not flashy or showy. She always had an air of restraint about her, even of embarrassment about her powers. Not that she wasn't friendly, but she rarely laughed at Sparkplug's corny jokes, and after a successful mission, while we held press conferences and celebrations, she'd disappear to her room. Gypsy was erratic—would party like crazy, then have bouts of crushing depression. But Huan, she just idled at a different speed. Her belief that we were doing good was an article of faith for her, a matter of serious conviction.

Huan's metamorphoses, she told me, were always painful. At first I took this to mean physically agonizing—capes are wired to think this way, to translate the spiritual into the bodily so that we can do something about it—but over the years I came to realize that her pain was twofold. In part this was because Huan's powers derived from a kind of superempathy. She literally felt her way into the skin of whatever she became. And after a while in any form, her humanity receded, and she became tortured by the instinctual urges that took hold. She was awed by their intensity. One time we were tracking Mr. Squid and Aquarius in the northern Pacific, off the coast of Washington. Huan transformed into a right whale, just to send out some sonar. When she finally returned—six days later—she couldn't stop talking about the irresistible pull of migration. "I nearly forgot who I was," she told me, and I could see it clearly, the gleam of regret in her green eyes.

Over time she began to spend more and more of her days as something other than human. "It's like being in a dream," she told me once toward the end. "Do you have any idea how fast a hummingbird thinks?"

Huan didn't so much retire as retreat. She'd had it with the human race and chosen the animal kingdom. After Titan bailed out and before the cops forced us to butt out of their affairs, there were a couple years when mostly what we did was track down ordinary criminals. With our supercomputers, superstrength, and superspeed—and without the restrictions placed on traditional law enforcement—we tracked murderers, exposed corrupt politicians, burned meth labs in the fields of Kansas, broke up a kiddie porn ring outside Detroit. As glorified heroes, we'd spent years seeing mankind as mostly grateful fans, and distance from them allowed us to believe in our own mythology. Dealing with everyday crimes helped us realize how little good we really did. Huan, the only daughter of Chinese dissidents who defected during the Cold War, had always been a devout believer in our cause. She fell hardest. Responding to a domestic disturbance one night in Jersey, she and I found an eight-year-old girl in a basement apartment. The child hadn't been beaten, just left alone while her father went out drinking. Supposedly for her own protection, he'd handcuffed her to the couch, abandoned her with the remote and a box of Cocoa Puffs. Soon after that, Huan left a note explaining her decision to take a retreat from the human race but saying that, if we were in dire need, we could seek her out at her new home, this zoo she loved so dearly. The remaining Guardians took a pact to keep her location secret and leave her in peace. For nearly eight years, we'd all honored that. Now, I wondered if she was still here, just how far gone she might be, and if I was justified in defining my harebrained scheme as "dire need."

A sign on the double glass doors tells us the butterfly exhibit is closed, though when Nate shoves his face against the fogged glass, he says, "I can see them!" Briefly I contemplate breaking in, but decide instead on another course of action. I lead the boys outside and ask if they're ready for some lunch. "There's the train ride!" Nate says, one chubby finger aimed at a sign overhead.

Thomas smiles, but I say, "Nate, that thing is lame, really lame. It rattles, and it's smoky, and all it really does is huff around the zoo. I'll take you on a real train later."

"This one's right here," Nate says.

"We should eat now."

"I could take him," Thomas says. "If you're, like, hungry and all."

"No," I say. "We stick together. We'll go on the ride and then find some chow, OK? It's family fun day."

We cut through a food court overrun with pigeons, even seagulls somehow, and then have to pass through a tunnel of sorts, one lined with glass-walled animal enclosures. On the right side, the boys get interested in a komodo dragon; meanwhile, I wander along the left side, reading about the koala bears, which aren't really bears at all. There are three in the exhibit—two huddled up high on a PVC jungle gym, one below sitting in the dirt. The one on the ground is holding a single leaf, turning it in its paw and studying it with great concentration. It looks up and sees me looking. Then the koala smiles. Its eyes are bright green.

I glance over my shoulder to be sure the boys aren't watching and hold my hand between my belly and the glass. I give the koala a peace sign. It looks at its paw, drops the leaf, and slowly extends two fingers in a **V**.

"Hey guys," I say. "Change in plans." I cross to them, reach in my pocket, and fish out a twenty. "Take your brother back to the food court and get him a slice of pizza."

Nate says, "I don't want pizza. What about the train?"

"Then have a cheeseburger. We'll take the train twice after we eat. It's lunchtime now, OK. I don't want you guys getting overhungry. I'll be right there."

"What kind of a word is *overhungry?*" Thomas asks.

I scowl. "Would you just do as I say?"

Nate, sensing tension, folds his arms and strolls to a platypus display. Thomas cocks his eyebrows and says, "What's your deal? You seem a little more psycho than usual. This is hardly worth a spring break in Nags Head."

"That's how your mother got you to agree to do this? She had to bribe you to spend time with me?"

"I wouldn't call it a bribe," he says, then stares at the twenty.

I can't help glancing back at the koala, just to be sure Huan didn't shift into a gnat and slip away. But she's still there, with her jade-colored koala eyes aimed at my son. "Thomas, I need you to watch Nate for a few minutes. Just take him back there and buy him whatever he wants. Do not leave the food court. I won't be five minutes."

Thomas stares at his brother.

"Tommy," I say, something I haven't called him in years, "this is important. It's about work."

"Hero work?" He'd deny it, but for an instant, his eyes shine.

I nod and feel a tightness in my throat. This was the phrase we used when he was a child and I had to explain my many absences. I'd tell him he was old enough to know a secret and that he had to be man of the house, help watch his mom, whatever. I ask him the question: "Can I count on you?"

"We'll be in the food court." He snatches the money, turns to his brother and says, "Come on, we'll start with ice cream." Nate trots off with him, and I turn back to the koala pen. The two up high still cling to one another, but Huan is gone. I'm about to say her name when a couple enters the tunnel from the train end, pushing a stroller. "Look at the teddy bears," they say.

A monarch butterfly circles my head twice, hovers as best it can in front of my face. When it flits out of the tunnel, I follow. It floats and flutters around the side, leading me through some overgrown azaleas. But in a small walkway in the rear, between the back of the building and the zoo's outer fence, I find overturned milk crates, a patch of dirt littered with cigarettes. The butterfly lands on one of the crates, and its flesh stretches and grows into the shape of a Great Dane. The dog, green-eyed, says, "Don't tell me that was Tommy."

"He goes by Thomas now."

"Unbelievable. It's been that long?"

"Longer still in dog years."

The Huan-dog laughs. "It's good to see you again, Vincent." She closes her green eyes, concentrates, and shifts into an orangutan.

"Look," I say, "I know this is an intrusion."

"Not at all. I'm so glad you've come." The orangutan blinks before shifting into a horse, which says, "Terribly sorry, but I can't quite dial up human. It's been forever."

"Don't apologize," I tell Huan, who finally settles on a snowy owl.

"I've done it, Vincent," she says. Her emerald eyes are glassy and still. "I made contact."

Huan used to talk about becoming one with the bestial world, tapping into the unified spirit of the animal kingdom. Just before she left, she told me it was her destiny.

"I don't just mean communication within a species. That's easy. I'm talking about interspecies conversations. They may be very basic, but the animals, they all talk to each other."

She sounds fevered, blissful, like a preacher revving up a sermon. I sit on the milk crate opposite her. "What do the animals talk about?"

"The very things we do. The weather, food. Sickness and death and new life. And love, of course love. I don't think I ever understood love until I heard elephants murmuring in the predawn light. Their capacity for kindness, it makes me feel so small. Some of the animals tell jokes. You wouldn't believe how wickedly funny skunks are. Giraffe humor, I have to say, is more an acquired taste."

"I'm sure it is," I say. As I'm wondering if Huan has gone native, she turns her owl head completely around, 180 degrees, which reminds me of Linda Blair. When her face comes back around, she says, "Sorry, I thought I heard something."

I'm silent, wondering what she thought she heard and trying to decide just how crazy she is. At the same time, I can't help but admire the abiding faith she possesses in this absurd delusion of the animal kingdom. On top of all I'm feeling, pity for my friend, selfish concern for my plan, I feel envy. I wish I had something like this to believe in, something huge and important to be a part of. She seems to read my mind and says, "It's all right that you don't believe me, Vincent. Humans don't need to believe me for now. The day will come when everyone does. Maybe for now, we should concentrate on why you're here."

"Right," I say. "Let me think where to start."

"With the Techno-Horde, of course. They're the ones trying to stop me."

Something startles her, and she shifts into a mountain gorilla. Her huge hands split open a leafless azalea to her side. Two squirrels haul ass up a tree, and Huan lifts her ape face. "My apologies, dear sisters."

"Huan," I say. "We shut down the Horde fifteen years ago."

"We thought we did. They're back. And it only makes sense they'd come out of hiding now. They must realize how close I am to finishing my work. If I can unify the animal world, their plans for a society of pure technology will be in jeopardy. I'm astonished their surveillance teams didn't attack. I've seen their robotic operatives all over the zoo lately. Clearly, they've improved their designs—these new androids are almost undetectable. Yesterday one came by the seal tank that was an exact duplicate of Jacques

Cousteau. I suppose they've developed a sense of irony. You took a great personal risk coming here. On behalf of the animal community, I thank you." The gorilla closes its green eyes and bows.

I know Huan's rap on the Techno-Horde is nutty—those lame androids and their robotic creations were long ago recycled or turned to scrap metal—but her sense of lurking danger infects me. I can't help but picture my two sons, sitting on a bench with ice cream cones, alone and unprotected. I feel an urge to get back to them, but I need to finish what I started. I'm not too proud to use her paranoia against her: "This all makes sense," I say. "We knew King Chaos was planning something big, but we didn't know he was in bed with the Horde."

"Chaos," the gorilla says as she nods. "A human behind this after all."

"We're closing in. If we can bring him down, my guess is that the whole Horde scheme will collapse on itself. Can I count on your help?"

"Guardians forever," she says. Once, this credo was nearly sacred to me. At night, to ward off the anxiety that comes before sleep, I'd repeat it like a mantra to ease my mind. Now I can't even bring myself to say it back to Huan. I reach into my pocket and pull out my Danger Ring, thinking I'll swipe another from Ecklar. But Huan shakes it off with a thick paw. "When you need my help, merely whisper my name. As long as one animal can hear you, word will get to me, brother."

"All right," I say, not sure what to believe. "I should go find my boys."

"Of course," the gorilla says.

I turn to go, and she says, "I assume there's some connection between all this and what's happening to the sky."

I look up.

"Directly above the city," she says.

I nod. "That's radiation from Ecklar's people. It's the start of some kind of interstellar space bridge. They're coming back for him."

The gorilla considers my explanation, and I realize that I sound as crazy to her as she does to me. "Whatever it is," she tells me, "the birds don't care for it."

"OK," I say, not sure how else to respond. That her abilities allow her to perceive the vortex doesn't surprise me. Can't animals sense earthquakes before they happen?

My former teammate morphs into a squirrel and follows the two she spooked earlier up that tree. I walk away, wondering which side she'd take in a planetary war between beasts and man. Ecklar once speculated that Huan might not be human at all, that her abilities operated on a different plane from everyone else's. He was always frustrated that he couldn't account for the increase in mass when she changed shape. The ability to create and shape matter at will, that kind of energy, he explained, was something even his people couldn't conceive of.

When I reach the food court, I don't see my sons. Packs of children chew on floppy slices of pizza. Parents puncture juice boxes with plastic straws. In the branches of a sycamore, a red-and-yellow parrot sits, clearly an escapee. But my children aren't where they should be.

I maintain my breathing and try not to think of Huan's wild claims, that the park is overrun with sworn enemies of the Guardians, sinister androids intent on destroying mankind. That bird is just a bird, not a robot replica. But my pace quickens as I move through the Tex-Mex Chuck Wagon, the American Grill, and even Veggie Garden. Outside once more, I scan again each table, studying the faces, hoping maybe they fell in with some kids. All I get is a scolding look from a suspicious mom. I recheck the benches scattered along the perimeter, but there is nothing. Even though Thomas is angry with me, he'd never have taken Nate to those trains, and he'd have no reason to leave the court. By now my heart is starting to get away from me, and realizing what I'm about to do quickens my pulse further. I stride to the center of the court and do the thing that no parent wants to do, publicly admit abject failure. I cup my hands to my mouth and yell, "Nate! Tommy!"

The pigeons take flight, and everyone turns my way. I crank my head left and right, expecting to see them coming my way from some isolated eating spot, embarrassed but safe. All I get are the stares of strangers. I take a few steps toward the train and repeat my cry, and that suspicious mom stands from her table. "I saw two boys with a security guard by the fountain," she says. I look where she's pointing, but nothing is there. "He had a walkie-talkie and sunglasses."

I can't say why the image strikes me with such terror, but it's like a spark on gasoline. Without making a conscious decision, I'm instantly aloft, fists clenched, eyes sharp, forty feet in the air above the civilians of the food court.

There's an audible group gasp, fingers pointed, and a few smart parents evacuate, shoving strollers away from the area at high speed. I slowly rotate like a wrestler at the center of the ring, scanning for trouble, expecting it to come at any moment. A single scream from behind spins me around, and coming over the sycamore is a man-sized creature with an insect body, reptilian wings, and a bull head complete with horns. Now everyone is screaming.

I don't think about what to do. When you see a monster, you hit it. I bolt toward the beast and cock one fist, thinking *center mass, center mass,* eyes on its shiny thorax. Just before impact, something happens to my body, and my head whips forward and back. A tightness around my ribs makes me look down, and I see a slimy coil squirming around me, squeezing me like a boa constrictor. I follow it back to the creature, which now has tentacles, feathery wings, the head of a goat—and deep green eyes. "Vincent," it asks, "what are you doing?"

"Fuck," I say. "My kids are gone."

"The Horde," Huan says, and her head becomes an eagle's. She squints down at the scene below, where the civilians have all scurried for cover.

"I'm calling for backup," I say, but I can't get to the Danger Ring in my pocket because she's still got me wrapped in her tentacle.

"Wait," she says. One of her other tentacles points to the far side of the restaurants, where Thomas and Nate stand next to each other just outside the restrooms. Thomas has his arm around his brother and is looking my way. He does not seem afraid.

"False alarm," Huan says. "Thank the goddess."

I want to fly down and sweep them up, zoom off to a safe place and never leave, but Huan clenches me tight. I look her in her eagle eyes, and she says, "Vincent, you'd better go ahead and punch me. Not too hard."

I don't move.

"My cover," she says. "I can't just fly away. The Horde is surely watching. Knock me into the lake, slam me straight up into the clouds. I need to disappear."

I don't understand my friend's logic, but when she uncoils that tentacle, I grab it in one hand. I gather two other ones, enough to have a good grip, and I say, "You with me?" She follows my thinking and begins flying around me while I anchor the center. From below, it looks like I'm spinning the creature against its will, and I twirl to build momentum. When I let go, she accelerates, and her body arcs over the zoo, out toward the south river. Maybe she'll work her way to the sea.

I quickly float down and land next to my boys, ready to apologize and take the blame for leaving them, screwing up this special day like it seemed I was fated to. But before I have a chance, they rush into my arms and embrace me, together. The three of us hug, and it's Thomas who speaks first. "That kicked ass," he says. Nate squeezes my side, and I feel the spike of pain that likely means a broken rib, but I don't push him away. Then comes a sound from behind us, something I almost don't recognize. Cheers and applause.

The zoo patrons come out from hiding. They emerge from beneath the food court tables, step out from behind the boulders lining the lake. They clap and take pictures, and one of those old folks rises out of her wheelchair as if she'd just received a miracle cure. The faces beam at me with thanks and admiration and awe. It's like yesterday at Titan's stadium, only better. In the minds of these people, I've protected them and their children from a vicious monster. They think they owe me their lives.

"You did it, Dad," Nate says. "You saved everybody."

I think for a moment about how to answer. "Just doing my job, son," I say, and I feel wonderful, and I feel disgusted, but I go on. "I'm a hero."

# NINE

*Accounts of the Incident with the Hideous Beast. The Beginning of Something Sinister. Power beyond Reckoning. A Bedroom Scene. The Thrill of Being Desired. The Threat of Spontaneous Combustion. Fear of Falling.*

---

There's nothing quite like being surrounded by appreciative fans. But when you've got a four-year-old with you, there's a danger of being crushed if things get out of control. To avoid such an event, and to get out of the cold, I led both my sons through the first open door I could find. And so, five minutes after my grand victory, I'm sitting now with both boys at a corner table inside the Tex-Mex Chuck Wagon, a restaurant with wall murals of tepees and buffalo. They dip corn chips in melted cheese, slurp complimentary sodas brought by the staff.

"It had six arms," Nate says.

Thomas chews and says, "Must've been an alien, don't you think, Dad?"

"Maybe so," I tell him. The longer you let a lie go uncorrected, the harder it is to get out of it. But both my sons seem so happy, so bright with belief in me. Telling them the truth would be cruel. This is what I keep telling myself.

A man with a two-foot-tall red sombrero delivers something he calls "Enchanted Enchiladas" on a square plastic plate. The boys dig in, and I grant the man a smile so he can walk away. He passes a zoo security guard, one of a dozen men and women dressed in odd zebra-striped uniforms who showed up only moments after the fight. They are armed only with what look to be cattle prods, and I wonder if they aren't trained in animal control more than crowd control. Still, I can't argue that they aren't doing a fine job.

Through the oversized window, just past a line of these peace officers, I see the grateful civilians who didn't leave as soon as the action ended. Their eyes are wide with wonder, and their mouths move quickly. I can't tell exactly what they're saying, but I know who they're talking about. As a group, their attention shifts suddenly upward, into the sky, and those at the center of the courtyard scatter for the perimeter. I hope, for an instant, that this signals the return of Menagerie, come back as a griffin perhaps, ready for a second fake beating.

Instead, a hovercar descends into the open space. Blasts from the air jets whip up trash and leaves, sending citizens for cover behind trees or making them turn their backs. As it descends, I'm surprised to see Ecklar at the wheel, armored up in his battle suit. It's been years since he's had it out in the field, though maybe he was inspired by Nate's late-night adventure. Sheila is also in the hovercar, and she vaults over the side like she's heading into combat. She somehow knows where we are and runs straight to us, but when she bursts through the doors, the three of us just sit where we are, strangely still. She bends to embrace Thomas, who hugs her back and says, "Mom, everything's OK. Dad was way awesome."

She looks at me, and the fear for her son's life melts away.

A second hovercar, this one piloted by Clyde, touches down. Dressed in her Venus costume, Deborah bolts through the courtyard and lifts a hand. The doors swing open before her, and she joins us inside. Nate scoots off the bench and charges into her arms.

So each of my boys is now in his mother's embrace, and each of the women holds me with her eyes. They look on me with relief and gratitude.

Clyde appears behind them, wearing his geeky yellow-and-white All-Star costume, and says, "Ice Queen and Ecklar are securing the perimeter. Report."

"There was a monster," I say. "I kicked its ass. After that, nachos."

He cocks a look and says, "Did you recognize it?"

Thomas squirms out of Sheila's extended hug and goes back to his food. I shake my head at Clyde and offer Sheila a sip of iced tea. She waves it off.

Clyde rubs his chin. "First those college kids hypnotized into thinking they were cavemen, then Bone Crusher reappears. Now an unknown creature. This could be the beginning of something sinister."

Nothing Clyde loves more than conspiracies. I say, "Those damn Kappa Alphas weren't under anyone's spell. They were drunk, that's all."

Clyde looks at me askance, like I've spoken heresy.

Nate, still clutched to Deb's chest, tells her, "The okapi wasn't where it was supposed to be. It's missing."

Clyde's eyebrows arch, and I say, "Figure that's unrelated."

Deb stands, holding Nate like a baby now, and asks, "How'd you end up at the zoo anyway? What happened to the museum?"

"Change in plans," Thomas says. "Who wants to see dead animals when you can see real ones?"

Though he doesn't know it, my son is now an accomplice in my lie. Clyde takes out his handheld computer and starts inputting data. When he asks for a description of the creature, the boys begin speaking at the same time. Tentacles, they say. Horns and claws. Deb's and Sheila's expressions grow more disturbed as the danger their boys faced increases in their mind.

Clyde types for a minute, then says, "OK, I've officially designated the new hostile as the Hideous Beast. Did it exhibit any supernatural abilities?"

"Flight," I say. "Superstrength. Bad breath."

The boys chuckle. Nate says, "Laser eyes."

Clyde hesitates, not quite trusting the eyewitness testimony of a four-year-old. But before I can correct him, Thomas nods. "You bet. Red lasers."

I wish I were alone with him, so I could ask if he's just protecting his brother or trying to exaggerate his father's heroics.

Ecklar's seven-foot robot walks in and approaches us. Nate cringes and curls against Thomas. Then the shield flips up like a welder's mask, and Ecklar's face appears. My friend's eyes drill into mine with a meaning I can all too easily guess. He reports to Clyde, "No unusual readings on my scanners. Ice Queen's rounding up witnesses, but their accounts are somewhat divergent. We've got some photos, though."

He holds up a civilian's cellphone, and there on the screen are Huan and I, locked in deadly combat.

Clyde says, "Thing looks like an amalgam. Any chance the Grand Geneticist could be involved? Maybe he's got an experimental lab on the zoo grounds somewhere."

Ecklar gives me that intense look again, waits for me to answer. When I stay silent, he says, "I suppose anything's a possibility."

Clyde decides to evacuate the zoo and conduct what he calls a "Level-7 Full Sweep." He informs the zebra-striped rent-a-cop waiting by the door, who nods, depresses a button on his cattle prod, and heads out. Within moments, the zoo patrons—my adoring fans—are being ushered out of the courtyard. They seem reluctant to leave, and a few of them wave at me through the window, like we're old friends being separated against our will. Clyde asks Ecklar to take Sheila and Thomas back home in the hovercar. "Stay with them till we've ruled out a code 72."

I don't know what this means, but Ecklar nods.

Thomas says, "I want to stick around."

Sheila drops a look at him.

"Can't I even finish my food?"

"Get a to-go box," Sheila says.

I should tell my ex-wife that our son is entirely safe, that he never was in any jeopardy, that this is all a fantasy I'm not man enough to break out of. When she puts her arms around me to say good-bye, I say, "I'm sorry about all this," and in a way, my apology is entirely sincere.

She sniffles and says, "I'm just so glad you were here."

Behind my breastplate, I feel the rising. But this glorious moment is diminished somewhat when I see Deb watching my face, seeing how much the words of my ex-wife mean to me.

I walk them out to the hovercar. Though Thomas is sixteen, Sheila buckles him in. Ecklar comes up behind us, his robotic limbs whirring and humming with every step. He leans over the side and says to Sheila, "I won't be but a minute." Then he walks away, toward the pond with the fountain. I know I'm supposed to follow.

I'm surprised to finds ducks skimming the surface, unimpressed by all the excitement. Ecklar stops walking, becoming a seven-foot statue, and I say, "Good to see you in the old suit. Still fits, huh?"

Ecklar asks, "At what point in time do you think we should talk about precisely what the hell's going on?"

The ducks paddle away from us. I watch the ripples fade, then say, "I suppose now would be the answer you're looking for."

"Now works for me. Let's start with the truth of the Hideous Beast."

Still facing the retreating ducks, I say, "You know the truth."

"Huan?"

I nod and turn away. Only the original Guardians know she's been hiding out in this place. Sunlight cracks through a break in the clouds, and something at the bottom of the pond sparkles, like lost keys. I lean over the rail for a better look. The sparkling objects are scattered beneath me, and of course they aren't rare gems or jewels, but coins. Those are somebody's dreams down there, tossed wishes half-covered in mucky duck shit.

Ecklar says, "I always suspected she wasn't really drawing on altered DNA patterns. She's relying only on her imagination. There's no limit to what she could turn into. The power to do that, it's beyond reckoning."

"She's also a little bit nuts, I should tell you."

"That seems to be going around. You two planned this little charade?"

"No," I say. "I just got lucky."

Ecklar glances at the hovercar. "I don't especially care what you tell Clyde. An exercise like this has definable advantages for the team. But Sheila, Debbie, they need to know the truth. That seems nonnegotiable."

"Why does this suddenly sound like a hostage crisis?"

"Just go tell them."

"I can't. Not right now. Other things are happening."

"So Titan tells me."

I feel again my friend's deep hurt. As the day of his departure from our planet grows near, he and I are going through what feels like a kind of divorce. "It just came to me yesterday morning," I tell him. "If you haven't noticed, I've been kind of busy. Plus, with your own plans, well, I didn't want you to feel obligated."

"You are my *naddeo,*" he says. "I will stand by your side."

I've always envied Ecklar's resolution. "We can get this done before your people show up," I say. "If we do it right, we can pull it off in a couple days, tops."

"If Bone Crusher is aware of the current location of King Chaos."

"He'll know."

"And if he agrees to surrender that information."

"That's why I need Gypsy."

For a moment, Ecklar is silent and still. We both got the same letter from her when she was in rehab, the one chronicling all her addictions, asking for forgiveness for past wrongs and support as she strode boldly into the future. At the bottom, beneath hearts and kisses, Grace signed her name in big loopy cursive. Even her signature seemed under the influence. Ecklar says, "Gypsy was part of my phone call with Arthur. He thinks it's unwise to involve her."

"Arthur can kiss my caped ass."

Ecklar says, "Hee hee hee." When his fake laughter ends, he looks at the hovercar, where Sheila sits with one arm around Thomas. "It would be better if you spoke with her now. Since I'm certain of the truth, I'll have to tell her."

"Andromedans don't perpetuate falsehoods," I say. This is a line he's dropped on me a dozen times.

"Indeed. But beyond that, lying's just a shitty way to treat someone you care about."

I know my friend is right, that he is speaking with the voice of my better self. I know I should be grateful to him instead of angry. But anger is what I feel as I follow him to the hovercar. Sheila and Thomas turn to me as one, and in their eyes I see the same look—the thing I know will soon be gone, stolen by the truth—their belief in me as a man.

Ecklar says, "I'll give you all a few minutes."

Thomas picks food from an unfolded Styrofoam container. I say, "Look you two, something needs to be cleared up before you go."

Sheila's eyes narrow, and before I lose my nerve I just say it. "There was no Hideous Beast. That was Menagerie, and I had to pretend to fight her because she's kind of lost her mind and thinks the Techno-Horde is stalking her. I had no choice."

Thomas speaks with his mouth half-full of corn chips. "Menagerie can't turn into things like that."

I shrug. "I guess her powers have evolved some in eight years."

Sheila holds her silence, but I can tell by her face she's calculating something. Thomas says, "So she just picked this time to come out of hiding and pretend to attack you? That was a coincidence?"

"Yes. No. It's more complicated than that. After we got separated, she heard me shouting your name."

Sheila says, "You were shouting?"

"The boys were lost," I say. "What else would you suggest I do?"

Thomas folds the box and says to his mother, "We were in the bathroom."

She turns to me like a prosecuting attorney. "Vince, where were you when the boys went to the bathroom?"

"We're getting way off track here." I hold both hands up. "Huan heard me yelling and thought there was danger. She came to help, and I didn't recognize her, so I thought she was a threat."

They both look at me, incredulous. I say, "Look, these things happen. I'm just trying to come clean and be honest with my family."

Sheila starts thinking of a new question, but Thomas has heard enough. "Bullshit," he says.

Sheila snaps, "Thomas Stephen!"

"No other word for it," he says. "This whole day. Everything he says. All bullshit. This is so typical."

"Tommy," I say, "you can't believe that. I love you."

"You want to come clean and be honest with your family? That's cool. Tell Mom here about how you got drunk and shoved Nate into Ecklar's armor, nearly sent him blasting into outer space."

Sheila stares at me, and when I don't speak, she asks the obvious question. "Is that true?"

I look over at Debbie and Nate, still inside the Tex-Mex. He's sucking on a straw shoved into an enormous chocolate shake. He's alive and unhurt, but what I did that night, it could've gone very wrong. I grip the side of the hovercar for balance and say, "I wasn't drunk." I don't offer that I was under the effects of some high-end muscle relaxant.

"Christ Jesus," she says. Then she yells, "Ecklar! Let's go."

Thomas says, "I told you, Mom. Bullshit."

She ignores him. I say, "Obviously, I didn't mean for the suit to activate. I'd never put him in harm's way."

Ecklar opens the door and climbs in, then the ignition sequence starts. I say to Sheila, "I'm telling you this because I don't want any more lies between us all." This too, of course, is only partly true.

My ex-wife shakes her head. "Even for you, this is pretty fucked-up. I think it's best if we take some time to sort this out, OK? From a distance."

I nod, then step back. With a whoosh, the hovercar lifts into the sky, and Ecklar speeds away with a family I have most certainly lost.

After the zoo, I head back to the HALO with Nate and Deb. Bubba and J.D. meet us in the hangar, and each gives me a high five for my monster stomping. They want to take me out for a drink, but I've got bigger plans. Nate demands we open birthday presents before he goes down for a nap, and then he insists we put together the model rocket ship he picked out for me. After we're done, Deb leads a reluctant Nate back to his room, carrying the fragile rocket ship, and I sit at the computer in the corner of the living room. I start forcing myself through the questions on Clyde's "Incident Requiring Intervention Report." I keep an eye on the clock and try not to get too upset when Ecklar doesn't return when I expect him. I imagine him in Sheila's home, trying to convince her not to sever all ties.

Just when I've decided Debbie has passed out with Nate, our son's door opens, and she tiptoes out. She crosses the living room without looking my way and silently slips into our bedroom. Last night nobody got any sleep in that cramped bed, and I assume my wife has decided to lie down herself. That this further postpones my obligation of telling her what really happened at the zoo does not upset me. I go back to the form on the screen. Field 14A asks me to "Compare the unknown combatant's abilities to known paranormals."

The thing to do, I decide, is wait until tonight, when Debbie and I are alone on patrol. I'll bring her to one of my secluded rooftop haunts, tell her how excited I am about the future, tell her she means the world to me. I'll tell her that at forty I have perspective enough to realize that she has made my life have meaning. Then I'll explain how I tricked her into thinking her son was in mortal danger. Afterward I'll tell her I need to find Bone Crusher so I can track down my mentor's nemesis and kill him or die trying, in part to avenge the death of the man who cuckolded me.

Thinking through my plan only makes it seem more absurd, and I can't help but wonder just what the hell I'm doing. This kind of thing, it occurs to me, wasn't part of my early days as a hero, when I didn't know the meaning of doubt. It's pathetic, but I tap a few computer keys and bring up some archival footage. The screen flickers, and in grainy images, the original Guardians stand back to back, surrounded by dog-size paramecia mutated by Micro Maestro. It's hard not to notice that, though our lives are in mortal danger, I'm smiling. Smashing monsters doesn't require a great deal of deliberation or moral conjecture. Then the camera catches something truly disturbing. Micro Maestro watches the battle from atop a bacterium big as a bulldozer. Gazing down on the mayhem he created, he seems happy. Even more than that, he looks certain. But his smile is no different than mine.

My fingers clatter on the keyboard, and file footage of King Chaos comes up. He and the Insidious Six wade through the defenses of a government weapons facility hidden in the mountains of Wyoming. Rockets explode, dust swirls, and the Guardians descend from the sky. Quickly everyone engages an opponent. And I see it there in Chaos's face as he commands his minions—I pause the film to study it. No hesitation. No doubt. Only the conviction that this course of action is the one he is committed to.

Good is a lot more complicated than I thought it was as a kid. But evil, it seems, is basic as black. On Earth 1.6, the moral order was inverted. The Guardians ruled Kingdom Town like a superpowered mob. With iron fists, we meted out our will and took whatever we desired. That world's Commander Invincible had just assassinated Titan to become leader of the team. Just before I was sucked through the portal to yet another parallel reality, I confronted that Vincent and pleaded with him to mend his ways. I told him that deep down he was good. I told him that with power like ours, we could make the world a better place for all humanity. He looked at me in disgust and shook his head, then gave me some advice of his own. "Get your head out of your ass."

A squeaky hinge lifts my head. The bedroom door swings slowly open. The latch doesn't always catch, and Deb's asked me to fix it a dozen times. I don't want to wake her with my typing, so I get up and approach quietly. I reach inside for the knob, but a flickering glow stops me. When I peek through the doorway, I see lit candles on both nightstands. On the bed, my young wife bunches the covers up under her chin and smiles. Ripped wrapping paper has been tossed onto the floor, where I see a small rectangular box with the words "Vickie's Top Drawer" in elegant script.

"I opened your present," Deb says. "Hope you don't mind."

"I need to talk with you," I tell her. I will do the right thing.

She pulls down the blanket, exposing her bare slim neck, the graceful slope of her shoulders. Across her chest, white lace—delicate and lovely. I close the door and move toward the bed, unbuttoning my shirt. The wrongness of this does not escape me as I crawl onto the mattress, plant a kiss on my wife's sweet lips. I know I should be honest with her now, beforehand, that later this will make my confession all the worse. But she is beautiful, and I am weak, and the promise of sex, of rolling my body into hers because she wants to roll her body into mine, is too much of a temptation. The thrill of being desired never fades.

Deb hitches my pants past my knees, uses a foot to kick them free of my ankles, and guides me down next to her. She kisses my neck, tells me she loves me, and my vision goes white with the wonder of it all. I feel excited and aroused, and only thinking this thought makes me realize I am not.

When I go still, Deb's eyes zero in on mine. "Vince?" she says. My expression of failure must be pretty obvious, because Deb immediately snakes a roaming hand to the source of the problem. She begins caressing me and whispers encouragement into my ear.

"Stop," I say.

She does. There is a sigh, and she releases me.

I climb off her, settle down on my back. Deb pulls up the blanket to cover herself. We center our heads on separate pillows and study the ceiling, side by side and silent. The HALO's antigravity engines hum. Shame begins settling over me, not because I couldn't perform, but because I tried to. My body, which I've battered and abused over the years, took the moral high ground and betrayed me. But in doing so, it's given me a chance to set things right. I'm wondering if I should start with my big lie about the zoo or my grand redemption plan or, of course, what really happened with our son and Ecklar's armor. Before I can make a choice, Debbie says, "It's not fair to Nathan."

"What?"

She keeps her eyes fixed on the ceiling. "Denying him a little brother or sister. You see him with Thomas—the kid loves family. He deserves a sibling that isn't twelve years older."

"That's why you want to have another baby?"

"One of the reasons. You think it's a bad one?"

"You told me you didn't want to be done being a mom."

"That's true too. Now that I've done it once, I know what to expect. I think I'll be better at it."

"You couldn't be better. You're a great mom."

She inhales, then sighs. "So great that the idea of getting me pregnant makes you limp." My wife curls on her side, away from me. The candles on both nightstands extinguish on their own.

During one of our sessions, Dr. Janet explained that when you know you should say something, but aren't sure what to say, you should start with a simple emotional fact, something that's nonconfrontational and candid. I think for a minute, then reach over and lay a hand on the blanket covering Deb's shoulder. "I'm afraid."

She stirs, but does not turn. "Afraid of what?"

"Of screwing up with Nate like I screwed up with Tommy. Of having another kid to love like hell but not be a good father to. Of retiring from the one thing I know how to do. Of losing you like I lost Sheila. Of being the kind of man who lies to his family to make himself feel good."

This last one makes her roll over, and I force myself to meet her eyes as I keep going. "I'm talking about this morning," I say. "There was no Hideous Beast. It was Menagerie. We started fighting before I knew."

Deb holds her tongue. I say, "The people all were clapping. You should have seen Tommy and Nate."

I wait for her to react, but there's nothing. I say, "I know how screwed up this is. I'm sorry."

"You went to the zoo looking for her," Deb says, as if she's posing the answer to a riddle.

"Pretty much," I say.

"What did you want with her?"

When I don't answer right away, she cocks her head, and her eyes drill into mine. Sometimes, even when you know you can fly, it's a scary thing to leap from the top of a building or drop away from the side of a bridge. That childhood fear of falling never quite leaves you. And of course, with my abilities dwindling, one day it might not be there, and I'd simply plummet like a jumper. That's what grips me now, the sense that I'm on the edge of something, that everything hangs tenuously in the balance, but I know I can't step back from the ledge.

"I've been planning something on the side," I begin. "Something I was going to tell you about." As I go through the rough details of my scheme to use Bone Crusher to get to King Chaos, my wife's eyes narrow. The air in the room grows warmer, and I worry about the threat of spontaneous combustion.

When I stop speaking, she blinks hard and shakes her head. "Unbelievable," she says. "You're just unbelievable."

"It's a thing I felt I had to do," I tell her.

"Obviously," she says. "And how did all this lead to you and Menagerie fighting?"

I take a breath. "That was all a kind of misunderstanding," I say. "We weren't really fighting."

"Right," Deb says, as if my words make sense.

I start telling her about the part of the plan that involves gathering the original Guardians, but I see no sign that she's listening. The room is no longer heating up, but for some reason this worries me. Behind her eyes, it looks like she's coming to some conclusions about the man she married. I can't think of a thing to say, but the silence is choking me. "I'm sorry," I try. "For all of this."

"Yeah. You said that." She looks into my face for a while as if she's trying to place just where she knows me from. I don't know if she's considering forgiving me or trying to think of another question or wondering why she ever wanted to have a child with me in the first place. At times like this, my wife's face is a mask I cannot penetrate. I would trade all my powers—the flight, the strength, the not-quite-what-it-used-to-be-invincibility—to be able to read her mind like Gypsy, just once, to truly see what she thinks of me.

"Listen," she says, and I hold my breath. "I need to get dressed now, and I really want to do that alone."

This hits me like a punch to the gut, but I nod and try to smile. "OK," I say. I slip on my pants, grab my shirt, and head for the door. At the threshold I turn. "It feels like everything's coming undone, Deb. I feel like I'm losing a grip on everything that's good in my life. Something's dead inside me."

I wait for thirty seconds, and she says nothing, so I step out and pull the door shut behind me. I'm grateful when the broken latch catches.

In the bathroom, I bend and run cold water over my face, reach for my towel. I don't have to be psychic to know that Deb would prefer if I weren't here when she comes out. Right now I feel the same way. And when Ecklar does return, they'll be more recriminations and blame. I want to be away from all this. I consider working out, going for a drink, finding a matinee movie, seeking out Gypsy. I even think of flying out to Altoona and visiting Carl. None of these options appeals to me. Everything feels still, and that's when it calls to me quietly, more a whisper than a shout. I slide open the middle drawer of the vanity, shove my shaving kit to the side, and there's the pilfered bottle of Xonopexal. I rattle it and estimate there are a half-dozen left. I've never taken that many at once before, but it seems as good an idea as any. I start fiddling with the childproof lid, which gives me just enough trouble that I spit, "Motherfucker!" And it's the curse, the anger in it, the desperation, that makes me look into the mirror at the guy in his boxers, wet faced, who needs a fix this bad.

I set the bottle inside one hand, and when I close my fist, it's pulverized—the white dial of the top and the brown cylinder and the pills inside, all reduced to fine dust. When I brush my palms together, a little white cloud puffs into the air and settles on the sink top.

I grab one of my spare costumes from the front closet, change, and head for the hangar bay. And yes, that moment comes to me, on the lip of the flight deck, when I peer down on the city and wonder what it would be like to fall to Earth. What Arthur said about my Chaos plan being a death wish, sure, that struck a nerve. Being dead would resolve a lot of my problems. But I didn't go into the hurricane to kill myself. I'm not suicidal. Yet I can't deny how I've envied Billy all these years, the way people speak the name Sparkplug so reverently. It's ironic how no one knows but me, and maybe Sheila, why exactly he did what he did. Slick son of a bitch not only stole my wife. He claimed the legend I was supposed to inherit. Dying in combat, giving your life for the good of your friends and loved ones, that's the highest sacrifice there is.

The act of flight does take willpower. You have to think about it. Maybe if I stepped into the air now and let myself fall, they'd find my body and decide it must have been the Hideous Beast. Ecklar and Debbie would keep my secret. Nate would think I died a hero. For all the decades to come, his last image of me would be in combat, protecting him.

More likely, I'd just drive a crater into the concrete and temporarily break a few bones.

Instead of testing my hypothesis, I stretch out my hands and reach for the air above me, and my body floats up, lifts like it has a thousand times. Call it what you want—the freedom suggested by flight, the liberation of breaking gravity's hold, running away from my problems—it brings a certain exhilaration. I circle the city I've helped save a dozen times, and gradually my head clears. The dark mood that has a hold of me begins to fade. Nothing, essentially, has changed. Everybody forgets your screwups when you do something right. Ecklar and Debbie and Sheila, they've all forgiven me before, and they'll forgive me again. I decide that later I'll follow Jersey Devil and Bigfoot when they go to relieve Kid Cyclone and the Speedstress. I'll stake out their stakeout and figure out how to get to Bone Crusher.

I'm not feeling good, but my sense of hopelessness is diminishing. I decide that maybe the thing to do now is head for the zoo, come clean with Clyde and the rest of my Guardian comrades. Confession is good for the soul, and I want to go into my final mission with a clean conscience. This notion makes me feel even lighter, and I turn toward the sun and let it warm my face. But the sensation, though pleasant, is wrong somehow, and I reach for my cheeks. My fingertips touch skin. In my stupor earlier, I forgot to don my mask. For an instant I feel almost naked, and I think of flying back to the HALO. But then I remember what Titan said about nobody knowing who I am, and I think of all the cellphone shots of me, maskless, facing off against the Hideous Beast. Along with everything else, it seems the time for secret identities is coming to an end.

# TEN

*Questions from the Press. The Value of a Good Rooftop. Surveillance. The Problems with Accurate Prophecy. Brain Chemistry. Fixing the Future.*

Approaching the zoo from the air, I see quite the commotion in the parking lot. There's a small crowd of people held back by police barricades, four squad cars, a fire engine, and five news vans topped with satellite dishes. One is from KQEP, Sheila's station back in the day. Everyone's attention is focused on the entrance, where a gang of about a dozen reporters huddles. They're all waiting for something, so nobody's even looking my way when I drop to the asphalt behind them. A single figure emerges from the exit turnstiles, clad in gaudy yellow, and I take cover behind a freestanding porta-potty twenty feet back from the edge of the crowd. The civilians clamor, and the reporters surge forward to surround Clyde. Some snap pictures, while others aim shoulder-mounted cameras. They begin shouting questions, each one trying to drown out the next: "Where did the creature come from?" "Can you guarantee the public that the area is now safe?" "What do you know about the mystery hero?" Clyde holds up a hand to silence the reporters. A boom stick gets dangled just above his face. It looks like a baited hook.

"I have a brief statement, then I'll entertain questions. Earlier today, a being of unknown origin with unknown but presumably hostile intentions appeared in the city's skies over the Kingdom Town Zoological Gardens. It was repelled by a registered and licensed paranormal hero acting in close conjunction with—and under the authority of—the Guardians. There were no injuries and no loss of life. At this time our investigation is ongoing, and though we are on Stage Delta alert, there appears to be no immediate cause for concern. We have designated the combatant as the 'Hideous Beast.'"

As soon as he stops speaking, the questions pour in again.

"What powers does the Hideous Beast possess?"

"Well, it could fly, obviously. We have reports of superstrength and bioenergy discharges."

"Bioenergy discharges?"

"Laser beams," Clyde says. "From its eyes. That's unconfirmed."

"Is it true it ate an okapi?"

"There was no confirmed loss of life, human or animal."

"Are you saying the hero was one of the Guardian deputies?" This comes from Hal Hightower, the KQEP reporter who did that exposé on Gypsy at rehab. He included a hazy cellphone photo of her passed out next to a toilet.

Clyde knows the guy's hostile to our cause. "The hero's identity is confidential at this time. The Guardians train as a team and act as a team. He was here monitoring unusual energy readings and had tech support directly from the HALO. I want to emphasize that this encounter was not a random intervention but a carefully orchestrated and measured tactical strike. The public should be aware of our continued vigilance against unanticipated threats."

I'm enjoying Clyde's performance so much I decide to get in on the act. I step out from behind the porta-potty and start toward the impromptu press conference. Flying in would be more efficient, but I decide instead to walk among my people. I wade into the crowd, excusing myself politely. "That's him!" a woman shouts when she sees my face. "He's the one who saved us."

That turns everyone toward me, and the crowd parts as I move through it. I shake a few hands, give a high five to a dreadlocked teenager. Someone pats me on the back. Even the reporters clear out of my way, and I stride up beside Clyde, whose face sours. I say, "Sorry I'm late, everybody."

The reporters recognize my costume, and it's a short woman in front who asks the obvious question: "Commander Invincible, why aren't you wearing your mask?"

They wait for my answer, and I see the camera lenses aimed at me, feel the energy of the entire focused attention. "When the beast first appeared," I tell them, "there was no time to change into my costume. Preserving my secret identity would have meant endangering lives. It was no choice at all. In truth, it's been years since I maintained a civilian life."

Hal Hightower says, "So this means the two children reported with you at the scene were Thomas and Nathan?"

The tabloid press has long had a fascination with children of superheroes. Sheila sued *Weekly News* when they published a photo of her nursing a three-day-old Thomas in the hospital. "My boys were with me," I tell them. "But I'm going to ask you to continue to respect their privacy. I'm the public figure here, not them."

"But why would you bring your children on a dangerous surveillance mission?"

"I didn't," I shoot back. "What kind of father do you think I am? We just came to the zoo today. That's the kind of thing you do with your kids. It's my birthday tomorrow, and I wanted to be with my kids."

"Happy birthday," the tiny woman says.

But Hal presses immediately. "So you weren't at the zoo on the trail of the Hideous Beast?"

"No."

"We just heard from All-Star that you were here on official Guardian business."

I hesitate, and Clyde shoulders me to the side. He grins. "Ladies and Gentlemen, Commander Invincible and I differ on how much of our Guardian protocol should be made public. It's a fair difference of opinion. But we both agree that today's events show the need for continued vigilance, and we hope the Tucker Commission recognizes this."

A reporter with a pad and pen, dressed in clothes from a different era, says, “Commander, any direct comment on the Tucker Commission?”

I think for a moment, then simply say, “I came up in the old school.”

“Does that mean you advocate rogue and unlicensed paranormal action?”

Clyde raises his hand. “My good friend may have suffered a concussion today as a result of his heroic actions. Frankly, he refused medical treatment simply to be here to answer your questions. His comments do not reflect the official position of the Guardians. This ends our press conference. Thank you for coming.”

Clyde takes my arm and turns to go. I stand where I am. “I don’t have a concussion. My mind is clear as a bell. I’m the picture of health.”

He leans into my ear and whispers, “You’re screwing up royally. Come with me. That’s an order.”

“An order?” I say. “That’s a kind of interesting word.”

Clyde blinks a few times, flashes a forced smile to the wall of reporters. I know he’s right, but he’s so goddamn righteous and smug. I’m done following a man like this. It belittles me. I look up into the clouds and try to pick a direction. Hightower raises a hand and says, “So, Commander, you’ve fully recovered from what happened in Biloxi?”

This brings my attention earthward again, to the mass of reporters and civilian. All of their eyes are tense. “People’s lives were in jeopardy,” I say, though I know it is a lie.

Clyde says, “I remind you that any action Commander Invincible took during Hurricane Juno was not part of his duties as a Guardian. Mississippi falls outside our jurisdiction, and this is not a matter we wish to comment on. I also wish to go on the record as saying that if indeed children were present today, that was without the authorization of the Guardians. We do not advocate child endangerment.”

The shouted interrogatives come rapid-fire from the reporters, who crowd close around All-Star. But through the buzz of rage and dizziness I can’t decipher either their questions or Clyde’s answers, which register as gibberish. I wish I had my mask on. I know I’m going to fly away, and that this will make everything all the worse. But what I do first comes as a surprise. I pry off my Danger Ring and shove it through the throng of journalists at my fearless leader. "You're a world-class asshole, Clyde," I say. "And a shitty hero to boot. I quit."

As I drift up, I can hear the cameras clicking behind me, but nobody's asking any more questions.

This is a fine rooftop, here on this warehouse, neither too clean nor too dirty. Six stories up, I'm high enough that no one is likely to look up and see me crouching on the edge, and I feel removed and safe. At the same time, I'm low enough that I can pick up sounds, see the expression on people's faces. The roof hasn't been made over with gardens or turned into a fancy patio like all the tops on the north side, where once it was easy for a hero to find a temporary getaway. Graffiti stains the massive air-conditioning units and the concrete walls over by the entrance to the stairwell—huge, puffy letters that are all but unreadable. I can't tell if the nearest one says DIE or PIE. A few empty beer cans roll back and forth with the early-evening breeze. There's the skeleton of a solitary beach chair, the old fold-up kind with fabric strips woven together to form a seat. Beneath it, a pyramid of cigarette butts. I am not the only one who has found sanctuary here. But for now, thankfully, I am alone.

Below me on the street sits the black van that Jersey Devil and Kid Cyclone drove out of the parking garage I tailed them to earlier. When they left the HALO to begin their shift, I was waiting in the sky above them. There wasn't a lot of cloud cover, and fortune put the setting sun at my back. But neither of them cleared his flanks. Neither one circled back to be sure they weren't being followed on this supposedly covert operation. And after they picked up the van and arrived here, they honked the horn so that the Speedstress and Bigfoot, or whichever damn Guardian wannabe had the earlier shift, pulled their black van out and gave them the same parking spot. The younger generation has no style, no discipline. I shouldn't blame them, though. They were raised in peacetime, and their softness makes perfect sense.

It's been about an hour with no movement, and I wish I knew if the surveillance equipment in the stakeout van was recording Bone Crusher's voice. He may live in a building nearby. Perhaps he works as a bouncer at one of the bars, Rich and Ami's Party House, or Club Dixon, which is pulsing with music. Maybe Bone's taken a room in the towering hotel right across from me, the Metropolitan. Like most structures in this part of town, it's seen better days. Or maybe he's beating his way through an underground fight club nearby or acting as muscle for a local crime boss. A bruiser like Bone, just hitting his mid-thirties now, would still have plenty to offer to the right organization. Running through these possibilities, I find myself truly curious about how he's managed to stay off the radar all these years, how he's coped with life after being a full-fledged supervillain. But since I've all but lost the ability to see through bricks or tune in subsonic sounds, all I can do is wait, keep an eye on the surveillance van, and hope I get lucky. The only thing I want tonight is a glimpse of him, confirmation that the first part of my plan is within my grasp. I've been thinking of what Huan said about Gypsy, and I don't want to bother her until I'm sure I need her help. Although I'm eager to act, age has taught me some patience. Besides, once again I've found myself with nowhere else to go. So far today it seems I've severed ties with not only my team but both my families. Maybe it's pure momentum that led me here, feeling compelled to press on with a scheme I know to be fatally flawed. At this point, the notion that bringing in King Chaos could somehow bring order to my world is preposterous, yet some part of me clings to it. If I told all this to Dr. Janet, surely she'd finally decree that I am certifiably nuts. And I don't know that I'd argue.

So I wait here on a rooftop, a place that has always brought me a certain sense of ease, if not peace. Long before my powers came on, I took any excuse to crawl up on my parents' house—leaves clogging the gutter, a lost ball, a branch fallen from the oak tree. I'd sit in silence and enjoy the view. It calmed my spirit. Some of the most important experiences of my life have taken place on rooftops. Early lessons in how to be a hero from Titan, back in the days before he forgot. My first kiss with Sheila, who I'd just saved from the clutches of Killer Frost. Long philosophical discussions with Ecklar during breaks from nightly patrol. And of course, it was on rooftops just like this one where I had so many scenes with Debbie, who miraculously fell in love with me when I was supposed to be training her. I proposed at the top level of the Kingdom Tower, the tallest point in the city.

I'd been thinking that tonight, when we were supposed to patrol together again for old times' sake, she and I could tap that faded magic, get back to a place where we could be honest with each other about the things that are wrong between us, maybe begin coming together again. That was all part of the plan. By now she's heard from Clyde that I've quit the Guardians. In a way, she's getting what she wanted. I've thrown in the towel, and soon enough I'll be out of harm's way, available for full-time dad duty. Of course, after today's other revelations, I'm guessing she's not so sure I'm the guy she wants to make babies with after all. It could be that as I sit here looking for an old adversary, she's making phone calls inquiring about filing for divorce.

A stretch Hummer turns onto the dark street below, makes its way through the corridor of parked cars. It cruises past the bars and slows in front of the lights of the Metropolitan. A female driver jumps out and hustles around to the door, and for a moment, I think I'll get entirely too lucky and Chaos will emerge. But he's too smart for such an attention-getting vehicle. Instead, I get a gaggle of girls in lime dresses, followed by a tiny bride in a white gown. The bridesmaids hustle to bunch up the tail, and the doorman bows when he pulls back the door. And it's right then, something about the way he hunches, the curve of his shoulders, that makes me realize who I'm looking at. Bone Crusher, who once took a bazooka shot to the head, who punched his way through the walls of Alcatraz, is now a doorman.

It occurs to me that Bone is likely content with this life. The manager explained the job to him. Simple—wait here for a car to pull up. Open the door and say hello. Carry in any bags. I'll bet he makes great tips. And when he goes home at night, surely to some ratty one-bedroom within walking distance, he turns on the TV and watches old sitcoms and drinks beer. I'll bet he has a girlfriend who rubs his shoulders. I'll bet his neighbors know they can call on him to help with moving heavy things. I'll bet at night, he sleeps the sleep of the just.

Some part of me is envious of the life I imagine for Bone Crusher. But one way or another, his days as a doorman are coming to an end. Somewhere in that thick head is the secret I need, the location of King Chaos. But I'll have to get Gypsy to find it.

I read somewhere that when it was first built back in the eighteenth century, the New Horizons Addiction Recovery Center was a monastery. It was constructed on land donated by one of the town fathers, on what was at the time farmland well past the eastern edge of the city. As decades rolled by, the farms around it were transformed into factories, which were torn down to make space for condominiums, which were torn down for strip malls. A high stone wall encircles the center, a last attempt to fend off the reality of Dollar Stores and drive-thru pharmacies. But change, just another word for time really, won't be kept out by rock and mortar. So I'm not surprised by what I see when I descend through the early evening cloud bank—a huge message posted on the billboard just outside the main gate: THIS PROPERTY FOR SALE.

Because only two of the billboard's three lights are working, the right third of the sign is cast in shadow, obscuring some of the letters. What does surprise me is that within that darkness, something shuffles. Gypsy rises from a seated position and steps briefly into the light, just long enough to wave me in.

I float down to the billboard's platform and find her sitting again in the darkened third, her legs crisscrossed beneath her. She's wearing not only her cape but her hood, so I can't see her face or her wispy white hair.

"Don't worry," she tells me. "Nobody is seriously injured."

*She crazier than I am,* I think, and she says, "Maybe so." But in the next instant, a blaring car horn spins my head down to the intersection, where a minivan slams into the side of a UPS truck.

"Paramedics'll be here in a few minutes. Right when we're heading out."

The driver of the UPS truck climbs out, holding a cellphone. I see movement inside the minivan. Gypsy says. "Really, there's nothing you can do. We should go ahead and get started."

"Sure," I say. I look around and try to think of where to start. "What are you doing up here?"

She keeps her face aimed downward. "Waiting for you, what else?"

Below us, traffic starts backing up. Some folks have come out to help, but others are honking their horns, trying to get turned around to skirt the accident. "But why are you waiting up here?"

She shakes her head. "Because this is where we were going to meet. If I weren't here, I might have missed you."

I've forgotten what it's like to converse with someone with severe personality issues and the ability to glimpse the future. I sit next to her, back against the board. My feet scrape broken glass, and my eyes fall on a smashed stage light in front of her.

"Damn thing was just about blinding me," she says. "How's the family?"

"Just fine," I say. "You seem to be holding up well. I'd heard you were in a pretty bad way."

Now she looks my way, and even in the shadows I can make out her sunken cheeks, dull eyes. "I've always been in a bad way, Vincent. You of all people should know you shouldn't trust what you hear on TV. Listen, I should tell you right now that I'm not sure what's going to happen. Don't waste your time asking me to tell your fortune. The future comes and goes these days, like a radio station I can't quite tune in."

"That must be weird," I say.

"It's a bitch," she says. "Like going blind. Take us meeting. About a week ago all I saw was us up here in the dark. I even had to break the light to get the image right. Sometimes the future needs fixing, that's the moral of the story. This is the third night I snuck out of my room and sat here in the dark, waiting. A curfew infraction means limited privileges."

"I'm sorry," I say. "I had no idea you were waiting."

"How could you? Besides, it's OK. I kind of like it up here. The people in that place are pretty messed up. Addicts have unstable personalities. Sometimes I have other people's nightmares."

"Right," I say. It's been a couple years since I spoke with Gypsy, and she always had a kind of witchy way about her, so I can't tell if she's stoned on meds right now, or coming out of a meditative trance, or 110 percent mental. Somehow, she seems more grounded than Huan. It seems impolite not to ask, so I say, "So how's it all going, the therapy and stuff?"

"Like therapy always goes. I'm addicted, Vincent. To alcohol and antidepressants and, if you believe the good Dr. Heiner, reality TV. They've also added anorexia to my list of ailments, but you know I never had much of an appetite. I collect diagnoses these days like Girl Scouts collect merit badges. I should get a sash."

The catalog of addictions was part of the letter she sent out her first week in this place. Addressed to "People I Love and Who Love Me," it was composed in shaky handwriting and photocopied. There were stickers in the margins and a sprinkling of glitter. The note, part of her therapy, explained the importance of accepting one's addictions and seeking forgiveness. These were the first two rungs of her Ladder of New Life. I'm wondering now—two months later—what number rung she's made it to. I hike a thumb at the billboard sign. "Are they shutting down?"

She nods. "Five weeks, and the lights go out. I'm not so bad off. Close to completing my mandatory term anyway. When they lock the doors, I'll go back to my cabin. With the foliage turning, the Appalachians are beautiful right now. By the time I get there, it'll be all bare branches and snow. But I'll be fine. Arthur's guilt seems without limit, like his bank account. He'll always send me checks. You should see Blackfire. Poor bastard spends most afternoons in the dayroom with crayons. He draws demons with flames coming out of their eyes, asks when he can go home to his aunt. Or Supersword. They put him on something so his arms would stop twitching, but now he hums constantly, even when he's sleeping. It's creepy."

I wonder what the plans are for these patients in the wake of New Horizons. An idea passes through my head—I'll become leader of a new team of superheroes composed only of retirees and addicts. The thought is so disturbing that I force myself back on task. "Grace, do you know why I'm here?"

"We're not there yet," she says. Now her eyes hold mine, and I wonder if she's casting a spell. "You have to let me say a few more things. Then it gets to be your turn."

"OK. No sweat."

"Sorry if I seem rude. It's just I've come to a few conclusions, and nobody in that place is sane enough to listen. I know all about your plan, Bone Crusher, all that. But first, I want you to hear me out and tell me if you think I'm really crazy."

"I don't think you're crazy."

"You haven't listened to me yet."

I kick at some of the broken glass. Down below, the drivers have apparently exchanged insurance cards. They've taken the customary accident-victim seats on the curb. I tell Gypsy, "I'm all ears."

"Well, for starters, I don't think any of us were supposed to get powers."

"Supposed to according to what?"

"To God. It wasn't God's will for human beings to fly and be able to walk through walls and see into other people's minds. It isn't natural. This nonsense about it being the next step in evolution, that's just absurd. We're freaks of nature, plain and simple. I'm surprised any of us can breed. My guess is that we got screwed up because of toxins in the air, particulate matter in the water supply, maybe solar radiation caused by the diminished ozone. I don't know. Doesn't matter. But none of this was supposed to happen, that's the moral of the story. These weren't the lives we were destined to lead."

The hair rises on the back of my neck, and I shiver.

"Think about it. I can see the future. I can read people's minds. That doesn't make me superhuman. It makes me inhuman."

"You don't need me to tell you you're human."

"I need somebody to, and you're the only other one on this billboard. I'm deadly serious now. Human beings, I've decided, need to not know in order to function. Knowing too much screws you up. We're meant to stumble forward, blindly."

If this is true, I may be the ultimate man. Gypsy goes on. "I remember your wedding day. Sheila with that antique veil, you in that atrocious tuxedo made of what back then—Lycra?—so your shoulders and biceps could fit. You were so young and bright. Bursting with promise. But while everyone was dancing and laughing, I was sipping my wine trying to force a single image from my mind: you on a high balcony, crying—she on the other side of a sliding glass door. I knew right then your marriage was doomed. I didn't know how it would fall apart, and I knew you'd have lots of happiness, even joy, before that day came. So what could I do? I kissed you both and wished you well and tried to enjoy the chicken marsala. Maybe that's the moral of the story: eat your dinner and forget what you know."

In the distance, sirens cry out. We both listen to them coming nearer.

"At my wedding," I say, "you taught me how to waltz."

"It was the foxtrot," she says. "And I didn't teach you. I tried. I used to love dancing."

"You were good at it."

"How would you know?"

I laugh.

"I'm still a virgin, you know. Closing in on seventy and never been laid. Every guy I got close to, I'd see what he really thought of me, and sure, plenty of it was lovely and touching, warm, kind stuff. But mixed in with it, always, was how I kind of made them nervous or how my legs weren't as fine as Miss Perception's or how what they really wanted was someone more like Mommy. People think knowing each other's thoughts would make it easier to communicate and understand, come together with other lost souls? It makes it impossible."

If Dr. Janet were here, she'd argue with my friend, who's making a whole lot of sense to me just now.

"After this, I'm going back on my meds for good. I'm going back to my cabin and waiting for my powers to fade completely. Then maybe I can have a decade or two to live like a normal person. Then, I'll be ready for the old-age home. At least I can learn to play gin rummy or something, not know what cards are coming next."

"You really think we'd all be better off as civilians?"

"Without exception. It's made us all addicts, don't you see? You, me, Arthur, the whole lot. God knows why, but we have these incredible freaky abilities, things no human should be able to do, and when we play hero we get a bona fide buzz. I'll bet your brain floods with dopamine, just floods, every time you go into battle. I'm talking now about brain chemistry, Vincent, the most powerful and mysterious force on Earth."

I nod and say, "Brain chemistry, I'm with you."

"By comparison, the rest of life flattens out. It's dull and dead, and it's hard to even find meaning in it. You ever check the suicide rates of combat troops after they come home? Why do you think boxers keep going back in the ring till they nearly get killed? Whether they wanted it or not, they became addicted. And once you're an addict, you lose the ability to make the best decisions."

"But think of all the good we do. You can't deny that."

"You're rationalizing. Maybe once you could argue that, but really, how long has it been since you did battle with a supervillain?"

The sirens are louder now. "Gypsy, are you saying you won't help me?"

"Oh no, I'm with you. I'm in. Bone Crusher might lead you to Chaos. It's a grand plan. But I'm not deluding myself. This whole thing is a charade. I'm willing to play my part. After tonight, though, I'm out."

"But tonight?" I ask.

She stands, peels back her hood, and shakes out her white hair. "Tonight I'm a Guardian."

I rise, and below us, the paramedic trucks arrive. "Right on schedule," I say.

She nods, fluffs out her cape. "One more thing. About that little show at the zoo this afternoon. Some mom with a camcorder's got you and Huan on tape, talking about how you shouldn't punch her too hard."

"Shit," I say. "This came to you in a vision?"

"CNN," she tells me. "It's all over the news."

I shake my head. "Perfect."

Gypsy steps into the light. Her eyes are glassy and far-off. "Something's coming to pass," she says. "The future is shifting right now."

"Shifting how?" I ask.

"I'm not sure. Until a few minutes ago, it was clear that we'd apprehend Bone Crusher. All of a sudden, that seems like an uncertainty. We'd better hurry."

"Right. We're talking about four, five miles back to the Metropolitan. Can you fly?"

She nods and extends her arms, hands up. But then her wrinkled eyes pop wide open, and she stares at something over my shoulder. I turn.

In the middle of the city's silhouette of skyscrapers, a pillar of fire scorches the dark sky. It's as wide as an office tower spire and extends up a thousand feet, disappearing in the low clouds. Brilliant yellow and red flames roil, entwine. The things seems angry, almost alive. "Merciful Jesus," Gypsy says, "that looks like the wrath of God."

"Close," I say. "I think it's my wife."

# ELEVEN

*A Wife on Fire. Projectile Wedding Cake. Kid Cyclone Overreacts. Public Perception. The Weight of the Sanctified Christ.*

"This may not be helpful," Gypsy says from my side as we fly. "But the possibility of capturing Bone Crusher is rapidly diminishing. The spectrum of outcomes collapses as we approach any given moment. Every second the future becomes more certain."

"Bone can wait," I tell her. A mile ahead of us, the column of flame torches the night.

"The whole plan depends on him," she says.

"Debbie could be in trouble," I answer.

In my heart, though, I know my wife does not need to be saved. Whatever is causing this fiery display, my guess it that it has little to do with her being in any jeopardy or distress. Clearly, my wife's abilities have evolved in some way; she's found a new level of intensity. I wonder how civilians are interpreting this event, if some are thinking it's a strange natural phenomenon, while others guess it's some sort of publicity stunt. No doubt many whisper prayers, seeing this as a sign of the end of days. As for me, my greatest fear is a simple one: in the same flat tone that Sheila once used, Debbie will explain that our union has reached its regrettable conclusion. The fire in the sky is an omen of the end of our marriage.

As we near the pillar, I expect to see it rising from a parking lot or rooftop, but I'm wrong. The column hangs in open space, a hundred feet above the nearest skyscraper. The heat warms my face, even a quarter-mile out, and I slow down, hover beside Gypsy. The base of the inferno is too bright to look into, white-hot and broiling. Gypsy says, "So now what?"

I'm thinking of an answer, trying to concoct a strategy, when the whole thing extinguishes, just blinks out like a blown birthday candle, and in the wake of such illumination I'm temporarily blind. But as my vision comes back, I see my wife hanging in midair. She is two hundred feet above me, glowing, her arms spread as if she were being crucified.

"Stay here," I tell Gypsy. She starts asking a question, but I don't listen.

As I ascend to my wife's side, she watches me. Her eyes express no emotion and barely register recognition. Clearly, she's in no danger. I say, "Impressive fireworks."

"I have to tell you something," she says.

"You must be exhausted. You want to pick a rooftop?"

"I'm fine, Vincent. I feel strong."

"So all that was just to get my attention?"

"Obviously, I couldn't call you on the ring."

"Right."

"Look, the thing is, the truth is out about the zoo. A woman videotaped you and Menagerie. The footage is grainy, but it's all over the news, along with your drama at that press conference. Nobody's been able to find you, and people are saying you've gone off the deep end. Clyde is furious, says the team needs to divert attention before the news cycle ends."

"I don't care about any of this," I say. "I want to talk about us. Before, when we talked in bed, I didn't—"

"Clyde is going after Bone Crusher. Right now. And he's not alone. Titan came in, suited up and everything. Plus Bigfoot, Kid Cyclone, Jersey Devil. All of them. It's a goddamn circus, and Clyde is making noise about calling in some third-stringers. Ecklar and me, we tried to stop them."

"You tried to stop them?"

"When we couldn't, I didn't know what else to do, so I just hoped you were somewhere you could see the burn."

"Why did you try to stop them?"

"We've got to go, now. There's still time. That's Gypsy down there?"

"Time to do what?"

"Does she need to be in physical contact with Bone Crusher to read his mind?"

"Ideally. But if she's close, it'll do."

"Then come on." She extends an arm my way, weightless, for me to tow her.

"Hold on," I say. I don't reach for her outstretched hand. "Just wait. Why are you doing this?"

"There's no time, Vincent. We've got to move."

My head is dizzy with the implications of all this. "You could've gone with the team. But you're here."

She's silent for a moment, then another. Her arms cross. "And what does that tell you?"

"I'm not sure. That's why I'm asking you."

She looks disgusted. "And somehow my explanation, my words, that's going to mean more to you than the act itself. I need to spell this out?"

Behind my wife, the crescent moon seems close enough to touch. I tell her, "I'm tired and confused. I think spelling it out isn't a bad idea."

Something flickers in her eyes, and my neck heats up. "Fine then." She takes a breath. "You are my husband, and the father of my child, and I love you. I love who you are, I love the man you want to be, and I think the two are a lot closer together than you think. This plan you talked about—you and the original Guardians bringing in Chaos—is insane."

"Right," I say.

"But I believe in you."

My head goes light, and I have to concentrate to keep from tumbling from the sky. She's said these words with a kind of defiance and anger, like a confession. I can't imagine anything I would rather hear from her, but hearing them only makes me wonder why she feels this way—why, in the face of everything, she loves me still. Asking her for further explanation now would only bring about the return of the conflagration.

Gypsy appears at our sides. "I hate to interrupt. But the time stream's becoming quite firm."

I turn to her and say, "What?"

"Bone Crusher is getting away."

"All right then," Debbie says. She nods at Gypsy. "Let's go." She holds out a hand, and I reach for it. Deb can only levitate; she can't fly on her own. But somehow it feels like she's the one keeping me up.

As the three of us approach the Metropolitan, we see the street is blocked off in both directions. On the sidewalk, police barricades hold back a small crowd, and two Guardian hovercars sit parked out front, right where you'd expect the limos to be. There are also a fire truck, three ambulances, and an armored assault vehicle.

There are no masks outside, so we land close to the entrance and immediately head for the revolving doors. Uniformed police crisscross the lobby. Guests mob the front desk, and paramedics tend to a dozen people sitting against the far wall. Most of the wounded, I notice, are in tuxes or lime-colored gowns. It looks like that wedding party took the brunt of the excitement: the tiny bride holds an ice pack to her swollen face, and the groom's ripped pants expose his bloody leg. Strange, but he's wearing a Red Sox cap. A firefighter sits in a high-back chair, ax at his side, reading the newspaper. I grab the elbow of a passing cop. "Who's in charge around here?"

"Captain Jennings. But if you're looking for your pals, try the Mallard Ballroom." He points to his left.

Debbie strides ahead and leads us down a hallway, past a series of elevators. Fist-sized char marks spot the wall, burns from All-Star's starbursts, if I had to guess.

Bigfoot's at the doorway in his denim overalls, bulky arms crossed in front of his chest as if he were with the Secret Service or something. On a tripod next to him, a placard displays a plump red heart with the words STACY AND BRENDAN. When Bubba sees us approaching, he looks around, hoping for someone to help him decide what to do. He holds up a calloused hand. "Hang on, now. I probably need some authorization for this."

"Authorize this," I say, and I bump him out of our way with a shoulder. Bubba's a punk but not stupid, and clearly he recognizes Gypsy. Everybody in the business knows she can twinkle her fingers and turn someone's mind to mashed potatoes.

The ballroom looks, quite literally, as if a tornado struck. Round tables and folding chairs are overturned and scattered everywhere. The carpet is littered with instant cameras, shattered plates and glasses, hunks of food, exotic yellow flowers that I suppose were centerpieces. A group of capes are huddled around the head table; they don't notice us. As the two of us cross the dance floor, we pass a huge disco ball dead center like a cracked metallic egg.

Titan's head lifts, and he steps away from the pack to meet us. "Grace, you shouldn't be here."

Gypsy waves a hand dismissively. "Arthur, you can be so precious."

After throwing Bigfoot a dirty look across the ballroom, Clyde locks eyes with me. "This is a restricted area. You'll have to leave."

"Where is he?" I ask.

All the fight goes out of him. I look at Titan, who turns away, then to the other two capes in the room—the Jersey Devil and Kid Cyclone, who says, "It's not my fault. The guy threw an ice sculpture at me. What was I supposed to do?"

Titan can't hide his disdain. "How about duck?"

"You're responsible for all this property damage?" I say. "Not bad for a rookie."

"The windstorm only lasted a minute or so," J.D. explains.

"Long enough," Titan says.

Debbie scans the room, shakes her head. "Tell me I'm wrong, Clyde. Tell me that with half the heroes in Kingdom Town, you didn't lose one man."

Gypsy closes her eyes and tilts her head back slightly. It looks like she is praying.

Clyde says, "We were diverted from our primary mission. Civilians were in danger."

"Right," I say. "Flying debris. Projectile wedding cake."

J.D. gives me the finger. Debbie says, "Grow up."

"So why aren't we in hot pursuit?" I ask.

Titan shrugs. "He vanished in the chaos. The wedding guests stampeded out all four emergency exits, and he slipped away with the crowd. The Speedstress and the Ice Queen are sweeping the area, but face it, once he hit the street, he was gone. There's three subway stops within two blocks."

Gypsy opens her eyes. "He's not in this building."

"Where is he?" Clyde demands.

"Gone," Gypsy says. "Like Arthur said. That's all I'm sure of."

"Shit, guys," Kid Cyclone says. "I'm really, really sorry."

"Nobody cares," I tell him.

"Let me get you home," Titan says to Gypsy, stretching an arm over her shoulder.

She sidesteps it and keeps her distance. "My home's a long way from here," she says.

Clyde raises his Danger Ring. "Ecklar, can you give me a ten-twenty on Blue Bloodhound?"

Ecklar's voice crackles through. "His taxi is stuck in midtown traffic. Currently at Fifth and Adams."

Clyde shakes his head. "Budget cuts are killing us. Titan, could you fly out and pick him up? That trail grows colder every second."

Titan hesitates, looks over at me and Gypsy, and I say, "I'll get him."

"Negative," Clyde says. "You're no longer affiliated with the Guardians. This operation is not your concern, and I'm going to have to ask you to leave immediately."

"He's so sweet, Arthur," Gypsy says. "Where'd you find someone who sounds so much like you?"

I try to stay grounded. "Look, Clyde, let's put our bullshit to the side and catch the bad guy. You want to meet me after school in the parking lot, that's fine. But for now, you need my help."

"Our help," Debbie says, and her voice makes me go weak with tenderness. We are a team unto ourselves.

"What I need," Clyde says, "is for you to see the big picture. That stunt you pulled with Menagerie is being broadcast all over the country. The civilians already don't trust us. Now they think we're running hoaxes to win sympathy with the Tucker Commission. Fair warning, tomorrow I'm putting out a statement that disavows you entirely. I may even call your mental capacity into question. Stay as far away from the Guardians as you can. You're through, you're through, you're through. I officially accept your resignation."

I start cataloging all the ways I could inflict bodily harm. Then a hand settles on my shoulder. I turn, and Debbie says, "Come on, we're done here."

Though the idea of leaving with Deb, reunified by our righteous indignation, thrills me, we have to keep someone on the inside. "Stay with the team," I say. "I'll see that Gypsy gets back where she belongs."

My wife shakes off my suggestion, and she looks a bit betrayed. I tell her, "The people still need the Guardians. And the Guardians need you."

Titan steps forward. "I'm sorry about all this, Vincent. I had to do what I thought was best."

"Save it for your fans. You've always been a glory hound."

As I'm walking away with Gypsy, Clyde says, "Any attempt to interfere with the investigation will be considered a criminal act."

Just past the crashed disco ball, Gypsy bends and stretches for one of those yellow flowers. But her other hand, close to her body, reaches for a small hunk of ice, something that used to be a sculpted hand or wing. She touches it for an instant, lets her fingers rest on it with her eyes closed, then releases it. At the door, Bigfoot scowls at both of us. She gives him the flower and says, "Lighten up, son. You'll live longer."

As we exit the hotel, I think we're under attack for a second from the assault of flashbulbs and shouted questions. At least two film crews have begun rolling, and journalists I recognize from CNN aim microphones at me like weapons. Gypsy has a mind-sweeper spell, but these folks are just doing their jobs. She's actually the one who takes flight first, and I follow, leaving behind an unhappy mix of paparazzi and press. It's only after we're in the air that I realize we're heading north instead of south. I pull up beside her, and she cracks a sly smile. "This way."

At every intersection she pauses, closes her eyes, and faces each direction, as if feeling for the sun's warmth on her cheeks. Then she floats one more block, pauses again. After three or four turns, she says, "I'm surprised I can still do this. Of course, we may end up at the caterer's for all I know."

Just a couple blocks later, she finds herself turning back down the way we just came.

"Did you lose the trail?" I ask, worried about how strongly an aura imprints on ice.

But Gypsy shakes her head. "Bone's here. Somewhere on this street."

We descend to the sidewalk and go building to building. At each doorway she hesitates, holds out one open palm, then moves on. We pass a boarded-up brownstone, a two-story Syrian restaurant with harp music floating out, a building with scaffolding rising up its exterior and a sign promising COMING SOON, TRUE BANKING FOR THE PEOPLE! An old stone church with a tall steeple occupies the corner lot, and it's here that Gypsy stops. We push back the creaking black gate, follow a path through unkempt grass, overgrown bushes. On the message board is the name Church of the Sanctified Christ, and black, blocky letters:

PRAY FOR REVEREND PITCHFORD

FOR SALE

For a minute I think it's some clever play on words, like "What's missing from ch——ch?" but then I realize that the place really has been abandoned.

We climb the dozen stone steps, watched by a larger-than-life statue of Christ directly overhead. He stands in an alcove with His arms raised. One hand holds up two fingers; the other is missing altogether. Above Him is a huge circular window, stained glass. At the double doors, something like you'd expect at a castle, Gypsy points to the fresh wood of the splintered lock. She nods at me once, and I hold up my hand. "Stay," I mouth. I ease back the door and enter the church.

The floor is completely dark, as if I'm walking in black space. But along the walls, streetlights leak through the stained glass, illuminating dim, colorful saints in acts of great kindness or torture. The images seem to be projected into the air.

I wait for my eyes to adjust enough that I'm sure he's not sitting in the pews or kneeling in front of the statue of Mary. I work my way down the aisle like some timid bride, squinting along the kneelers, eyeing the chandeliers overhead. When I reach the altar, I turn back, scan the choir loft, and stand still. The idea that maybe Gypsy had it wrong drifts through my head. Then I hear a low murmuring off to the side, the hushed whisper of prayer. I turn to the twin curtains of the confessional, twenty feet away.

"Bone?" I say. And the murmuring stops. "I don't want to fight in a church. Let's agree to step outside."

The curtain gets yanked back, and Bone emerges. He is wearing his doorman's outfit, complete with epaulets. He looks like a steroidal bellboy. "Didn't see you back at the hotel, Commander."

"I wasn't with them. An ambush like that, it's not my style."

"Is everyone all right?" he asks. "There was a wedding party."

"I saw a few bloodied heads but no covered bodies."

"Thanks be to Jesus."

The sincerity in his voice is obvious, and I wonder when he got religion. Like Magus, another ex-villain turned true believer. I move down the pew he's standing by, so that its scrolled wooden end is all that separates us. "I'm sure God would want you to come peacefully."

He gazes into the empty ceiling, waiting perhaps for word from the Almighty. "I don't think you're strong enough to make me do that."

We take stock of each other, gunfighters in the dusty road. "That's what we'll find out, I guess. Out front?"

"Sure thing. Mind if I finish my prayer first?"

"What are you praying for?"

"My kids."

"I didn't know you were a dad."

"I got three. Two girls and a son. My boy Clayton is sick, but he's a fighter. Way tougher than me." Bone eases back a kneeler and settles down, tips his thick head into his folded hands.

I feel a strange urge to join him, to raise my voice to the god of superheroes and seek absolution and guidance. But I'm afraid he might think

I was mocking him. So I wait in silence. When Bone rises, he thanks me and says, "So out front, then?"

I nod, and we start down the aisle together. "Gypsy's out there. Don't think it's a trap. I'll tell her to stay out of it, and if you beat me, to let you go."

He regards my face in the shadows. "I miss the old ways."

"Tell me about it."

"Best of three falls?" he asks.

I tell him, "I'm too old for three falls."

We smile together, and it seems like maybe we'll laugh even. The door is just ahead, and it feels impossible that we're about to engage in combat. More likely, we'll head for a neighborhood bar, share a pitcher and shoot pool and fill the jukebox with quarters. I even find myself wondering if a drunk and friendly Bone might not simply volunteer what he knows about King Chaos. But then comes the faint whistling sound, growing louder, and soon the piercing shriek resembles what you hear on the wrong end of an incoming mortar. I raise my eyes to the circular stained glass window over the choir loft just in time to see it shatter. Shards rain down on us, and I cover my face with an arm. When I look again, Titan is blocking our path, arms crossed, feet set. He's in full hero pose. "Bone Crusher! You're coming with me!"

Bone charges, catching Titan under the arms like a linebacker. He drives him back, and they crash through the wooden doors, spilling outside. I run out and find them upside down on the stone steps, Bone kneeling on Titan's stomach with both hands digging into his throat. Titan punches him in the ribs, but it seems to have little effect. I rush past Gypsy and leap onto Bone's back, slide my arms around his neck hoping to slip in a choke hold of my own. Over Bone's shoulder I can see Titan's face, upside down and turning red. Bone is managing to bang Titan's head into the stone steps without releasing his grip on his throat. Titan's eyes bulge. Inside my forearm lock, Bone's neck is like the trunk of a tree. I'm not even sure he knows I'm trying to cut off his air supply. Then I hear him gasp once, and he shrugs his shoulders, so I know I'm at least providing an annoyance.

My right side lights up with a burning sensation, and I turn to see Clyde standing with Deb and Gypsy up against the black metal gate. His hands are open, and starbursts sizzle from his glowing palms. He's bathing the three of us in a storm of them. Next to All-Star, I see the Blue Bloodhound, complete with his ridiculous long-nosed mask. I hide my face beside Bone's, then sink my teeth into his ear, tug, try to pull tighter on his neck. Nothing's distracting him, but I swear his breathing is growing more shallow.

Below us, Titan's eyes have closed.

"Vincent," Debbie yells, "get clear!"

I turn and see my wife holding her palms up, a glowing ball of flame between them. "Hit us all!" I shout. Bone's face turns to her. She and I lock eyes for a second, and the fireball swims and spins in the air, then she pulls her arms in and pushes out, like she's heaving a basketball. There's a bright flash of heat, a burst of sound, and we tumble sideways on the steps. We end up with me on my back and Bone atop me, both of us facing skyward. We're smoldering, and the air smells like singed hair. Titan is fifteen feet away, very still. I've still got Bone in that choke hold, and now I'm sure I'm doing some good. His massive fists flail, punching holes into the stone steps on either side of us, and he tries to reach back for my head, but I keep it tucked in tight to his. Clyde tries to come in close, probably to try to laser him at point-blank range, but he can't get past Bone's kicking legs and swinging arms. The beams he blasts Bone with only seem to be making him more angry. Remarkably, Deb's already recharged. She's yelling for me to get clear and glowing with energy, brighter than I've ever seen her before. If I release Bone, though, he'll come up swinging and could really do some damage. A few lucky shots could topple the whole church. I can't let him go, but my adrenaline boost is fading, and when Bone finally settles down enough to grasp my forearm with both his hands, there's only so long I can hold on. My eyes fix on the rising steeple and follow it downward, to the alcove with the one-handed Christ.

"Gypsy!" I manage to yell, hoping she can read my mind from this distance. Whether she uses her powers or just follows my eyes, she understands. As she begins to contort her fingers, summoning a spell, I hear her voice in my head. *This will hurt. Are you sure?*

I think back, *Drop that fucker.*

Thirty feet above us, the statue begins to wobble. Below the sandaled feet, a crack appears, and for an instant it seems like Christ is walking toward us. Bone stops flailing and says, "Shitfire." He tries to roll free, but I hold him tight, and a two-ton Jesus drops down on us both.

When I come to, covered in rubble, my forearms are still wrapped around Bone's neck. The other heroes are clearing the chunks of rock off us, like a rescue team after an earthquake. Bone's gone limp. I crawl out from underneath him and see that he's groggy as hell, but still conscious. "Son of a bitch, Commander," he says.

"I didn't know they were out here."

Clyde kneels with a syringe, eyes on Bone's veiny neck. This is standard procedure in the new era—doping up the villain till we get him transported to a secure holding cell. I hold up a hand and say to Bone, "Tell me where King Chaos is."

Clyde looks shocked, but waits with the needle.

Bone's eyes focus a bit, and I know he heard the question. "Gypsy," I shout. She's still kneeling over Titan. "I need you now."

Clyde says, "What's going on here, exactly?"

I slap Bone across his cheek. "Come on. You don't need to say anything, just think it. Picture it. Where's King Chaos?"

Bone blinks and pushes his bloodied tongue out between his lips, tastes his own blood. "That's why you came after me? You want to know about freaking Chaos?"

"Just tell me," I say. "Where is he?"

Bone tries to spit, but the blood only slips onto his dusty cheek. Then he grins. "It matters that much to you? Then I'm happy to tell you. Last time I saw that crazy bastard he was talking about India. Maybe Kuala Lumpur. This was eight, nine years ago. By now he could be anywhere."

The grin cracks into a full-blown smile, and he raises his eyebrows at me, satisfied that though he lost the fight, he deprived me of what I wanted most. Clyde steps in and jabs the needle into Bone's neck, depresses the plunger, and drops him into unconsciousness.

I step away, glance up to the empty alcove where Christ once stood. Deb and Gypsy come along beside me, but I don't need the psychic to tell me that Bone spoke the spiteful truth. Chaos is gone. All this has been for nothing.

# TWELVE

*Ending a Century of Violence. A Show of Good Faith. The Difference between Incarceration and Atonement. Resurrection within Our Lifetime. Unfinished Business.*

The morning of my fortieth birthday, I'm lying in bed awake, waiting for the sun to rise. The space next to me, where Debbie should be, is empty, and I've been reminded of the months after Sheila and I called it quits, how I hated sleeping alone again. I'm hoping that soon Nate will wake up, and the two of us can spend the morning on the couch watching cartoons. In the hours since I woke, I've laid here trying to deny that at middle age, I am on the verge of becoming the thing I most feared—a man without ambition, direction, or purpose. But it's impossible now, with the Chaos Plan in shambles, not to tally up the first half of my life and draw some conclusions. In my two decades as a grown man, I've racked up one failed career as a second-rate hero, one ruined marriage, one on shaky ground, one son embarrassed by me, one too young to know better. That I am a failure strikes me as more of a statement of objective fact than a judgment.

I simply can't bear being alone with myself any longer, and I flip back the covers, swing my feet to the floor. My head pounds from last night's battle. I think of the Zone in my bathroom, then remember I destroyed it on a better impulse I now regret. When I stand, my back aches, and a wave of dizziness nearly topples me. I wonder again how long I have until my recuperative powers disappear entirely.

On Earth 1.7, I found my doppelganger, and he had no special abilities at all. That Vincent Shepherd had married a woman named Cindy I don't even remember meeting. They had toddler triplets—Casie, Carol, and Jessica—and he sold ads for a radio station in Maryland. I'd tracked him down in hopes that he could help me get back to the right dimension, spied on him from the safety of a bridge a quarter-mile from his suburban home. As I watched him mow his lawn, sweat, run a hose into a faded plastic pool, sip at a beer while sitting on the edge of a deck in need of cleaning, I realized he'd be no help at all. I never spoke to that version of me, so I can't say for sure if I was more content in that universe. Maybe he dreaded his crummy job and dreamed of saving the world. But from a distance, my ultrahearing heard him calling out his laughing daughters' names as they splashed in a few inches of cool water, and he seemed happy. Maybe, from a distance, everybody does.

I sneak into Nate's room, fully expecting him to wake at the hinge's squeak. He is a light sleeper. But today, he doesn't shift as I cross the floor. The curtained window allows morning light to filter in. I stand over his bed and look down upon him, twisted in his blankets, at peace. As I often do at times like this, I wonder about the life he has ahead of him, the long stretches of challenges and disappointments, of triumphs and defeats. I wonder what role he will let me play.

He may be the only reason I have left to live. This, I realize, is an unfair burden on the boy, and something he can never know.

"Pssst," I hear from behind me. When I turn, I see Ecklar's green head leaning through the open door.

I tiptoe into the living room, closing Nate's door behind me. My alien friend follows me to the far table, where we sit and speak in hushed tones. He tells me, "They want you down at St. Clementine's."

"They who?" I ask.

"Clyde is the one who called. But I could hear Deborah in the background."

"Is Arthur all right?"

Ecklar nods. "Gypsy's healing spell is working wonders. He'll be laid up a day or two, but he'll be right as rain."

I can't imagine what Clyde would want with me. But if Ecklar knew, he'd have told me already. He says, "I'll keep an eye on Nathan. I just have computer files to back up this morning. Information I want to take with me. He can help."

I picture an Andromedan rescue ship floating through hyperspace. "The vortex is nearly open, isn't it?"

He blinks at me and smiles. "The radiation is intensifying. It could be any time now, I think."

I imagine the HALO without my friend. "Ecklar," I ask, "what will you do when you get back?"

A thin finger rises to his chin and taps. "Spend time with my family. Then return to work, find a way to serve my people. I have learned much in my time here."

"Will the war with the Malkovians still be going on?"

"I hope not. But it is likely. A century of violence won't be brought to an end easily."

I nod, think about my son in the room behind me. The rooftop notion that he may better off without me—that his life would be a better one fatherless—returns. Alongside it, I feel the swelling under my breastplate of being engaged in a war with a race of deadly aliens. Ecklar has described the Malkovians as ruthless—huge reptilians with advanced technology and a taste for flesh. Evil. I tell Ecklar, "I'm handy in a fight, you know."

His huge eyes aim at me, unblinking. "What are you proposing?"

"I could come with you," I say. "These Malkovians have never seen a man who can fly. At the zoo, you looked just fine in the old battle suit. The two of us, we could raise a little hell, eh?"

Ecklar looks frightened by what I'm saying. "The vortex is unstable, Vincent. It won't function like a permanent bridge. It is possible, even likely, that you would never be able to return."

"That might not be the worst thing."

Ecklar doesn't speak for almost a minute. I wonder if this man, ripped away from his three wives and seventeen kids by an accident, is weighing the morality of helping me ditch my family. Finally, he says, "I searched through all the available databases and didn't have any luck with Kuala Lumpur. No reports of unusual criminal activities or suspicious phenomena. If Chaos is there, he's buried deep."

"Chaos wouldn't stay in one place this long. I doubt he'd even tell Bone the truth about his plans. Why would he?"

Ecklar shrugs his thin shoulders.

"I guess I'll head down to the hospital."

As we move through the living room, Ecklar says, "Vincent. You are my *naddeo,* and I am forever in your debt. I am honor bound to protect your life, even from you. Leaving Earth would be an act of surrender and disgrace. You would come to hate yourself for abandoning your family or change into the kind of man who does such things and accepts them. Neither outcome is worthy of you. I can't endorse such destructive behavior."

I sigh but can't think of anything to say. His logic, as always, is irrefutable. But that doesn't mean I'm not still thinking about going with him. We reach my door. I say, "I appreciate your honesty."

"Indeed," he says, still sensing I'm not convinced. Then a slim smile appears on his lipless mouth. "I almost forgot—happy birthday."

Because it's overcast, threatening rain, and I'm tired as hell with no coffee, I swipe a hovercar and fly down to St. Clementine's. I float past the helipad, leave it clear in case they have a genuine emergency, and land on the upper deck of the parking garage. I wander through the hallways, which seem unusually busy for this early in the morning. After I finally locate an elevator, I step inside and press the button below the one reading "street level." This should bring me to the subterranean floor we constructed for superheroic medical cases. The elevator doesn't move for a minute, and I see the security camera in the corner narrow its eye at me. With a jolt, the elevator begins its descent. When it stops and the doors split open, Debbie is waiting for me, and she greets me with a hug. "Did you sleep?" she asks.

"Yeah," I say. No reason to tell the truth. "What's wrong with Bone?"

"Nothing's wrong," she says as she leads me down the hallway. "He's recovering just fine. Doctors say he's stabilized and will be OK to move by tonight. We'll take him to Megajail to await trial. But we had an early-morning visitor, and we're not quite sure what to do with him."

Deb doesn't offer anything else about the mystery guest, and I don't push. It's enough that she's holding my hand, a signal I'm not quite sure how to interpret. I wonder how she would feel if I told her I was considering leaving not just our marriage but the planet. This isn't because I don't love my wife. I just can't figure out how to do it right.

We round a corner, and she opens a door to a conference room. Clyde turns from a row of three television monitors, but does not greet me. On the far left screen, I see Arthur asleep, Gypsy sitting at his side. The middle monitor shows Bone Crusher in a bed, groggy but awake. I can't help but notice the IV drip and the thick chains attached to his wrists. God only knows what kind of sedation he's under. On the last screen a figure sits in a straight-backed chair before an empty table. Just as I recognize the top hat he's wearing, Clyde speaks. "It's your pal, Magus."

Magus looks up into the camera and smiles. He knows I have arrived.

"What's he doing here?" I ask.

Deb says, "Apparently, he was the one call Bone decided to make when he came to this morning. Claims to be his spiritual advisor."

"Yeah," Clyde says. "And I'm the Easter Bunny."

"He could be telling the truth," I offer. "The other night Magus told me he's doing some work along those lines."

"And you see this as mere coincidence? Him showing up at a secret Guardian function while we happen to be running surveillance on one of his former partners in crime?"

"They never worked together," I say.

"Not that you know of," Clyde counters.

Deb shrugs. "The old guy seems harmless to me."

"I don't buy any of this," Clyde says. "We let him in there, he could magic up some escape."

"According to his files," Deb says, "by himself he's only capable of garden-variety illusions and tricks. He's no threat without his wand, which was confiscated when he was arrested back in '88. The computer says we've got that under lock and key in the Vault."

"Those files may not be entirely accurate," Clyde says. "His powers may have changed. This is too risky."

Deb says, "We refuse to let him see counsel he's requested, the whole case could blow up later on. You know the rules."

"A spiritual advisor isn't the same as a lawyer."

"That's something you're certain of?" I ask.

Even Clyde can recognize when he's out of his depth. Everything we do nowadays has six layers of oversight. Panels and subcommittees review all our actions. To reassert his authority, he gives me a command. "Go in there and find out what the hell his story is. I'll call DA Repka and see what's keeping her."

"Anything you say, boss."

When I step inside the room, Magus rises from his chair on shaky legs. He removes his hat and extends an open hand, frail and not quite trembling, across the table. "Good to see you again so soon, Vincent."

We shake. "Guess we're just lucky."

He takes his seat, smiling, and says, "I think you know I don't believe in luck."

I sit across from him. "I didn't mean to offend you."

"I wasn't offended, dear boy."

I offer him coffee, mostly because I want some myself, but I'm not surprised when he turns it down. He seems content, at peace, like sitting under the light in this square, barren room is precisely what he wants to be doing right now. "So tell me," Magus says, feigning concern, "did All-Star send you in with brass knuckles?"

"Pretty much," I say. "He doesn't believe you're a spiritual advisor."

"And what do you believe?"

I stare at him over the table and feel suddenly like I'm the one being interrogated. He half-smiles, then says, "This is a question I've been pondering since the other evening, when you assured me you weren't in crisis."

"I'm not sure what I believe. But I trust you. I'm on your side."

"Good. That gives us a chance."

"To do what, exactly?"

"Help Andrew. Help each other."

I know he's not using his powers right now, but there's something mesmerizing about his voice. I feel like I'm falling under his spell. "Can you tell me anything to help convince Clyde?"

"I can tell you what I told him."

"Let's start there."

"Four years ago I went out for one of my night walks."

"Sure," I say. "Your strolls."

He nods. "I found Andrew in a park. He was watching an empty playground—swings and slides with no children. Those big shoulders were sagging low. I knew the Lord had led me to him, and I sat at his side. After a while, we began to talk." He pauses, as if he's explained everything.

"What did you talk about?" I ask.

"At first, if I remember, the playground. Andrew's son was quite ill at the time. He's in remission now, praise the Lord. But he was worried about his boy's life, wondering why such things happen, why God allows children to feel pain."

"Fair question," I toss in.

"I can't say that he'd lost his faith, because I think now he never really had any in the first place. Andrew had a difficult childhood, Vincent, the kind that no one deserves. That night in the playground, I convinced him to join a little Bible study I'd formed. After a few months, he began attending the Sunday service at Apostles Assembly, where I act as a kind of deacon. Now he's an active member, donates his time to help with charity work, that kind of thing. He's not the man he used to be."

"He still needs to answer for his crimes."

"I understand that, Vincent. But you need to accept there is a difference between being incarcerated and making atonement. One is inflicted upon you, and the other arises from within you. It's true that for me, one led to the other, but whatever the circumstances, each of us faces our demons alone."

"This is the kind of thing you and Bone have been talking about in between all the Bible study and charity work?"

Magus nods. "For months I've been trying to convince him to turn himself in. I thought it would be good for him."

Suddenly aware of the camera over my shoulder, I imagine Clyde mocking this. I say, "You thought spending the rest of his days behind bars would give him a better quality of life?"

The magician sighs. One of his hands roams over his upturned hat, as if he's about to reach in and pluck out an answer. "I'm talking now about the quality of his soul, Vincent. I'm talking about helping him leave one life behind and begin another. I'm talking about resurrection."

My confusion, or discomfort, must show on my face.

"Christ died on the Cross to wash away man's sins. But He rose from the dead to show us the way. To show us we can transform from one thing to a better thing. And yes, I believe in the afterlife. But I also believe in something more important than heaven. I believe in resurrection within our lifetime. That's what I'm talking about now. And that's why I came today when Andrew called me."

A tightness grips the sides of my head, and Magus seems to be tilting sideways. That he is speaking about more than Bone Crusher is obvious to me, as it surely is to him. He knows what he's doing. I've lost control of this conversation, if I ever had it.

"I've told you all I can. The rest, spiritual matters, is between me and Andrew. Now, though, I think it's important you tell me. What brought you here, to the other side of this table?"

I think about Debbie, leaning in with Clyde watching on the monitor. Do I begin with the night at Chili's? Or the day in Hamburg when Sparkplug sacrificed himself so I could live, or with the moment I realized Sheila's love had vanished? It's hard to know, after all these years, just where my story starts. But that camera is transmitting all this to the control room, where Clyde could be, at this instant, watching closely. I should've crushed the damn camera when I came in. Now, I don't have time to screw around. "I was trying to find Chaos," I say.

Magus nods, as if he were expecting this answer. "You're seeking retribution?"

"Justice."

"Call it what you want. Vengeance will not ease your troubled mind."

"Maybe it will, and maybe it won't. Whatever my motives, the point is moot. Bone says he hasn't heard from him in years. The trail is stone-cold. He could be anywhere."

Magus tilts his hat and gazes down into it. "You'd need a lot of luck, or some pretty good help, to find him."

I fix him with a hard look, knowing he doesn't believe in luck. "What are you getting at?"

"I'm sure they have plans to move Andrew to the Megajail soon, and I want to speak with him before he's shipped off. If a show of my good faith will help convince you to let me minister to Andrew, I'm more than happy to oblige. You could consider it my birthday gift. The only catch is, if I'm to be of any help to you at all, I'd need my wand."

Sixty seconds later, I open the door to the surveillance room, and Clyde hits me with, "Absolutely not. Out of the question."

Deb looks at me with drowning eyes. "It doesn't seem . . . especially prudent."

"We're in the prudent business now? I thought we fought bad guys."

She says, "Don't be mean, Vince."

Clyde rubs his head. "That we're even having this conversation shows just how unstable you are, you know that, Vince? No way I authorize this."

"Don't authorize a goddamn thing then. Keep your hands clean. I'll go back to the HALO, get the damn wand, give it to him for two minutes, and have him finger Chaos. If it doesn't work, what have you lost? I'm a disgraced rogue agent anyway. But if Magus comes through, think about where that puts us. Think about the Tucker Commission."

Debbie can't help but smile. She knows I've got Clyde cornered.

He glances around the room, as if searching for cameras himself. "I won't condone this. But I won't stop you from going back in to see Magus again in, say, an hour?"

Before I answer, Deb says, "Vince, are you sure about this?"

"One hundred percent," I tell her.

"Just so we're clear," Clyde says, "this is your baby. Officially, you are not a Guardian. The plan goes sour, in any way, and I'll burn you."

"Peachy," I tell him.

Deb looks worried, and I can't say I blame her. There are too many variables to calculate. But I want to tell her that there's more on my mind, that if we do catch Chaos, I can say the thing with Menagerie was part of the plan—even my blowup on camera—all of it a scheme to lure Bone Crusher out of hiding. It may sound like a crock of shit, but in the wake of a capture like Chaos, people will believe anything. I can still go out as a hero.

Back at the HALO, I make my way down rarely used corridors and an elevator that requires a DNA scan. I go to the innermost room of the central level and stand before the two-foot-thick steel door of the Vault. My code still works—a sign that Clyde hasn't had a chance to formally boot me from the ranks—and fist-size titanium rods slide back from above, below, and both sides. There's a hydraulic hiss, and the enormous slab of metal slowly cranks open a few feet. Inside, automated lighting snaps on, and I see that more than a few bulbs have to be replaced. The dusty room is the size of a basketball court, cluttered with war trophies from nearly two decades of Guardian battles. It's a kind of superpowered evidence locker, loaded with devices too dangerous to be left in the hands of mere mortals.

Moving down the rows, I pass the souped-up chopper of Rider X, the sacred shield of Zulu Blue, and the Venom Beam created by Dr. Cobra. There's the haunted Mayan mask that turned mild-mannered Professor Hasselmeyer into a bloodthirsty lunatic for two years, the underwater outfit that Arctic Orca used to attack Atlantis, and the parchments of Vsgiril, which Gypsy assured us should never be unscrolled by anyone who wished to live. Every item brings back a memory—of combat, of struggle, of standing shoulder to shoulder with my comrades and facing an unquestionable enemy. Not all our foes were evil, but they were each surely bad. That they had to be stopped was never an issue, and it was clear, too, that we were the ones who had to do it. I miss them all, these sweet adversaries.

In the center of the room, standing like a sentinel over all this history, is the grandest prize of all—a complete set of Chaos's armor. Right after Sparkplug's death, a tip led us to an abandoned base on the southern tip of Madagascar. We fought through a series of outer defenses—missiles and lasers and a cloud of purple gas—but when we reached the inner lair, it was empty. Gypsy did a quick reading and told us no one had been there in weeks. The attack against us had been automated by computers that self-destructed when the compound was breached, so there were fires burning and smoke in the air. Titan saw the armor first. Instinctually, he attacked, flying so hard into it that he drove through two concrete walls. That was all it took to realize he was dealing with a dummy. Nobody had ever tackled Chaos.

For weeks afterward Ecklar did nothing but stay in his lab and study the armor. He'd been moping around the HALO, feeling guilty he hadn't been in the field that day in Hamburg. So I wasn't surprised when Ecklar asked me to help him test a hush-hush project. Out on the salt flats of Utah, far from prying eyes, Ecklar had me don the armor pilfered from our greatest enemy, the villain who killed my best friend. To understand the technology, he had to see it in action. Did I have mixed feelings about this? Sure. Did I put them aside for the possibility of having an ally as powerful as Chaos? You bet.

Now in the Vault, I recall the weight of the great red helmet, three-horned, and the heaviness of the black chest plating. I admire the shoulder-mounted proton grenade launcher and the pulse cannons affixed to each forearm. He was a different class of villain, no doubt. That day in Hamburg, I could've taken him, though. I know it. Standing before the armor now, I'm reminded of its raw and awesome power. I think of Titan, who nearly had a heart attack last night. Even together, the two of us could barely handle Chaos's henchman. It's clear that if I manage to locate our old nemesis, he'll kill me. Once again, that scenario plays out in my mind—a vicious battle, a heroic last act, a glorious death. The grand funeral, streets lined with mourning masses. The eulogies, delivered with tears and silly jokes. The white stone memorial and the rectangular hole. It will be raining. My proud, weeping wife. The stiff-chinned, determined sons, arms at their sides as the horse-drawn hearse passes by.

In the wake of such a thing, the public outcry would be deafening. The Tucker Commission wouldn't touch the Guardians. My family would be protected from all my fuck-ups. And my memory would be dipped in gold forever.

And so I make the calculation: if Magus can pinpoint Chaos, I'll go after him alone. If somehow I can defeat him, great. But that's not the only way I can win.

I turn to locate Merlin's wand, and that's when I see that I'm not alone. A few feet back, Sparkplug sits cross-legged on the enchanted pirate chest of Jean Lafitte. With both hands he scratches at his red hair like someone just waking. He looks through his arms at me, almost embarrassed. "I'm sorry," he says. "I couldn't just let this go on anymore."

"Please, Billy, please just screw off."

"There's something you need to know."

"I don't want your help. I told you already that I forgive you. Can't you go back to limbo or purgatory or wherever the hell it is you came from?"

"I don't think this place has a name. Look, I wouldn't be bothering you if I didn't think it was important." He stands and shrugs.

"Fine, then. If you won't leave, I will."

With that, I turn my back on my onetime best friend and start walking toward the Vault door.

"Vince," he says behind me. "Chaos is dead."

This stops me cold. "No," I hear myself say. I turn back to Billy.

"Sorry, but it's true," he says. "Three years ago. Cirrhosis."

"That doesn't sound right."

"Doesn't matter how it sounds. Guy's name was Harold Cuttwater, and he lived in Tokyo. Owned a company that manufactured microprocessors. Probably one in your TV."

There's nowhere to sit, and my legs feel jittery all of sudden, something I can't blame on the absence of coffee. So I'm forced to join Billy on the treasure chest, where we sit like two old codgers on a park bench. I cradle my forehead in my palms. A bug crawls through my feet, big enough to leave a trail in the dust. Billy says he's sorry again.

"So he's in hell?" I ask him.

Billy lifts his open hands. "Nobody in here talks in terms of heaven and hell. Word got around that he passed through, that's all."

"Then you don't know for sure. If you didn't see him yourself."

The look in Billy's eyes stops me. Whatever his other transgressions, he wouldn't have told me this if he wasn't certain.

That bug skirts off into the shadows by the enchanted roller skates of Disco Queen. "Chaos is in hell," I declare. "There's right and wrong and a heaven and hell. And Chaos was evil."

"I'm sure you're right," Billy says.

"Cirrhosis," I say. "Son of a bitch."

He says, "That day at Titanland, I wanted to tell you. I mean, I thought I owed you that much. But you seemed so energized and happy to be on a mission."

I lift my face so he can see my eyes. I speak slowly. "You don't owe me anything. This is something I need you to be clear on."

"I owe somebody something."

"What the hell's that supposed to mean?"

"Unfinished business. That's the phrase most of the spooks around here use. I can't go on to my final resting place until I come to terms with my life on the mortal plane."

"Tell it to Oprah," I say. "Don't put your stalled career in the afterlife on my shoulders."

"That's not what I'm doing. I'm only telling you how it is. I mean, just because you don't need my help doesn't mean I don't need to atone for the wrongs I've done."

"I don't want to be anybody's penance, Billy. Besides, you took a bullet for me. I haven't forgotten that."

He stands up, scratches at the base of his neck, and drags his feet as he walks in a slow circle. From a shelf across from me, he lifts up a set of aviator goggles. "Remember the Baron?" he says.

I nod. He was a crop duster in Louisiana who somehow became possessed by the spirit of Manfred von Richthofen. He buzzed a Mardi Gras parade thinking he was strafing them with bullets, but in fact he was just dousing them in bug spray. Gypsy figured out the antique goggles he'd bought on eBay were authentic, actually belonged to the Red Baron himself.

Billy sets the glasses back. "That day in Hamburg," he says. "I wasn't trying to save your life."

I stare at him and try to make sense of what he's said, a statement that clearly took him some effort. "What were you trying to do?"

"I saw Chaos take out Titan. I knew the team was in trouble. But I was so confused then. So confused and upset and guilty."

He brings his eyes into mine, and I know what was making him guilty.

"I'm not saying it's a wrong choice for everyone. That's not for me to decide. But taking things into my own hands like that. Just giving up. For me that was a cowardly act."

"You're not making any sense. I've seen the tape a hundred times. Chaos aimed my way, and you flew into the path of his laser. You were saving me."

He shakes his head. "I wasn't trying to be a hero. I just saw a way out. I didn't even see you."

Now his meaning settles in my mind. He sees the epiphany on my face. "That's right," he says.

More than anything, I feel angry at my friend. "That was a dumb fucking thing to do."

"Tell me about it. I miss being alive."

"We could've talked. What you did with Sheila was . . . well, you did what you did, those choices were made. But we could've talked. I was your friend. I was your brother."

"I know what you were, Vince. I never doubted that."

"I'm not saying you didn't screw up royally. But there was plenty of fuck-up to go around that whole situation. If things had been right at home, Sheila, maybe she wouldn't have needed somebody else. It's taken me a long time, a whole second marriage, to figure this out, but apparently I'm not really Grade A husband material."

"You were a good friend," he offers.

"Not good enough," I say, a statement that has become my slogan. "I failed you both. Same as you both failed me."

We say nothing. The proton generators kick in, and the floor beneath our feet hums and vibrates. Surrounded by relics, I feel right at home. If someone sealed the Vault door and entombed me here, I wouldn't try to stop him.

"What'll you do?" Billy finally asks.

I tell him I don't know. Magus is waiting, not to mention Clyde and Debbie. "Thanks for telling me about Chaos. You saved me some trouble."

"Least I can do," he says, and he stands up. He doesn't offer his hand, and I don't offer mine.

"You think you'll head for greener pastures now? You finish up your business?"

"I hope," he says. "I'm ready for the next thing."

"Me too," I say. "I just got no idea what it is."

He takes a few steps away, toward the back of the chamber, wanting, I suppose, to disappear into the darkness. On the edge of the shadows, he pauses and turns back to me. "I been following you close lately. I mean, I know what's up and all."

There's something in his voice. "OK," I say.

"So far as I know, you're the only living person who knows Chaos isn't alive." He glances down the aisle toward the looming red armor, then shrugs. "I'm just saying." With that, smiling with friendship and brotherly love, he vanishes from my sight.

I sit there for a time, work through a few angles, worry over a half-dozen contingencies. The scheme, surely my last as a hero, is shaky at best, but the payoff would be unbelievable. The notion swells within me until I'm driven to rise. I should spend a month planning this, conferring with Ecklar and testing old equipment and having the HALO computer run battle simulations. But I don't have a month. I've got hours. So I quit screwing around and start searching the Vault for Merlin's wand.

# THIRTEEN

*Unexpected Contingencies. The Plans of a Madman.*
*A Threat to the Mission. The Man You're Going to Be.*
*A Constant State of Flux.*

After leaving the HALO, I touch down in the eastern field of Washington Park. Holding the long thin box in one hand, I start kicking about the oak leaves carpeting the grass, looking for a stick the right size. Pigeons take flight from the nearby walkway. Just beyond them, skate punks in hooded sweatshirts congregate at the bottom of a steep set of concrete steps. One of the kids is skidding down the railing on his board, but when he glances my way, he loses concentration. His arms flail, and suddenly he's airborne, twisting. When his face connects with the sidewalk, his head snaps back in a scary way. An instant later, I'm at his side.

Blood streams from his nose and a gash on his forehead. I say, "It's not broken. Tilt your head back."

"I know," he says, sitting up. "I'm fine."

His buddies huddle around us. "Nice dismount, douche bag," one of them says.

The kids look on me with a bit of apprehension, but not respect. More than anything, they wonder what I'm doing here. Just off the path I see a twig about a foot long. It'll do. I grab the stick, hold it against the black box. "Look, I need to go," I say, "but I'm on my way to St. Clementine's. I'll bring you to the emergency room."

He sits up and looks at the blood on his hands. "I've had way worse."

I look at their faces, just old enough that some of them shave. I think of Thomas. "You guys should really be wearing helmets," I say. "You could get hurt."

They smirk at each other, taking pride in how they face danger unprotected, as a tribe. And I envy them, sure, their youth and their confidence. Then the one who got hurt says, "I don't need advice from some homo flying around in his underwear."

I know, of course, that I've wounded his pride, that he's trying to earn some of it back by doing this. But his snarl, the way his friends snicker and nod in agreement, it gets under my skin. Still, I'm ready to bolt into the sky when I stop and think about what I'll be doing later. Getting into my role wouldn't be a bad idea. "Nice board," I say. I reach down and pick it up. Graffiti covers the top, a stylized word that is either *Cougar* or *Courage.* I flip my wrist the way you do when you toss a Frisbee, and the board spins into the sky, heading for the stratosphere.

"Dick!" the kid says, jumping up.

I find my hand on his chest, gathering his sweatshirt. A stone wall rises just past those steps, and it would take the slightest twitch for me to drive him into it. But this pretending comes too easily, feels too good. I release him and fly up, along the same angled path as his skateboard, trying to ignore just how good it felt to be bad.

At St. Clementine's, Clyde is waiting for me when the elevator doors split open. "You take the scenic route?"

I push past him, holding up the black box like a ticket. The stick from Washington Park is shoved in my boot. He follows me down the corridor. When we get to the control room, Deb is reading something on a computer screen. She turns, catches the box with her eyes, and smiles. "Success?" she says.

I nod.

Behind me, Clyde says, "All right. You sit tight, and I'll go upstairs and get Gypsy to come monitor all this."

Before I can speak, Deb says, "Let her sleep. She's been up all night." On the video screen, Gypsy is still in the chair next to Titan, her head tilted straight back, her mouth open.

I look at Clyde, who is shaking his head. "I want insurance on this. Someone with mystical abilities needs to be in that room in case something fishy starts happening."

"Something fishy," I say. "Magus is nearly eighty years old. He's a damned preacher. I vouch for the guy."

"Your word doesn't mean anything to me. I need you to make this thing go smoothly. But I'm not lowering my guard. I'm responsible for this operation, and I have to plan for unexpected contingencies."

"Fine," I say. "Go wake up an old lady because you're afraid of an old man."

Clyde and I turn, square off chest to chest. "This isn't lunchtime in the schoolyard, Vince. Mocking me won't make me do something stupid. I'll remind you that you're here as a guest." His left hand crosses to his right, holding the Danger Ring. "I can have a half-dozen Guardian Deputies in this room in three minutes."

I want to say, *You'd need a dozen,* but I get control of myself. Soon enough. I back away and dip my head as a sign of submission. "This is your show, All-Star. You make the calls."

"Good," he says, a bit surprised. "I'm glad we're clear on the chain of command. I'll be right back."

The moment the door closes behind him, Deb says, "Asshole."

It's hard to argue. She asks, "How's your back?"

"Hurts like a mother. But I'm fine. Last night was something else, huh?"

"Strange night. You're lucky you didn't get your ass kicked."

"I did get my ass kicked," I say. "Just nobody noticed."

She laughs, and it's a blessing. If I had time, I might tell her everything, about Billy and Chaos and Magus and all of it. I might tell her that my fear of being a bad husband has become so great lately that I've felt on the verge of quitting. But the way she burned in the night sky, the way she spoke of her faith in the man I want to be, that's given me a second life. "Deb," I say. "I've got to go in there." I'm looking at the interrogation room door.

She looks confused. "When Clyde gets back."

"No," I say. "I've got to go in there now. Before Gypsy's here."

Her eyebrows cock. "What's the deal, Vince?"

"I need Magus for thirty seconds. He might get rattled by Gypsy. For all we know, her presence may jam his abilities."

"Clyde will go ballistic," she says. "This is asking for a lot."

"No it isn't," I say. "I'm only asking you to believe in me, one more time."

She looks at the monitor, where Clyde is standing over Gypsy, hands on her shoulders. The sorceress stirs.

"Trust me, Deb."

"Go," she says, and I'm halfway to the door.

A minute later, when Clyde bursts in with Gypsy, I hold a hand up to still them. "He's close," I say. What the two of them see is Magus sitting very still, both hands on the base of his wand.

"Damn you, Vincent," Clyde says.

Gypsy says, "Hush."

Magus contorts his face, sways a bit to the left and right, even rolls his head, all of it for effect. He looks like he's close to breaking a sweat. Finally, he opens his eyes and shakes his head. "Tell me," I say. "What did you see?"

A sly smile starts to form on his lips, but he forces it away. "I can't tell you where Chaos is hiding," he says.

"Glorious!" Clyde shouts. "Give me that dumb wand." He reaches across the table.

But Magus pulls his hands back. "It doesn't matter. He won't be hiding for much longer."

"What's that mean?"

"He's on his way," Magus says. "Chaos is coming."

Clyde glances at Gypsy, who closes her eyes and stretches her mind into the future. I hold my breath. She says, "The magician speaks the truth. I can see it, a strong probability, an image of Chaos in battle with the Guardians."

"How far in the future?" Clyde asks. "Where?"

She shakes her head. "I can't see where. There's a highway. Flames. As for when, it's soon." She opens her eyes. "It's today."

Clyde turns pale, and his anxiety has him looking around the room for something to do. He finds me as a target and aims a finger. "I gave a clear, direct command."

"I'm not a Guardian anymore, remember?"

"Fine, then. You broke the law by entering this room without authorization. I'll have—"

I reach across the table and snap the stick from Magus's hand, break it in two before Clyde's face. "There was never any danger. You want to bitch about the past, or plan for the deadliest battle you'll ever be in? Today will define your whole career."

Something like fear settles in his eyes. "You're right," he says. "We've got to get ready."

Back at the HALO, we have to clear off the War Room's conference table, which had been covered with Clyde's latest draft of the team's semiannual self-assessment. He and I sit at opposite ends and are joined by Debbie, Bigfoot, Speedstress, Ice Queen, Jersey Devil, Kid Cyclone, and Ecklar, who begins by asking a fair question. "Why should Chaos return now?"

"Revenge?" Bubba says. "Maybe he's out to settle an old score?" Though there is no immediate threat, the young hero is enlarged to about eight feet tall, perhaps just as a precaution.

"If that's the case, then Titan may be in danger," Debbie says.

Ice Queen says, "But he couldn't know about St. Clementine's. He'd come looking here."

"From a tactical standpoint," Clyde says, "it's better to assume Chaos knows more than we think he does. Assume we have no secrets."

Ecklar shakes his head. "I find it unlikely that Chaos would risk so much for mere vengeance. There is no gain in that formula. The only other variable that has changed recently is the apprehension of Bone Crusher. That is the likely catalyst and his likely target."

Speedstress asks, "You think Chaos is going to try and bust his old friend out?"

"Chaos is a villain," I say. "Not a hero. His target may be Bone, but it's not out of loyalty, I promise."

"What then?" Bubba asks.

Ecklar's thin fingers are moving on the edge of the table as if he's playing the piano. "Perhaps Bone Crusher has knowledge Chaos is afraid we will acquire."

Clyde stands. "We need to split up. I want two full action teams to escort Bone Crusher to the airfield, stay with him all the way to the Megajail. A third squad has to remain at St. Clem's in case he shows up there. Can anyone think of another possible target?"

"Us," I say.

They turn to me.

"This station. I agree that he's probably not out for revenge, but if he's looking to cause maximum damage, the HALO's a big-ass target. And it's parked over nine million people."

"Bloody hell," Kid Cyclone says.

Clyde looks concerned. He knows I'm right. "Even if we call in everybody, splitting into four teams spreads us way too thin."

"I'll handle the HALO," I say.

Everyone looks at me, most of them taken aback. I tell them, "Don't get me wrong. Nobody wants in on this fight more than I do. But I'm not at full strength. Chaos never had to contend with Ecklar's battle suit. You've got to put me or him in the field, and it should be him."

Clyde listens and nods. "That's, uh, unusually sound thinking, Commander Invincible. And very big of you."

Across the table, Deb studies my face. She's not sure what I'm doing. Then again, in a lot of ways neither am I.

Ecklar says, "You can't defend the whole station."

"That's not what I mean. We have no idea what this madman has planned. If he launches an all-out attack—robot drones, proton bombs, a null field—he'll bring the HALO down. No matter how many of us are on board. I'll get Nate to safety, then park the HALO somewhere Chaos would never look."

The Jersey Devil looks astonished. "You're suggesting we hide?"

"I'm suggesting we initiate a tactical retreat. The HALO doesn't have the weaponry to repel Chaos. Defending it adequately would take all our other resources, which is just stupid."

"Vincent's right," Ecklar says.

Deb leans forward. "We could set up a temporary command base at St. Clem's."

"OK," Clyde says. "Venus and I will get to work on drawing up those teams. We'll meet on the roof at St. Clementine's ASAP. I need to check on one more option, then I'll meet you all up there."

"Affirmative," Ecklar says.

As the room clears, Deb rounds the end of the table and comes to me. She holds both my hands and rises on her toes to kiss my cheek. "I admire how you're dealing with this."

For the second time this week, it seems I've won my wife's approval by running from a fight. I don't know how things will play out, and I wonder if she'll ever know the truth.

Deb and Clyde start divvying up the heroes, and I follow Ecklar. He tells me he's going to try and rig up a radar cloaking field, as well as an ion cloud that should mask the HALO's energy signature.

An hour later, the Guardians congregate on the flight deck. Deb is leading the team that will cover St. Clementine's. She's got Kid Cyclone, the Jersey Devil, and the Speedstress. Clyde has the real muscle with him. Bigfoot is up to nearly twelve feet, and Ecklar's battle suit gleams in the midday sun. And the Ice Queen can be formidable.

Nate is standing next to Deb, one arm wrapped around her leg, listening to Clyde give a speech. It's about defending the helpless, defeating evil, rising to the challenge of a powerful enemy. He sounds a lot like my high school wrestling coach. But the effect is impressive. I can see it in the faces of the young heroes gathered here. Their eyes are wide with that crisp mix of terror and joy, the eager anticipation of battle and the chance to prove oneself. "Trust your training," Clyde says. "And trust each other. Go! Go! Guardians!"

They repeat his chant, and the feeling that I'm at a pep rally becomes palpable. There should be a band, tiny bouncing girls with pompons. Deb bends to Nate, gives him a kiss, then hugs him, stands, and passes him into my arms. She says, "See you soon," and I know this good-bye is meant for both of us. The heroes split off, either taking flight directly or racing to the hovercars. They storm off to face a danger that doesn't really exist, and I think about what a shame that truly is.

After they disappear from the sky, Nate follows me to the control room. "Why can't I go with Mom?"

"Mom's working," I say.

"But I want to go with her."

"You're staying with me. We'll have fun."

"I don't want to have fun. I want to go with Mom."

I can hear the tremor in his voice. "How about a snack?" I try.

"I want Mom," he says, starting now to sniffle. "I want Uncle Ecklar."

I stop, turn, and drop to a knee. "Hang on," I snap. "Don't you start crying. There's no reason to cry now." This, of course, brings forth a burst-dam effect, and before I know it, my son is wailing uncontrollably. I recall Dr. Janet telling me that denying the pain of another is no different from denying the person.

I reach out and pull him into me, try to soothe him, rubbing his back and shushing. "Come on," I tell him. "What movie do you want to watch?"

Now he's blubbering on my shoulder, a mix of snot and tears running down the indestructible material of my costume. I realize the mission may be in jeopardy. A tantrum was not on my list of contingencies. "How about if I let you fly the HALO?"

Like a shut-off faucet, the sniffles stop. My son looks at me with puffy, wet eyes. "OK," he says. And just like that, crisis averted. If you took away bribery, I'm not sure what parenting skills I'd be left with.

Half an hour later, I'm steering the command ship over the Susquehanna River. Nate's sitting cross-legged up above the controls on the dashboard, gazing out the panoramic windows and finishing off the chocolate ice cream I got him for lunch. He asks permission to lick the bowl, and I say, "Sure."

When he's finished, he sets it down and asks, "Did you figure out why you weren't telling the truth?"

He's got a drop of chocolate on his nose, and his whole face is bright with anticipation. "Things have been kind of busy lately," I say. "I haven't had a chance."

"Maybe you could think about it now. I'm really curious."

We enter a cloud bank, but radar shows nothing. So I turn and say, "Look, I may never know why I did that. Not everything has a reason. You'll learn this."

"That's not so. Everything does have a reason. You can't have a question without having an answer. It's like having an out without an in."

"You sound like Ecklar."

This makes him smile a bit. Again, I wonder if my son could choose his father, where I would be on his list. I check our ETA. Fifteen minutes. Nate climbs down carefully and says he's going to go wash his own dishes. This will mean lots of running water, half a bottle of detergent, and a sink full of suds. He's dropped the subject of why I lied and may never bring it up again. But that doesn't mean he won't think about it and come to his own conclusions. "Hang on," I say. My son comes back to me, and I activate the autopilot. I lift him back onto the control board so we're almost face-to-face. "I lied the other night because I was afraid. Fear is like the grouchy bug. It makes you do things you shouldn't."

"You get afraid?"

"All the time, son. But that's when it's most important to be brave."

"But what do you get afraid of? Monsters?"

I shake my head. "Sort of, I guess. But not like you're thinking of. Lately I've been afraid of getting old and not being a good hero. Not being a good dad."

"You're a good dad," he tells me.

Though he's smiling and sincere, I regret coercing my son into validating my fatherhood. Still, it doesn't suck to hear these words. "Thanks," I say. "I try."

"Do you try your very very best?" he asks.

Nate's eyes, huge and innocent, don't blink as he awaits an answer. I decide to go with the truth. "I try my best a lot of the time."

He nods, and on some level I realize he's appreciating my honesty. He says, "I think you'd feel better if you tried your best all the time."

"That's good advice," I tell him. And I think, *If I get through this, I'll try to follow it.*

Not long after, we descend onto the fallow fields on Sheila's farm. Between the valley's natural protection and Ecklar's camouflage screen, the massive ship will be all but undetectable here. I have Nate grab his backpack, and we head for an exit hatch on the lower level.

Outside, Thomas and Sheila are waiting for us. As we come down the ramp, she crosses her arms. "Vince," she says. "This is hardly what I call distance."

"I should have called," I say.

"You think?"

Nate tells Thomas that he got to fly the HALO. Thomas says "Cool," but throws me the same dirty look his mother is nailing me with. I say, "I need to talk with you two." Their expressions don't change. "Nate, go swing on the tire for a few minutes, OK?" My son hesitates for a second, gets a nod from his big brother, then charges up the hill. Once he's gone, I turn my full attention to my first family. "You guys saw the news last night?"

"Bone Crusher," Sheila says. "We saw."

"Was that staged too?" Thomas asks.

I pull up my shirt and show a grapefruit-size bruise spreading across my ribcage, unhealed. "My acting isn't that great. Listen, things are happening fast, and I don't have time to explain everything—"

"Typical," Thomas says to Sheila. She doesn't scold him.

"Bottom line," I say, "I need you guys to watch Nate for me. I needed a place where he would be safe, and I thought of you two. You're the only ones I trust. I'm also going to need you to keep a secret."

For the second time in an hour, I've spoken with absolute honesty, and again I can see its effect. The anger on both their faces melts a little bit. But it doesn't go away. Sheila says, "We can't go on like this. It's not sustainable."

"I know," I tell her. "That's part of why I'm doing what I'm doing today. I want things to be different, to be better. But I need your help."

She turns to Thomas. "This is your decision too. It's OK if we say no."

Thomas glances up the hill at Nate, then back at me. "So what's the secret?"

"I'll leave the HALO here, cloaked, essentially invisible. Then I have to go take care of something. If it goes well, I'll be back in a few hours. But no matter what happens, if anybody ever asks where I was, you need to tell them I was here with you the whole time."

"We're your alibi?" Sheila asks. "That's what we've become to you?"

"Screw this," Thomas says.

"You're my family," I say. And the words sound so strange. "The family I never would've lost if I hadn't messed up so much. But I did. I made selfish mistakes as a husband and a father, and they caused pain to people I love. But here's the thing—I can't entirely regret those mistakes now, because without them, I'd never have found a second family."

The two of them look at each other, not quite sure what to make of my rambling confession.

"So now we're all on the same page—I failed you both. And now, Sheila, you love me like a brother. And Thomas, you're done being a kid and don't need a daddy anymore. I can't go back in time. My chance with you two is over. I can't get it back. But with Deb, with Nate, there's still time. I know I can do better. But I can't do it alone."

Sheila can see Thomas is rattled, and she sets a hand on his shoulder. She says to me, "You think it's right, putting that burden on us?"

"I think I'd do it for you. And I think I'm out of options."

They turn toward each other, and I take a few steps away, give them a minute. When they break the huddle, Thomas strides over to me and holds out a hand. "Good luck," he says. "With whatever the hell you're doing."

I shake my son's hand. Studying his stoic face, I'm reminded suddenly of my father. He lets go and jogs up the hill toward Nate.

Sheila steps close. "All right, a few hours."

"Later," I say, "I'll tell you everything."

She closes her eyes and shakes her head. "We'll drive off that bridge when we come to it. Anything I need to know now?"

I think for a second. "Nate really only had ice cream for lunch, so he'll be hungry soon. If he uses the potty, he might need help."

"Standard procedure," she says. "That it?"

"Pretty much," I tell her. "But bring the boys inside, and for ten minutes or so, keep them away from the windows. Same for you."

"I thought you said we were safe."

"You're safe," I assure my ex-wife. "There's just something you don't need to see. Trust me."

There's no good-bye hug, no kiss on the cheek even. Sheila turns away and heads up the hill, facing her home and my two boys. And I walk back into the HALO, ready to try and pull off my greatest stunt.

# FOURTEEN

*Trashing a Junkyard. Bad Intentions.*
*The Keys to a Successful Ambush.*
*Damaged beyond Repair.*

The armor fits perfectly.

This is a fact that should upset me, that should suggest all kinds of things that make me doubt what I'm doing. Back on the Utah salt flats, when I first tried it on for Ecklar, the process took forever and was awkward as hell. Today it feels natural, like I'm slipping on a second skin. After I snap on the rocket boots, after I magnetically seal the massive red and black chest plate and slide my arms into the flexible metal-mesh sleeves, I stand with the helmet in my gloved hands, and I feel on the verge of a transformation. Earlier, I rigged up one of Ecklar's proton cells, so energy courses now through the exoskeleton. The whole thing hums with power as if it were alive. I raise the three-horned helmet and lower it over my face. The mechanism locks into place, and my flesh is entirely encased in the ebony and crimson shell. There will be no way to guess that I am an impersonator. I will be Chaos.

Outside the HALO, on the side away from Sheila's house, I emerge from a hatch into the open field. I remember how intuitive the armor's operation was, and I know full well how the brain-scanning control operates. Even so, when I close my eyes and concentrate on one word, *Up,* I'm shocked as hell to bolt into the sky.

After all these years, flying comes naturally for me, and the suit responds to my every move. I remember after a few minutes that I don't even need to picture the word. Seeing through the enhanced optical scanners takes some getting used to. Whenever I focus on something—a silo, a far-off airplane—a digital readout overlays and reports the exact distance. On top of that, the right eye port apparently has a thermal detector.

I don't have a great deal of time. If Clyde sticks to his schedule—and he always sticks to his schedule—they'll be moving Bone Crusher to the airfield soon. Once he's airborne and headed for the Megajail, everything becomes a lot more complicated. If at all possible, I'd like to avoid aerial combat with international enforcement officials. I have to ambush my teammates while they're on the way from St. Clementine's. An added benefit is that unless I'm wrong about Clyde, there'll be press at the airfield. Though I don't doubt he's taking the threat seriously, Clyde is too media savvy to miss the chance. He'll leak something. Action shots of one of the Insidious Six in custody—he knows the news networks will fall over each other to cover it live. What he doesn't know is that I'm going to give them all a show they never dreamed of.

I have about an hour until they're set to begin their operation, which means I have only the smallest window to give the suit a dry run. It's risky to take the time to practice, but if I don't invest a few minutes to reacquaint myself with the weaponry, all the wrong people might get hurt today. Using Chaos's devices in the open salt flats is one thing, but engaging friends in close combat is another.

On the way west, I used the HALO's scanners and found what looked like an abandoned junkyard in Potter County. It's a sparsely populated area and should be perfect for my warm-up exercises.

With the armor's onboard navigating system, finding the junkyard is no problem, but landing is another question. I streak in over the two acres of trashed cars and garbage and plow through the rusting carcass of a school bus. The impact crater is six feet deep, and when I climb out of it, I see the split halves of the bus. I pick up the rear end, toss it straight up into the sky the way you'd loft a tennis ball, then aim my right arm at it. I merely imagine it blowing up, and what looks like a thin flashlight unfolds from my forearm. There's a burst of white light, and the school bus becomes a ball of flame, raining debris on the junkyard.

A few chunks clink off the armor, and the exhilaration washes over me. It's not just that I felt no pain on the crash landing, though I didn't. And it's not just that the suit seems in perfect working order and reads my intentions, though it does. It's that I feel young and strong, returned to my natural state: invincible.

Effortlessly, I jump fifty feet to a stacked pile of cubes beside a compactor. I lift one and look at the metal, twisted and contorted. With palms in on either side, I begin to press—and I do my best not to picture Clyde's skull—but when the whole thing crushes inward, I can imagine the sound of his bones splintering. Other than his energy bursts and some superagility, Clyde is just like any other human.

These thoughts bother me, but just a bit. I start taking shots at distant targets with the palm lasers—a gutted refrigerator at 227 feet, an oven at 403—and I wonder if the brainwave reader in the helmet doesn't work two ways. Maybe the feedback loop is causing evil thoughts. Maybe such power corrupts the mind and twists the soul. Could be Chaos started off as just another megalomaniac supervillain but gradually went insane.

I take to the air again to coordinate flying and offensive maneuvers. From the shoulder-mounted grenade launcher, I sink three proton bombs into the compactor, and it goes up like a box of TNT. Once my thermal scans confirm no one's occupying the trailer office, a sonic pulse from my chest plate reduces it to quivering rubble.

With power like this, taking out the Guardians is well within my abilities. In the team escorting Bone Crusher, only Ecklar should prove a serious threat. And since he'll be wearing his battle suit, I won't have to be gentle. He's tough, he can take it, and this scrapyard has given me an idea for an edge. If the second team responds quickly, I may have to engage them too, which will be tricky at best. No, my primary mission objective today is merely to put on a good show, blow up a few things, let the civilians and the cameras catch me in the act. Bone Crusher is one thing, but the fact that he was living as a harmless doorman, no matter how Clyde spins it, won't have much long-term impact on the polls. The Tucker Commission will still go forward.

What the general public needs, what they've forgotten, is the genuine terror of a superhuman with bad intentions. Roughing up the Guardians—Clyde and Bigfoot especially—I confess, it'll be fun. But before I let them chase me off, retreat before an inevitable defeat, I need to scare the shit out of this city. In this suit, that won't be hard. These people have to be reminded about the existence of evil and violence in the world, and I'm just the man to do it.

The keys to a successful ambush are speed and surprise. Since I was part of Clyde's initial strategy session, it's not hard to see the gaping hole in his defense. The convoy is a parade of police cars, six armored vehicles, and a troop transport modified to be a mobile prison cell. Clyde himself will drive the transport, and Bigfoot will ride in the back with Bone; Ecklar and Ice Queen will provide air support. With as much of an advantage as the suit gives me in the air, it's the only logical place from which to attack. Similarly, the best location for the ambush is obvious: the heart of the city, close to St. Clementine's, before the convoy gets up on the interstate. The more civilians around, the more panic and distractions. But here, of course, is the difference between classroom battle tactics and the streets. Good villains never do exactly what's expected of them.

So when the convoy leaves the hospital, I'm not lurking nearby. I'm flying into a drainage pipe in the wastewater treatment plant on the outskirts of Kingdom Town. And as the heroes scan the empty skies, I'm navigating the city sewers. While Chaos's GPS directs me from tunnel to tunnel, I imagine my former teammates gradually growing more and more confident that indeed, Magus was wrong. Or at least that the attack won't come today. I know human nature, and all that initial anxiety and vigilance will begin to give way to relief once they come off the interstate, especially for the ones who've never been in real combat. With the airfield in sight and no sign of trouble, the notion of victory will rise in their hearts, and their guard will come down. Clyde will order Ecklar and Ice Queen forward to secure the plane. That's when I'll strike.

The sewage is a foot deep at my feet, and I'm glad that Chaos didn't install scent enhancers. Directly overhead is a manhole cover, four perfect dots of uninterrupted daylight. The streets are blocked off. While I'm waiting, I visualize the first few maneuvers I have planned, try to anticipate everyone's response. So much depends on Ecklar.

Of course, I've considered the possibility that I'll face defeat, or that things will go wrong and I'll find myself unable to escape. Back in the interrogation cell at St. Clem's, when I let Magus read my mind so he could know what I needed him to say, he must've sensed my whole plan. *Dear boy,* he projected, *this seems a bit dangerous.* And if things don't go my way in the battle, that's OK. For this too, I have a contingency that will mean a mission success. Today, I cannot lose. Thinking this, I wonder if all along I wouldn't have made a better villain than a hero.

I hear the sirens almost a mile off, and less than a minute later the police escorts race above me, scattering the light. I don't count the cars, but it takes a good thirty seconds before the heavy armor rumbles past. Then the big transport lumbers over me, and I wait for silence and the return of that light. I take a deep breath and plunge upward, exploding through the macadam and asphalt. In seconds I'm above the armored vehicle bringing up the convoy's rear, and I activate the sonic disruptor in the horn protruding from the front of the helmet. Every person within a quarter-mile should be driven into a fetal tuck with nausea—though thanks to Clyde, who I was betting would cordon off the runway, the area is civilian free. Most of the convoy vehicles dart left and right, skidding into a cyclone fence or crashing into a drainage ditch. Three of the police cars near the front pile up, blocking the road, and the armored vehicles and troop transports come to a halt.

Bubba climbs out of the back and begins to inflate into a giant. I storm at him and blast his eyes with magna beams, blinding him and stunting his growth. He's about thirty feet tall, strong enough to lift a tank, but freaked out by his inability to see. I launch a series of proton grenades around me, into the fields on either side of the road. This is mostly for a distraction, to rattle the younger heroes, make everyone wonder just what they're up against. As the grenades explode, Bigfoot looks left and right, and I fly shoulder first into his gut. He doubles over, and I aim my magna cannons straight up, delivering an uppercut with the force of a freight train. He spins, stumbles, and sits back on an armored vehicle, crushing it like a cardboard box. I'm worried about the driver but then see Clyde climb out, drop to his knees while puking his guts out.

In the sky ahead, three figures are clear. Ecklar's out in front, followed by Ice Queen riding a frozen slab of ice. Above them both is something that makes me grin. It's the KQEP news copter, exactly 1,123 feet away. Inside the helmet, I smile for the camera.

I fly straight at Ecklar, slipping past his barrage of stellar bullets and a poorly aimed neural net. He's been in the lab for too long, and his battle instincts are rusty, aiming where I am and not where I'm going to be. I pass beneath him and launch a proton grenade his way. He dodges it as I expected, but when it explodes just above him, the ionic shrapnel bathes his suit. This should wreak havoc with his guidance system. Sure enough, he starts flying straight up, out of control on full burn, and I realize I'll have to catch my friend to save him from going into orbit.

I don't have time to play with the Ice Queen, so I knock her sideways with a thermal blast, and she falls unharmed into the stubbled field below. I rocket upward in pursuit of Ecklar, thinking *Go go go* in hopes the suit will translate my urgency into speed. This was one of my calculated risks, that this whole stunt wouldn't endanger someone else. We pierce a bank of clouds, and as I close in, the curve of the Earth becomes clear on the horizon. Above us, the stars begin to emerge. Of course, he thinks I'm out to finish the job, so he launches a titanium torpedo down at me. I blast it with the palm laser, fly straight through the center of the explosion. From my hip, I pull free what I'd call my secret weapon, a chunk of an industrial magnet I swiped from that junkyard. I close in on Ecklar as if we were Blue Angels in synchronized flight, plow through another hail of stellar bullets. I slap the magnet onto Ecklar's chest plate—in the same spot I knocked them from just before I put Nate in harm's way—and all his systems just shut down; the flames from his rocket boots flicker and die. His battle suit, one of the most powerful weapons on the planet, becomes an impressive statue. The suit slows its upward ascent, rotates facedown, and plummets.

I match his free fall and grab him by an ankle, activate my retro thrusters to slow our descent. I scan the sky back toward the interstate, wondering where the second team is. My little drama has taken too long, and I need to find an endgame. Soon the damn Air Force may scramble F-16s, and I'm not good enough yet in this suit to defend myself and keep from injuring civilians. The problem is that my assault was too effective. There are no heroes on the ground who could imaginably defeat me. In the distance still, that KQEP copter is surely transmitting a live video feed now. Much as I hate it, I'll need to let Clyde chase me off.

Ecklar and I are close to a thousand feet when something lights up the radar on my readout. It's the size of a 747, which doesn't make a damn bit of sense because the airport is shut down and the object is moving too slowly to be a plane. When I turn and look through the clouds, though, it's moving plenty fast. A jade-eyed dragon—leathery bat wings, long flailing tail, scaly belly, gaping jaw with razor teeth—bears down on me, leading with an outstretched claw. The impact knocks the wind out of me, and I nearly pass out in the grasp of the huge beast. The concussion knocks Ecklar's ankle out of my hand, and my best friend tumbles toward the ground. The dragon corkscrews in a tight nosedive. "How dare you attack him!" Huan screams. "His is a kind and timid soul."

Her grip around my chest plate is impossibly tight, and all kinds of pressure alarms start clanging in my ears. I can't open fire on her until she catches Ecklar, and it occurs to me that she could, conceivably, crush this armor like a Coke can. Fortunately, she's a swift dragon, and she plucks my friend from the sky with a hundred feet to spare. Holding both of us, one in each claw, she lands on an empty runway, feet down, wings extended like sails. She sets Ecklar down gently and turns to me with piercing dragon eyes. Her nostrils flare. "I consider myself a pacifist, villain, and all life is sacred to me. But if you have hurt him, I will pluck your limbs like petals from a rose."

With Ecklar safe, I can reengage the fight. Both my arms are free, so I unload a burst of magna beams straight into her reptilian face. She roars and snaps her head back, but she doesn't let go, and suddenly we're aloft again, winging skyward. Her head, smoldering from my attack, turns back to me, and she says, "If you want to fight fire with fire—you should know your opponent better." With that, her mouth opens, and for an instant, gazing into the enormous toothed cavern, I think my former teammate may eat me. Instead of tossing me into her jaws, though, she engulfs me in white flame. Coolant hisses on my face, but still the sweat pours down, stinging my eyes because I can't wipe it away. The thermal detector registers the outside temperature at 225 degrees and rising. The optical readout is going nuts, running a series of flashing numbers that don't mean a damn thing to me. The message "System Overload" keeps blinking before my eyes, and no matter what I think—*Proton grenade, Mega beam, Thermal blast, Fly me the fuck out of here*—nothing happens. The suit may be damaged beyond repair. A strange smell makes me think of grilling hamburgers, and I worry that I might be cooking. It occurs to me that indeed I might die, and I find myself strangely at peace. Forcing Chaos to retreat would be a public relations windfall. Actually defeating him, causing his death even, would guarantee the Guardians public support for another generation. The Tucker Commission would surrender, maybe even disband. The dream would go on.

As I'm thinking this, a new message flashes before my eyes: "Failure Imminent. Emergency Initiative Omega Activated." Something like electricity crackles around the suit, blue lightning twisting and snapping. Huan's flame shower stops, and her grip on me goes slack. The dragon drops from the sky, and I fall right beside her.

When we strike the tarmac, for an instant I think I've passed out. Then I realize it's just that everything's gone dark inside the armor. I hear what could be muffled voices outside, distant and anxious. After a minute or two, a single beep gives way to a series of them, and the blackness in front of me is illuminated with this flashing message: "System Error. Reboot. Reboot."

Soon I hear the low hum of energy, and a flood of system checks scrolls down the side of the readout. Some read "Repair Under Way," some "Nominal," almost half are followed by "Terminal." I'm just glad when the lights come back on.

I stagger to my feet and think *Up,* but nothing happens, so I guess flying out of here isn't a current option. On hands and knees, I climb out of the still-smoking hole and find three heroes waiting for me—Bigfoot, the Ice Queen, and Clyde. Fifty feet away, a naked woman lies on the runway at the center of a crushed asphalt crater. It takes me a moment to realize it's Huan. Over by the cyclone fence and on the rim of that drainage ditch, most of the cops, coated in their own puke, have recovered enough to take shelter behind their cars, draw their weapons, and take aim with their peashooters.

"Surrender, Chaos!" Clyde yells. "Make no offensive maneuvers and you won't be harmed."

The Speedstress zips past me and stands at Clyde's side. Her appearance means the second team's arrival is imminent.

With the suit in the state it's in, I can't escape. I'm also probably not in any shape for real combat, even with these second-rate heroes. The only choice I have is to give up. And I'm ready for that, I suppose. I accomplished what I came here to do. Given all the possible outcomes, this isn't the absolute best, but it's far from the worst. Later, when I pry this helmet from my head, Clyde and Ecklar will be stunned. But they'll keep my secret. What choice will they have? Sure, we'll need one more charade when we transport Chaos to the Megajail, but it won't be hard to fool folks. Maybe it'll even be better if I "escape." Today could well be the beginning of my second career as an evil criminal genius. All this is clear to me, and despite some lingering disappointment, I am resigned to my fate.

But when I raise my hands over my head, I see the troop transport holding Bone Crusher, and the onboard computer places a blinking crosshair on the chest of each of the Guardians between me and my original objective. It's just a thought that slips by—*I could do it*—but I guess it's enough for the brain scanner. From my open palms three lasers flash. Bigfoot, Ice Queen, and the Speedstress go down, hard. Clyde cartwheels free and starts firing starburst clusters at me. He's between me and Bone Crusher, a guy I should be trying to free, so I march toward him. One more show for the cameras, I figure, what's the harm? The clusters slow me a bit now, sizzle off the armor. My force field must be down.

"You're no match for me," I shout to Clyde. The mechanized voice he hears is impossible to recognize. I wish the news copter were close enough to record my evil dialogue.

"Don't be so sure, Chaos!" Clyde yells back.

I swat the starburst clusters away like fireflies, advance on him as he backs away. "Your pathetic fireworks can't stop me!"

"Who said anything about stopping you?"

He grins slyly toward the troop transport, and I engage the thermal detector in the optical scanner. Other than the engine, the truck shows cool blue, no warm body in the back. It's a decoy. I have to admit, I'm just a bit impressed. With genuine curiosity, I ask him, "Bone's still at the hospital?"

But he shakes his head. "I stashed him on a fake news helicopter," he says. "Last place you'd ever look."

I shake my fist, because it's what a villain should do. Then I glance to the far side of the airfield, where the plane waits to bring Bone Crusher to the Megajail, and I say, "You're clever, but your arrogance has made you sloppy. I will dispose of you easily, and then no one will be left to stop me from freeing my minion."

Smiling now, Clyde holds up one hand, and his Danger Ring flashes. In the sky behind him, two figures streak our way. In seconds they come into focus, and I make out my wife in tow behind Titan himself. They touch down on the cratered runway behind me, twenty feet apart, and I find myself at the center of a triangle of heroes.

"It's been a long time, Chaos," Titan says. His skin is pale, and I suspect he's got a fever on the far side of 102, but he's clear-eyed.

Debbie's breathing hard, nervous, but her hands glow white with energy. I am so proud of her.

"Don't make us finish you," Titan says. "I can see you've already taken a beating today. You're not up for all three of us."

I face him, see that his costume is still dirty from last night's fight. I say, "Maybe you haven't looked in a mirror lately, old friend. You should've stayed in retirement."

I turn to my wife. "We haven't been introduced. Let me guess—Flame Girl? She-Torch?"

I expect her to say something snappy like *Call me Venus!* but her reply is even better. "I'm Miss 'About to Melt Your Armored Ass into a Slag Heap.' Not much else you need to know."

I do my best villainous laugh. "I know who you are, Venus. You're the one who took in that stray dog, Invincible. Hubby's kind of been falling apart lately, hasn't he?"

"Leave Vincent out of this," she says.

All-Star yells over me, "Don't let him taunt you."

"I'm not taunting," I say. "I'm just pointing out that even to a casual observer, the guy's got problems."

"He's a better man than you'll ever be," she says.

At this, of course, my heart swells thick. The belief in her voice makes me want to say, *It's me, honey. You were right. I found a way to show everyone you were right.* But of course, everyone can't know. That's the part of the plan I actually take the most pride in. This isn't about me getting accolades or being praised. It's about me getting back to basics, saving the day. To do that now, though, I need to press on, and what I need to put Deb through makes me sick. "He wasn't better today," I say.

Deb's expression shifts. Titan says, "He's toying with you. Don't engage him." But Deb has to ask, "What are you talking about?"

"You could ask your husband yourself," I say. "If you can find him. Try looking at the bottom of Lake Erie."

"Liar!" she says, and smoke begins to smolder from her fists.

"The fool somehow detected my approach and thought he could stop me alone. He put up a better fight than I imagined he would. My condolences."

"Bastard!" she yells, and when her hands come together, there's a burst of light, and a lava blast slams into my chest plate. I stumble back, but only a step. Then Titan's laser eyes burn into my back. The impact of the two forces actually holds me up for a second, but then the pain drives me to a knee.

"Pour it on," Titan commands, and Clyde releases a storm of his starburst clusters, which sparkle and explode off the armor like miniature grenades.

My palm lasers, the weakest but only weapon left in my arsenal, bounce off Titan's chest like Ping-Pong balls, but I keep returning fire because I need to remain an active threat. I don't want them to stop. Now I can see the finish line of all this, and I'm committed.

I've stumbled back into one of the better outcomes, maybe the best, of my scheme. It was a long shot that it would come to this, but I knew it might, and I'm ready. With the cameras running, the Guardians will defeat Chaos. They will avenge Sparkplug's death with a killing of their own, an act forced on them by a deadly opponent who would not surrender. And with the lie I told earlier about a battle between Chaos and Commander Invincible over Lake Erie, no one will ever know my full part in today's drama. I'll go down in the official records as a loser who stayed around too long. But the Guardians's legacy will be safe forever.

As they advance on me, intensifying their attack, I double over, press my hands together, and activate the lasers. The recoil is incredible, but I strain the armor's servomotors and my own weary muscles, keeping them locked tight. There's a white-and-red alarm light strobing in my face, and it feels like I'm holding an explosion pressed between my palms. In all the smoke and radiance, I doubt the Guardians—or the cameras—can even see what I'm doing. On the battle armor's readout, one last flashing message, "Detonation Imminent."

I want my final words to mean something. I've played this scenario out so many times, but my death was always as a hero, urging my teammates to victory, telling my wife I love her. I can't say any of those things now, so I'm forced to play the role I've chosen. I glance toward Deb, shimmering in her own heat, her hair lifting up and aflame. I see the ferocity and love in her eyes, and I yell, "You haven't seen the last of me! I'll be back. Nothing can stop Chaos!"

And then the armor explodes.

# FIFTEEN

*Live Coverage. The Salmon from Monhegan. Being Needed.*
*The Significance of a Closed Nightstand Drawer.*
*Bad Dancers. Fire in the Sky.*

I watch the armor burst in a fiery ball—surely bearing witness to my own death—on a huge flat-screen TV. Impossible as this is, I can't turn away from the spectacle—red and orange blooms, flowing billows of black smoke. It's enough to knock Clyde on his ass, which pleases me just a bit. Titan, who's got to be exhausted, deactivates his laser eyes and collapses forward in a heap. But Deb refuses to let up. I'm amazed to watch her charge into the debris, incinerating any piece bigger than a shoe box. She is furious and lovely, and I know she'll make an impressive widow. I imagine her dressed in black standing over my grave. As tears slip from her eyes, they sizzle on her cheeks.

Then I feel a tingle in the back of my brain, and I hear, *All that's a tad premature, don't you think, dear boy?*

I turn to see Magus sitting next to me in a plastic chair just like mine. Somehow I'm wearing civilian clothes, and we're in what feels like a large hospital room: white tile floors, cream walls, curtains drawn. There are two twin beds with rails. Next to Magus, a bald man with sunken cheeks slumps over in a wheelchair and gawks at the television. The words *Live*

*Coverage* appear in the lower corner. The man turns from the TV to me. Magus says, "Don't mind Julius. His mind isn't what it used to be. But he knows how to keep a secret." Julius winks at me and turns back to the TV, where Kid Cyclone and the Jersey Devil descend from the sky. The Ice Queen is extinguishing the flaming bits of the Chaos armor.

Debbie has her face in her hands.

From his lap, Magus lifts the wand. "That poor girl truly thinks you're no longer among the living. I'll send you back to the HALO, and you can call her."

"Wait," I say.

He holds the wand in midair, like a conductor with a baton.

"What the hell just happened?"

"I rescued you, dear boy. After you gave me the Merlin wand, when our minds touched in the interrogation room, when you asked me to play along with that part of your little game, I saw the whole plan. I didn't mean to, but it's like overhearing something. You can't very well unhear it. Anyway, that's why I've been watching. I couldn't let you get injured. Nice bit, too, snapping that fake stick in half. Very dramatic."

"Oh," I say. "Thanks."

Julius points at the screen and opens his mouth. What comes out isn't quite a word. Huan, covered in a blanket, is sitting on the back fender of a paramedic truck. Magus strokes the man's worried face and says, "I told you she'd be all right." Turning back to me, Magus explains, "He's always had a fondness for animals."

I nod as if I understand.

A nurse walks in pushing a squeaky-wheeled cart. After maneuvering a slim table between us and the TV, she transfers two covered plates, ugly yellow plastic, from the cart. "Slice of white bread, meatloaf, green beans, apple juice. I didn't know you all had a visitor, Mr. van Alkemade."

"An old friend," Magus tells her.

She glances at the action on the screen. "They finally get you a new television?"

"I suppose they did," he says.

"Fancy-schmancy." She smiles at me, wheels the cart on to the next room.

Magus says to Julius, "You remember the salmon we shared on Monhegan?"

Julius licks his lips and nods. Magus lifts the plastic lid, and the smell rises with the steam. There on a china plate is a slab of pink fish, nested next to asparagus coated in butter, alongside a short glass of what might be sherry. Magus unfolds a white cotton napkin and arranges it in on his friend's lap. Julius reaches for a fork with a trembling hand.

"I'll tell you," Magus says, tapping the wand on his lap. "It's good to have this back."

I wonder what the two of them are doing here. Perhaps my thoughts are too loud, because Magus says, "Julius wrote me every week while I was in prison. Somehow he'd guessed my true nature, something I'd never really come to terms with myself. After I got out, we had nine amazing months, then the Alzheimer's began to come on. Even with the wand, it seems I can't mend some things. But the nurses here, they take care of Julius and me both. They're good people, doing the best they can."

"That's all you can do," I say.

Magus considers my face. "I wasn't sure you realized that. I hope you do. Truly, my boy, that despair I felt when I touched your mind. You can't live that way."

I worry about what exactly he saw. "Hopefully that's behind me now."

"You don't have to hope," he says. "You have to decide. It's always easier to find a noble reason to die. Finding one to live for, that's the trick."

On the flat-screen, Debbie is helping Titan to his feet. They stagger toward a hovercar. "I have plenty to live for," I tell Magus. "More than most."

"All right then," he says. He holds the wand up like a question.

"What'll you do?" I ask.

"Same thing I've been doing. Going on my strolls, finding people who need me. It's important, I've decided, to feel needed."

"I'm in your debt," I tell him. "If I can ever help . . ."

"You can always help, Vincent. There may not be a global crisis every day, but somewhere, someone always needs help. Some days you might rescue the whole planet from disaster, and that's a grand feeling, I'm certain. But others, you might just save one person." He takes Julius's fork and cuts up the asparagus, returns it to his good hand. "The harmony you feel when you're using your gifts, that's God's way of telling you you're in the right place. Julius taught me that."

On the TV, the hovercar lifts off and whisks into the clouds, leaving the news copters in its wake. I know the place I should be. "Send me to my boys," I say.

Magus smiles, and I'm staring at crooked boards nailed into the trunk of an oak. Above me in the battered tree house, voices whisper. "But there's no way we could survive traveling into a black hole," Nate says.

"Sure there is," Thomas insists. "We'll protect the ship with a quantum-six bubble shield."

"There's no such thing," Nate tells him. "Uncle Ecklar says that anything going into a black hole is squished down to a molecular level. It's called spaghettification."

There's a silence, then Thomas says, "You can't talk like that when you go to pre-K. You'll freak the teachers out. Just pretend, OK?"

I glance toward the house, and like a blessing, my ultravision returns for an instant. I spy Sheila in her study, asleep on the couch with a textbook on her chest. Above me, Nate answers his brother. "Affirmative. Our research mission will go forward."

I would love nothing more than to climb the ladder and accompany my sons as they venture into the vast unknown. But this is their world, I recognize that, and I have no business interfering. Besides, I have a phone call to make.

Inside the HALO, I find the first communications portal I can and dial up the hovercar. As the connection is made, I think of the things I might say to her. *You were amazing. I'm so proud of you. I wish I could've been there with you.* Then comes her voice. "Hovercar Delta," she says. "This is Venus." And I think about what I want her to hear most, the most important thing. "It's me, Deb," I say. "I'm alive."

* * *

Three days after the death of King Chaos, Bigfoot and the Jersey Devil are grilling steaks and drinking beer, listening to the Ice Queen recount her part in what's already been declared the greatest battle in the history of the Guardians. When she finishes, Bubba says, "Chaos told me he had to take me out first because I posed the biggest threat." Those nearby, Kid Cyclone, Speedstress, a handful of others, nod as if listening to Scripture.

Deb and I can hear them clearly, though we're far from the crowd. "Bunch of bullshit," she says to me, both hands around one of my arms. Of course she's right, but I've reached the point where I don't mind the blending of history with fiction.

My sons, predictably, are flanking Ecklar, the guest of honor at this farewell party atop the HALO. Clouds drift above us, and my friend glances skyward now and then. His calculations are complete, and he's confident that sometime this afternoon, the vortex to Andromeda will open. He expects a one-man craft, probably a fellow scientific explorer, maybe even a drone rescue ship. Regardless, today he will see his home world. I wonder how he'll be greeted by his trio of wives, and how many grandchildren his seventeen kids have produced during his exile on Earth. At his side, Nate says, "Come on, I was just starting to get the hang of it."

"Absolutely not," Sheila cries. "Uncle Ecklar is taking his battle suit with him. That's final."

She stands behind the boys. Deb, right next to her, says, "Amen. We've had enough excitement around here." She smiles at me, and I grin. She is radiant, even more confident and bold since the victory over Chaos. The video of those final moments has been in constant play, and the whole world recognizes her now as a hero of the first order. At the official press conference, reporters focused their questions on her, asking what inspired her to such ferocity. "Love for my family," she said. "The people of Earth."

At the following photo opportunity, held on the airfield itself, Titan was a class act, giving credit to Clyde for thwarting Chaos's evil plot. Titan, a spinmaster without par, explained that it was Clyde's idea to fake a rift in the Guardians, have me pretend to quit the team, to make Chaos think we were weak. "All-Star knew a division might help lure Chaos into the open."

The only thing that stunned me more than hearing this on the TV—I watched the whole deal live from my sofa—was the way the reporters nodded and took notes. One more insane fabrication that no one's doubted.

Ice Queen turns up the volume on Bubba's karaoke machine and starts singing "My Way," dedicated to Ecklar. She's off-key, but it's sweet. Gypsy, on a day pass from New Horizons, walks with Titan to the middle of the helipad, where they begin slow dancing. Deb tugs on my arm and tilts her head toward them. "No," I say. "Let them have this to themselves. We'll have plenty of time later." And this, impossibly, is exactly how I've felt these last few days, like the possibilities before me are suddenly without limit. This strange elation began when Deb returned to the HALO, found me and the boys playing in that open farm field. Maybe it was the adrenaline of the battle. Maybe it was the glow coming off her. But when she floated from the hovercar and into my arms, when she embraced me inside a burning hug, I wasn't afraid—of her love or of failing or of not being good enough. I wasn't afraid of anything. Without speaking, we left the boys to their games and went to our quarters and locked the door. And so soon after, it wasn't a big deal when I didn't reach for my nightstand drawer. It barely occurred to me, but it was a decision I made even in the midst of the physical ecstasy, a moment when I chose to go on, to try. On the nights since, and in the early mornings when we wake tangled together, we haven't had any grand conversations, no formal declarations of our intentions. But we both know what it is we're doing.

Ice Queen finishes the song, and scattered applause breaks out. Bigfoot abandons the Jersey Devil at the grill and grabs the microphone. "This one goes out to a little buddy of mine with a big head and a bigger heart." Bubba starts belting out "We'll Meet Again," and I bring my eyes to Deb's. We stroll onto the helipad, joining Titan and Gypsy. All-Star has taken Ice Queen's hands, and Speedstress has hoisted Ecklar into her arms. Huan, wholly human and dressed in a long, lovely jade gown, steps over to Nate, and Thomas drags his mom onto the impromptu dance floor. Smiling and light, we are all swaying to the song's rhythm. Deb squeezes my shoulder and looks into my eyes, and I know she wants to be alone with me. She knows my desire matches hers. And this will come later, I'm certain. She puts her head on my chest. This is as real a thing as I've ever felt, this silent understanding between us about our new project—nothing less than making a new life.

Then, in the midst of the chorus, a crackling sound rattles the clear blue sky, like a thunderclap. Bigfoot stops singing, but the music goes on. As everyone turns, I find Ecklar's face, and he grins at me. We nod at each other, and all of it—the friendship and the love and the sadness—is understood. Directly above the HALO, a darkness begins to swirl, like a tiny hurricane at high speed. Rainbow-colored lightning flares within the pitch-black core. People applaud and whoop as if we were watching fireworks. As the phenomena expands, the size now of a football stadium, Ecklar's eyes narrow with concern. He climbs out of Speedstress's arms and weaves through the clapping crowd, over to me. I lean down. "Vincent," he says. "Something's not right."

At that moment, a long metallic needle pierces the spinning storm. It is the prow of an enormous gray spacecraft, sharp and angular. Along the sides are what look to me like turrets with cannons protruding from them. This ship is not a rescue vessel but a battle cruiser.

"Malkovians," Ecklar says, and he's charging toward his armor. Two more ships emerge behind the first. "It's an invasion!"

From torpedo holes in the ship's underbelly, twin rockets streak our way. Automated lasers from the HALO blast them from the sky. Everyone turns from the explosion, diving flat-bellied to the deck, and shrapnel rains down on us. Deb and I scramble to our feet, and already a few heroes are in flight, led by Titan and a pissed-looking dragon. Deb says, "Come on!"

But I hesitate. "I'll get the boys to safety. You go kick ass."

She shakes her head. "Sheila knows where the shelter is." I follow her gaze and see my ex, shepherding Thomas and Nate, crouching low but charging toward the shield doors.

Deb says, "They'll be safe when those ships are destroyed." She extends one hand, palm up. "Get me up there."

I reach out and take my wife's warm hand in mine and feel her go weightless. Next to me, she floats, and flames engulf her hair. Above us, a series of explosions shake the air like sonic booms. More menacing ships pour through that vortex, the beginning of what must be an armada. With my free hand I make a fist and raise it, aim it toward the battle raging in the darkening sky. I tighten my grip on Deb's hand, and she squeezes back. Finally together now, side by side, we'll go help save the world.

# *Acknowledgments*

For core support, I'm grateful for my wife, Beth, as well as our boys, Owen and James. I hope this book helps them both understand why Dad's at his desk when they wake up. I also recognize the keen eye of Warren Frazier for encouragement and instrumental feedback on early drafts of this story. For their camaraderie, I thank my many good colleagues at Shippensburg University, among them Zach Savich, whose generous response to a whiny phone call led directly to this manuscript finding a home. I'm grateful for the many comic book writers and illustrators who delighted me in my youth and taught me so much about the art of narrative: Peter David, Neil Gaiman, Frank Miller, Alan Moore, Chris Claremont, John Byrne, Art Adams, Jim Starlin, John Romita Jr., Kazuo Koike. Lastly, my deep thanks to Michael Griffith, an editor who earns that title on every page.